24 WOMEN

short stories

by

Lisa Wright

First published in 2022

Copyright © Lisa Wright 2022

All characters in this book are fictitious, and any resemblance to actual persons living or dead is purely coincidental.

ISBN: 9798352521779

Cover photograph of the author at Lanhydrock reproduced by kind permission of the National Trust

Contents

Play a Song for me	1
A Bit of Fun	10
Bedsit no. 2	21
Babysitting	25
Something Wild	39
Alice Bridger	44
Calypso Red	80
Film Night	86
Talking to Laura	90
Deirdre	102
The Man He Used to Be	114
Death Wish	124
Making it Better	135
Sarah's Visit	142
First Steps in Kyrenia	151
Nicola	163
Ready For Rapture	168
Do Me a Favour	178
Alison in Marbella	189
Daniel's Mother	203
Christina	208
Ruth and Ruby	211
Maureen	224
My Next Life	227

Play a Song for Me

I look forward all week to Thursday mornings. I position myself at the back of the dance studio, and little ripples of pleasure trip up and down my spine as I try to follow the routine shouted out by Jodie. She has spiky blond hair and boundless energy. 'Now stretch to the right!' she yells above the thumping music. 'Grapevine, mumba, jazz box!' To my delight, I understand now what it all means, and better still, I sometimes find myself anticipating what's coming next. I feel almost graceful and supple and, for the first time in my life, good at something. Also, because the music is young and modern and quite unlike anything I listen to at home, I feel, for an hour a week at least, positively trendy.

    After the class, I force myself to go for coffee with some of the girls. Jodie calls us girls, which is kind of her, because we are all over 50. I'm sure the girls only invite me out of politeness, and actually I don't enjoy it much, but I persevere, sure that on some level it's doing me good. I spend far too much time on my own – or rather, with Mother, which is practically the same thing – and I badly need to work on my social skills. It'll get easier with time, I'm sure of that. I just need to watch the girls carefully, study how they do it, how they manage to think of something to say and say it at the right time and in the right way. There's one woman in particular, Lucy she's called, who is so pretty and confident. Watch and learn, I say to myself, as I perch nervously on the edge of my chair and try to look interesting.

    So the keep fit class is great, and the coffee session very educational, but my favourite part of the weekly trip into town is walking under the underpass and catching the eye of the man who is always there, playing his guitar and singing. His repertoire is enormous – I've never heard him sing the same song twice. I'm amazed that anyone can know all those songs, and it seems very strange that someone so gifted doesn't have a proper job. At least I presume he doesn't. I presume that he's busking because he has no money and no home. We've never spoken to each other, so I actually know nothing at all about him. Every Thursday I drop the coins in his open guitar case, he gives me a little nod, and that's that. But for some reason this little act of exchange makes my heart sing. It's not that I feel virtuous; as far as I'm concerned his singing gives me so much pleasure that he's doing me the favour, not the other way round. It's more that there's a connection between us, something that feels real and important.

Yesterday was Thursday, and yesterday everything was different. I still can't quite believe it happened. The day began badly, because Mother had a bad night and I was in and out of her room half a dozen times before I gave up trying to sleep in my own bed. It was much easier just to doze in the armchair next to her, so that I was right there when she called out. She was in one of her anxious moods and just needed a reassuring stroke and plumping of her pillows, and only once the bedpan. She is actually quite loveable in the wee small hours, very different to how she is during the daytime, so it doesn't seem too much of a chore. But because we were both so tired, we overslept the next morning, and it was past 8 when I woke up. Normally this wouldn't matter at all, but it was Thursday, my special day, and I was going to be late. I had to get myself dressed, Mother washed, and the breakfast ready before Diane arrived at 8.30 to sit with Mother. Diane is the only person apart from me that Mother will tolerate. I've tried and tried to get her to accept other helpers, but she is so rude to them that they wouldn't stay even if I doubled their wages. The last one left in tears after only half an hour and I haven't had the heart to try again since then.

Diane, though, is what is known as a treasure – dependable, thick-skinned and utterly unflappable. She won't take any nonsense from Mother and I think is secretly respected by her because of that. I wish I could be more like Diane. And I wish Diane could manage more than Thursday mornings and Monday afternoons. It would be wonderful if I could have an evening off once in a while. Though I'm not sure what I would do with it.

Anyway, yesterday morning I managed to get everything done, but only just, and I was feeling distinctly flustered and disorganised, and really rather grumpy as I sped along the narrow lanes. I got stuck behind a tractor for at least 2 miles before he let me overtake him, and I was almost crying with frustration. I hated the thought of the girls all looking at me as I disrupted the class by arriving late. Luckily I found a parking space in Wilson Road and then I hurried along to the underpass. As I reached the steps I heard the guitar, and my heart gave its usual ridiculous flutter. I am 56, a spinster, living at home with my invalid mother, and I've got a schoolgirl crush on a busker. There. I've gone and said it. It's pathetic but it's the truth. I reached into my coat pocket for the coins I always put there in readiness, but my fingers closed on nothing but a folded tissue. In my haste that morning I'd forgotten to put my money there, ready for throwing into his guitar case. It wouldn't do for him to see me counting out the money, as though I were calculating how much I felt he was worth that day. It seemed important to appear nonchalant, to look as though I just gave him whatever money came to hand.

But now I had a more serious problem. I was standing at the top of the steps which led down to the underpass, rifling in my handbag, and I felt my glasses case, my car keys, my cheque book, my diary – but not my purse. Come to think of it, my bag did feel lighter than usual. So I'd left my purse at home. I had nothing to give him.

'Scuse me!' A plump young woman holding a small child by the hand was trying to get past me. In my haste to get out of their way, my left foot slipped off the step, and I reached out to grab the handrail. I missed it. I was completely off balance and I was falling forward now, my hands outstretched and helpless. I landed heavily on one knee before rolling on again and coming to an undignified sprawl at the foot of the steps.

'Jesus, are you alright?' The young mother was breathing her coffee and cigarette breath into my face, her eyes wide with alarm.

'I – yes – I think so,' I said, wincing as I tried to get up.

'Don't move!' The voice was so commanding that I immediately sank back down again. It was him, I'd have known that voice anywhere. 'You've had a shock, better rest a little before you try to stand,' continued the busker. 'Let me just move you against the wall, so nobody trips over you.'

He placed his hands under my armpits and eased me sideways until my back came to rest against the wall. I wanted so much to be light as a feather for him, but he seemed strong enough to manage my bulk.

I didn't know what to do. I'd never been so embarrassed in all my life. I took the easy way out by closing my eyes.

'That's right, just rest a minute,' said the busker, and he placed my handbag in my lap.

'Are you okay with this?' the mother asked him. 'Only I'm running really late. I'm really sorry, but it wasn't my fault, you know, she just slipped.''

'We'll be fine,' he replied and relieved, she disappeared into the underpass.

'That's all, folks, show's over,' he said to the three women and a young lad who had stopped to look.

'Should I call an ambulance?' asked one of the women but my busker said no, he'd do it later if necessary.

I opened my eyes then and smiled at him. He was wearing the scuffed brown leather jacket I liked, with a green jumper underneath. He looked very clean; he must have found somewhere to have a shower that morning. Perhaps he'd spent the night in one of those hostels for the homeless.

'Thank you,' I said. 'I do feel an idiot. I don't think I'll be making my keep fit class today.'

'How about a cup of coffee instead? I'm Rob, by the way,' he said, and his smile was warm and friendly. He had a lot of wrinkles round his eyes, from laughter maybe, or more likely from worry, and I realised he was older than I'd thought, late forties at least. His hair was receding from his temples and his face was very thin.

I instantly pictured myself taking him to the café in the market, and treating him to a bacon sandwich. He must be so hungry.... But then I remembered that I hadn't got any money. And of course I couldn't let him pay.

'Here you are, it should be nice and hot still.' Rob was crouching down beside me, holding out the beaker from his thermos flask.

I quashed any qualms about cleanliness.

'You're very kind,' I murmured, and took a sip. 'I'm Marion'. The coffee was instant, sugary and lukewarm, but I managed to drink it down.

'I play the guitar here on Thursday mornings,' Rob informed me and I couldn't help it, I gave a little gasp of disappointment. Three months, I'd been coming to my keep fit class. Twelve weeks of catching his eye and giving him money every single time and he didn't even recognise me.

'I know,' I said, amazed at my boldness. 'I really enjoy your singing.'

'Cheers,' he said. 'It's good to know someone does. Some weeks it hardly seems worth the effort. Most people just hurry past and don't even seem to notice I'm there.'

Then they must be idiots, I thought. Stupid, blind, deaf idiots. 'That was lovely,' I lied, handing him back his beaker. 'And now I think I'm ready to stand up. Could you....?' Rob helped me to my feet and stood with his hand under my elbow.

'Where does it hurt?' he said. With him holding my arm nothing hurt at all. I was fizzing with delight. I concentrated hard, and felt a faraway throbbing in my right knee.

'Just my knee,' I said. 'It's nothing, really.'

'Will you be going home now?' he asked. 'I think you should if you can manage it.'

I thought about my home. The big old house in a country lane with five bedrooms, three of them empty. I wanted to ask him if he had a home. And if not, would he like to come back with me to mine? Mother hadn't left her room for years and the rest of the house was far too big for just me. Rob could have the room in the attic. He could help me with Mother. She might behave herself if there was a man around. He could sit with me in the kitchen in the evenings and it would feel less cold and draughty with another person there. We could play backgammon and drink red wine, and he could play his guitar to me and sing while I cooked him nourishing suppers.

He was waiting patiently for me to answer. He was waiting patiently for me to go away so that he could get back to his busking. I was costing him his lunch money. I knew that but I didn't want to go. This was my chance to make something amazing happen and I grabbed it. 'I might just rest here a minute,' I said, leaning back against the wall. 'I wonder – do you think you could play me something? I love to hear you sing.'

'Course I can,' he said jovially. 'After all, you're probably my biggest fan!'

He fetched his guitar and case and stood in front of me, strumming. 'Any particular song?' he said.

'What about 'Hey Mr Tambourine Man,' I suggested, feeling positively lightheaded at my temerity. It was my favourite song in all the world.

'Nice choice,' he said with a smile. 'But I haven't sung it in a while. I don't know if I can remember it.' He played a few chords, and he was off. I smiled at him. For just a minute I forgot that I was a foolish middle-aged woman who had fallen down the steps. I felt young and free and unencumbered by life. And completely happy. Rob started on the second verse, and I couldn't help it, I had to join in.

'Take me on a trip.....' I had been singing these words to myself for years – in the bath, in the kitchen, in the vegetable garden - but never had I sung them as I sang them now, my voice getting richer and surer with each line.

He followed my lead as I sang, letting my voice be the dominant one, while he backed me up and gave me confidence. It felt quite wonderful. I kept my eyes fixed on his face, but behind him I noticed that several people had stopped to listen.

Simultaneously we both softened our voices for the last lingering jingle jangle line and I smiled at Rob and then and stared down at the ground, elated and stunned by what I had just done. Someone started clapping, and the others joined in.

'Encore!' shouted a bald young man, and I managed a bashful smile. Rob was grinning from ear to ear as he watched the coins spin into his guitar case.

'You have an amazing voice!' he said to me. 'Where did you learn to sing like that?'

'Nowhere,' I said. 'I just sing to myself, that's all.'

'Well not any longer you don't. That voice is much too good not to share it about a bit! How would you like to come and sing with me on Thursdays – after your class of course, just for an hour or so. I've booked the underpass for Thursday mornings to try and raise some money for the Children's Hospice, and I can see that with you helping me I'd raise much more.'

He lowered his voice and came closer. 'My sister's little boy died there last year,' he explained. 'My wife and I spent a lot of time with him at the end, and it's a very special place. I thought I could do my bit to help by taking one morning a week out of the office and busking.'

My over-stimulated brain was struggling to digest this new information. So he wasn't homeless or jobless. He worked in an office. He had a wife. He wouldn't be taking up residence in my attic room. My stupid daydream fizzled away into nothing, and I wanted to weep with disappointment. But I looked up at him, standing there with his eager smiling face and I managed to smile back. After all, he had asked me to sing with him. I hung on to that extraordinary fact and nodded my head vigorously.

'I'd love to,' I said. 'If you give me a list of songs, I'll make sure I'm word perfect by next Thursday. Nothing too modern – I only know the old ones.' He fished a pen and a scrap of paper out of his pocket and scribbled down some song titles. I looked at them and nodded. I would be fine. I knew most of them already.

'I must be getting back,' I said. I thought I would explode with happiness and excitement and I needed to be by myself, so as to calm down. 'Do you think you could just help me to the top of the steps?'

Walking slowly up the steps with Rob was the second best thing I did that day, after the singing. I moved my feet as slowly as I possibly could, to make the experience last longer. He had his arm bent and I was holding on to it. I shall always remember the feel of the muscle of his arm under the leather.

'Thank you,' I said. I couldn't stop grinning, so I made myself look away from him. I studied the clock toe=wer in the distance as I gently slid my arm out from under his.

'No problem. Are you sure you're okay to get home? There's no one you should call?'

'Oh no, I'll be fine. Thanks again. I'll see you next week then?'

'I'll be here! Bye.' And with a wave of his hand he was gone.

I limped back to the car, my mind already racing ahead to next Thursday. I would bring chocolate brownies and piping hot proper coffee. I would wear my new fleece jacket – it could get pretty draughty in that underpass. I would walk extremely carefully down those steps and smile at Rob as I passed him. 'Back in an hour!' I would say, and he would grin and nod at me. I would attack my keep fit routine with great energy, and when the girls said, 'Coming to coffee, Marion?' I would reply, 'Sorry, I can't today. There's somewhere I have to be.'

A Bit of Fun

It was supposed to be a bit of fun. Recreational activity, that's all – like playing tennis, only more exciting. It was supposed to boost my confidence, make me feel more attractive, more alive, more womanly, after years of being ignored by my kind but inadequate husband. Roger is ten years older than me and has wound down in every department.

'Go on!' urges my best friend Stella, who is unmarried, super-confident and very sexy. She seems to be able to leap from one man to the next with great enjoyment and not a single qualm. Her current squeeze, Brian, has been on the scene longer than most, but she enjoys her freedom too much to consider sharing her flat with him. She declares to anyone who will listen that monogamy is unnatural - but then, she has nothing to lose except her dignity, whereas I have my marriage to consider, my children, my reputation. 'It'll do you good!' she promises. And I want to believe her, to share, just a little bit, in her sunny world where life is permanently exciting and promising. Stella is always smiling and full of energy, and she makes me feel dull and careworn. Especially since I had my fortieth birthday a few weeks ago and realised that I am now into the second half of my life. The old, tired, good for nothing half. The slow descent to the grave with nothing to look forward to except an increase in aches and waistline and forgetfulness and boredom.....

So you can see that I was in a pretty bad way, the Tuesday before last, and ripe for persuasion. Stella must have sensed a shift in my resistance, because she suddenly became very bossy.

'You're coming for supper at Antonio's with me and Brian on Friday,' she announced, as she placed a stack of invoices on my desk. 'I've already booked the table.' She held up a hand for silence. 'No protests, no excuses, and certainly no Roger! We'll pick you up at 7.30, and I want you looking sexy please.'

I eyed her suspiciously over the rim of my coffee cup. 'Why? If it's just you and Brian?'

She gave one of her wicked little laughs. 'Aha, you're on to me already! Okay, I admit it, I'm setting you up on a blind date with a really gorgeous man. I'd be after him myself except that he's a good mate of Brian's and I have a 'no friends of current man' rule.' She gave a mock sigh and grinned at me. 'His name's Simon and he's sooooo fit.'

'And I'm sooooo married,' I reminded her.

'Oh come on Suze, we've been through this a thousand times. Just give it a go, will you? Give yourself something to sit and grin about when you're an old lady in a rocking chair, with only your memories for company.'

This was one of Stella's most effective lines of attack. And suddenly I was tired of resisting.

'Oh alright,' I said. 'I'll come. But if I don't like him I'm going home early with a headache. So don't pick me up, I'll meet you there.'

****

It took me all my free time in the next three days to decide what to wear. I tried on just about every item of clothing I possessed, and in the end settled on my red flippy skirt with a black t-shirt, and my lucky earrings. I didn't want to look as if I had tried too hard, and that much I certainly achieved. I left Roger making pancakes with the kids, a scene of such domestic harmony that every bone in my body was crying out to me to stay at home with them.

'Have fun, Mummy,' called Rachel, who had been told I was having a girl's night with Auntie Stella, and I felt so full of love and guilt that I had to run back and kiss her flour-streaked cheek.

I couldn't find a parking space near Antonio's, so I was ten minutes late by the time I eventually made it through the door of the restaurant. I heard Stella's laugh and located them at the far side of the room. She gave me a jaunty wave, and I stuck a brae smile on my face and made my way over. The two men had their backs to me, but I could see from their heads which one was Simon. Stella had made no mention of the fact that he was bald, and I didn't know whether to be relieved or disappointed. I relaxed. This would be okay. There would be no danger of me fancying him. I would have a pleasant evening and then go home to my husband and children.

So calm was I, so unsuspecting, that I was able to smile happily at Stella as we kissed. 'Hello Brian,' I murmured, kissing him as well, and then and only then did I turn to face my blind date. My bald blind date. My bald beautiful blind date with a face that made my tummy do a flip.

'You must be Suzanne,' he said, and I know it sounds ridiculous, but the way he looked at me made me feel as if he and I were the only people in the room. In the world even. My lips had gone dry and I licked them. He held out his hand to me and his fingers squeezed mine, and I honestly thought I was going to faint. My knees gave way and I plumped down in the chair next to Stella. I still hadn't spoken to him, but it didn't seem to matter. Nothing at all mattered, now that I was sitting opposite the most drop-dead gorgeous man I had ever seen. I was in a bubble of pure happiness.

Stella was chattering away and Simon poured me a glass of wine. I managed to speak then. I managed to say 'Thank you,' while I absorbed his face. If I never saw him again after this night I wanted to be able to remember every detail. His brown eyes were warm and clever and full of humour. His lips were thin but made beautiful shapes as he spoke and I wanted to kiss them. His head wasn't bald, but shaved, with a covering of tiny hairs which I longed to touch, to see whether they were soft or bristly. His voice was low and sexy and stirred feelings in me that I hadn't known were there. You may be surprised that all of this registered in a few seconds, but you couldn't be more surprised than I was. This, I realised, was what was meant by 'love at first sight', something I had always thought only happened in chick flicks.

It took a huge effort for me to focus on the menu and tell the waiter what I wanted. I don't suppose I would have noticed if he had brought me a bowl of cornflakes. Simon wanted to know all about me, and whatever I said he seemed to find fascinating. I heard myself saying things I didn't even know I thought - apparently I had an opinion about Mozart! By the time the food arrived, I was leaning across the table, totally absorbed. Stella had to elbow me hard in the ribs to get me to pass her the bread basket, and her eyes were dancing with delight when I finally responded.

'Didn't I tell you?' she whispered. But I didn't have time to speak to her, and she understood. She and Brian talked to each other and left us alone and I was in heaven. At one point Simon got up to go to the loo and as he passed me he ruffled my hair, smiling, and I felt a jolt of pleasure, right down to my toes. Stella tried to talk to me then but I still couldn't pay attention. I just wanted Simon to come back, and when he did I wanted him to touch me again.

Somehow the food was eaten and the bill was paid and it was time to go. Stella and Brian tactfully melted away, and Simon walked me to my car. I was so glad that I hadn't parked nearer. My hand felt small and cherished in his strong grip. I unlocked the car door and hesitated for a minute, wondering what came next.

The Kiss was what came next. Oh my god. I didn't know kissing could be like that. So gentle at first and then bolder and finally urgent. I gave myself up to it and I didn't want it ever to end. My entire body was tingling and expectant, and when he drew back I felt bereft. 'Don't stop!' I wanted to wail, but instead I just stood there staring at the ground, overcome by what had just happened to me.

Simon lifted my chin and gazed into my eyes. 'I live pretty close,' he said. 'How about giving me a lift home and coming in for a coffee?'

I didn't hesitate for a second. It seemed to me that I had already gone far beyond the point of no return. I didn't think about Roger, I didn't think about anything really, except about how much I wanted this man. I was, I suppose, temporarily unhinged by such lust as I couldn't remember ever feeling. Well, obviously Roger and I had had our moments way back when, but it was like comparing a nice cup of cocoa with a bottle of Dom Perignon.

We didn't bother with the coffee. He undid my bra with a deft movement of his fingers the minute we were inside the door, and we stumbled into the bedroom. I didn't have to think what to do, because he took complete control and it all just happened, and it was incredible. He did things to me that I'd never experienced before. It was so overwhelming in fact that I found myself sobbing without understanding why. And Simon had a cigarette and waited for me to calm down, and after a little while we did it all over again and this time I didn't cry.

It was after midnight when I let myself into my house, very quietly so as not to wake Roger. I ran a bath and soaked in the bubbles, reliving the whole evening from start to finish. Then I climbed into bed beside my gently snoring husband and for a long time I lay there in the dark, smiling.

****

That was last Friday. Simon and I had exchanged mobile numbers, and I waited on tenterhooks all day Saturday, but he didn't phone. Stella rang to pump me for details, but I didn't want to share my magical experience with her in case she spoilt it. I was horrid to the kids, snappy and tense, and Roger took them off for a long walk to pick blackberries. His thoughtfulness, of course, only made me feel worse. Finally, after supper I couldn't stand it any longer and I dialled Simon's number, despising myself. It went straight to voice mail and I had seven goes at leaving a message, erasing the one before until I managed to sound almost light-hearted. But he didn't ring back, and that night I cried myself to sleep. I don't think Roger noticed.

On Sunday we had friends to lunch, so that I was fully occupied all day, cooking and entertaining and then clearing up. It was only when they had gone home that I was able to check my phone and I saw then that he'd left a text message. 'Hi Suzie,' it said, 'Thanks 4 a gr8 evening! We must do it again sometime. Simon x'

I must have read that message thirty times, trying to inject it with some tenderness. I drank a glass of whisky to give me the courage to phone him again. This time it didn't go to voice mail, but was answered on the third ring..

'Hello!' giggled a woman's voice. 'Simon's phone!' She sounded young and silly and hugely sure of herself. I hung up.

****

It was supposed to be a bit of fun, but over the next few days I was more miserable than I had ever been in my life. I hated myself for being so weak and disloyal, I hated Stella for getting me into this mess, I hated Roger for never trying to waken me the way Simon had. The only person I couldn't hate was Simon, because I still thought he was wonderful. I couldn't sleep, I couldn't eat, and I couldn't stop checking my phone. I confessed some of how I felt to Stella, who obviously thought I was completely loopy. She said she would make sure the next one was less dishy, less fall-in-loveable, so that I could do what I was supposed to do and just have a good time for a few hours.

But there would never be a next one, I knew that. I couldn't inflict that pain on myself ever again. My one evening of passion may only have lasted one evening, but to me it was very real and far too precious to soil with imitation. It was like a tiny delicate flower growing in the desert of my life and I wouldn't let anything kill it. I would nurture it with my tears and my love and I wouldn't let it wither away. I told myself that when I was an old lady in my rocking chair I would hold it tenderly in my hands and maybe, by then, I'd be able to smile at the memory.

****

And that was the ridiculous stage I'd reached a week after That Evening. I was tearful and maudlin and drowning in self-pity. The kids tiptoed around me and Roger suddenly found lots of jobs he needed to do in his shed. And then today, Saturday, something happened. It was such a little thing that ordinarily it would have passed me by, but in my super-sensitive state I grabbed it with both hands like a drowning person would a lifebuoy. I was sitting in the café in Tesco's, staring into a cup of tea and trying to summon up the energy needed to push a trolley up and down the aisles. Two young women, full of fun and laughter, were sitting at the table next to me. One of them started scrabbling about in her shopping bag, and I couldn't help seeing that she was showing her friend some knickers she'd just bought. The next bit of conversation, conducted in a stage whisper, was sufficiently animated to rouse me from my puddle of misery, and it went something like this:

'God, you wouldn't catch me wearing those! I tried a thong once and it was really uncomfortable – I had to take it off after an hour and go round with no knickers on till I got home.'

'Oh, they're not that bad! You get used to them after a while. Anyway, Gary loves them and that's a good enough reason for me to wear them.'

'You mean, you wear them just for him? That's crazy!'

'Is it? Why do you think he's still so mad about me?'

They dissolved into giggles then, and left the café. I sat on at my table and thought about the knickers I was wearing. The most positive thing I could think to say about them was that they were comfortable. Sexy they definitely were not.

'She wears a thong just for Gary,' I muttered to myself as I piled bags of apples, potatoes and satsumas into my trolley. 'And he's mad about her.' It was so easy to blame Roger for the lack of passion in our marriage, but maybe it was time I took a look at it from his point of view. When had I last tried to look sexy for him? When had we last had dinner by candlelight? When - and this question made me feel so ashamed - when had I last told him I loved him?

I was loading the shopping into the bags when I heard someone calling my name. Lindy from down the road was at the next checkout, with her husband, waiting their turn to be served. I waved at them and turned back to my bags, but not before I had noticed that they were holding hands. When had Roger and I last held hands? Would he like it if we did? Was he just waiting for some encouragement from me, or had he given up on us too?

I drove home very slowly. The house was completely quiet and I remembered that Roger had taken the children round to his parents for the day. To get out of my crabby way, for all our sakes. I couldn't remember, probably because I'd never asked, whether he was going to just drop them off or stay with them.

'Rog?' I called, suddenly wanting him to be there. But there was no answer. I unloaded the shopping and carried the loo rolls through to the bathroom, and stopped in the doorway. Roger lay in the bath, his head cushioned on the plastic pillow, and his eyes closed. I smiled. Roger had a habit of falling asleep in the bath. I sat down on the loo seat and had a good look at him, this man I had been married to for 12 years. The hairs on his chest wafted gently in the water as he breathed, and he looked so peaceful, so relaxed. One hand lay cupping his penis and I pictured how it would look under it. He had a beautiful penis. I used to tell him that, often, when we were first married. I hoped he wasn't getting cold. I leant forward to feel the temperature of the water, and it was barely lukewarm. I touched his knee, and he opened his eyes.

'Hello darling,' I murmured, and his eyes widened a little in surprise.

'Sorry, I fell asleep,' he said unnecessarily, and we both laughed.

I reached for the bath towel on the radiator. 'Let me dry you,' I said, and he climbed out of the bath and stood in front of me. I slowly dried every inch of him, front and back, and when I'd finished he pulled me into his arms. We stayed like that for a long time, and when I drew back to look into his face his eyes were wet.

'Hello you,' he said softly, and then he kissed me.

What I hadn't appreciated before is that a kiss is made up of two halves. If one half doesn't respond much, the other half gets discouraged. Well, I responded. I said sorry with that kiss, and thank you, and I love you and please let's try again. And when we broke apart he said,

'I'll just call Mum and get her to keep the kids overnight.'

****

It was supposed to be a bit of fun, my evening with Simon, and it was a lot of things, but fun wasn't one of them. It was scary and exciting and it gave me just the jolt I needed. It's no good drifting through life vaguely wishing things were better - you have to grab happiness with both hands and that's exactly what I intend to do. Roger won't know what's hit him.

No more boring nights slumped in front of the telly and then flopping into bed, too sluggish and indifferent to manage anything more than a quick peck on the cheek. From now on life will be full of surprises and loving attentiveness and even some passion, if what happened after Roger's bath tonight is anything to go by. I'm going to live in a flower-filled garden, not a desert, and when I'm an old lady in a rocking chair I intend to have chalked up so many delicious memories that I'll probably be grinning all the time.

Bedsit no.2

Tuesday January 6th

I'm writing in my new pad today, in honour of the New Year. It has lovely smooth pages, and my pen is gliding over the surface. My writing, as a result, is suddenly more fluid, more dreamy, perhaps more truthful? I should get quality paper more often. Usually I buy the cheapest A4 pad the supermarket has to offer, but this time I treated myself to an up-market version, with a beautiful photograph of pink roses on its thick cardboard cover.

And by some strange coincidence pink roses are what Jack gave me yesterday. He appeared at the kitchen door clutching the most enormous bunch, so that I couldn't see his face behind the flowers. Pink roses in January! They must have cost the earth and they won't last of course, but they're lovely just the same. Perhaps they're all the more lovely because they've been forced to grow out of season, forced to be something that isn't natural for them, and they're doing their best to hide their confusion and be gracious about it. There's an edge of sadness to their beauty. And they have no scent at all.

Expensive flowers can only mean that after these last few tetchy weeks, he has finally embarked on his new affair. As I carefully arranged the roses in my largest vase I thanked her, whoever she may be, for winging the flowers my way and for giving Jack what he wanted. The chuckle in his voice is back, the lightness in his step, the bubbling good humour which fills the house with cheerfulness. The kids love it when he's like this. And so do I. He's like the man I married. It's just a pity she didn't succumb before Christmas so that we could all have been spared that distinctively unfestive crabbiness.

The man in the room next door has just come back from somewhere - probably the pub today, judging by how hard he's finding it to fit his key in the lock. I wait for the familiar sounds: the thud of his boots as they hit the floor, the telly leaping into life, the squeak of the springs as he collapses onto the bed. I love the fact that I've never met him; it makes me feel light and airy and insubstantial. No one in the world knows where I am. If I died in this shabby little bedsit, no. 2 it's called, if I died right now, it would be days, even weeks, before anyone knew. The strange little landlady would come to collect the month's rent from the drawer and find my corpse instead. That is just so liberating. This is the only place in the world where I feel perfectly free to be me. Not the loving wife, the perfect mother, the efficient secretary, the dutiful daughter-in-law – just me. For two whole hours twice a week I can do exactly what I want – write my novel or my stories or my journal, read, day-dream, paint my nails, sleep – and nobody knows or cares.

I think I'll just pop my earplugs in to muffle next door's telly. The canned laughter is a bit intrusive. There, that's better. That's perfect in fact. I wonder if, out of all the residents, I'm the most satisfied with my room in this battered old building. Apparently its official title is 'House of Multiple Occupation', which I think is delightfully anonymous. Obviously I'd feel differently about it if this was my home, rather than my bolt-hole. When I took it on I imagined I'd make a few improvements – find a pretty bed cover, replace the tatty curtains – but as the months have gone by I haven't altered a thing. I like it just the way it is. And the contrast with where I am and where Jack believes I am is hilarious.

'Had a good afternoon?' he'll say to me this evening with a knowing grin. 'Not bad at all!' I'll reply, modestly lowering my lashes as I pretend to be recalling the delights of romping all afternoon with my lover in his luxury flat. Martin is his name, I can't remember why. I wonder if he's been going on too long? Is it time I moved on to a new man? But I wouldn't want Jack to think Martin had tired of me. He loves the idea that I have a man, that somebody out there wants his wife, with unflagging consistency, twice a week. It's funny how different we are – I have to block all thought of him with his latest conquest, or else I dry up like a prune, whereas he's totally turned on by the idea that another man has been intimate with me only a few hours before.

And of course this regular arrangement of mine must mean that I find our 'open marriage' very satisfactory, that I can't possibly get upset by his behaviour and demand fidelity or anything unreasonable like that. After what happened to Angie when she issued her ultimatum to Max, I knew I could never risk making demands on him. It's just not in his nature to be monogamous, I know that. And I would so much rather have some of Jack than none of him. This way he's happy, the kids are happy, everyone thinks we have the perfect marriage. I don't think he wants to be married to anyone else, and I know I don't. It's pretty good to be able to say that after ten years of marriage. Isn't it? Lots of people haven't got what we have. I just wish I didn't feel so utterly miserable sometimes. Like right now.

I've just checked the time and I've only got five minutes left. It's extraordinary how the hours speed by in bedsit no.2, even on one of my least productive afternoons. I've just got time to splash my face in the plastic sink and re-do my mascara. Then I must pick the kids up from school, and speak to Becca's mum about the sleepover next Friday. We'll call in at that new deli on the way home and pick up something special for dinner; perhaps a large wedge of creamy dolcelatte to have after the casserole. I'll wear my black velvet dress and light the candles and we'll go to bed early. Jack's always extra loving on Tuesdays and Fridays and I do so adore it when he's loving. Whatever the reason.

Thank you Martin xx

Babysitting

It was fortunate that Sally was standing at the kettle with her back to me when she delivered her bombshell, as there was no way I could have hidden my look of horror. I have never been able to disguise my feelings, and learning that poor little Emma had got herself pregnant by that moronic boyfriend of hers filled me and my face with disgust at the stupidity, the carelessness, the utter wrongness of it all. In the time it took Sally to fill the teapot and return to the table, I had done my best to adopt an expression of calm concern.

She plumped herself down opposite me and poured the tea, still chattering away as if the situation were perfectly natural. 'Do help me finish up the Christmas cake,' she coaxed, passing me a wedge. She was willing me to be nice.

I cleared my throat and attempted a smile. 'Does she want to keep it?' I enquired in the most level of voices, and then stared fixedly at the chip on the rim of my mug as Sally said, 'Oh yes! She and Darren are really excited about it, now that they've got over the initial shock.'

Excited! I took a large bite of cake and chewed away. What right had they got to be excited about bringing another baby into the world, when they were little more than babies themselves? Emma was sixteen, for heaven's sake, and Darren not much older. Who was supposed to pay for this baby when the parents hadn't even begun to think about how they might earn a living? The whole thing was ridiculous, and had Emma been my daughter and not my neighbour's, I would have lost no time in marching her straight off to have an abortion clinic, , so that she could get on with her life.

'I knew you wouldn't approve,' Sally said with a rueful laugh. 'And of course it's not exactly the way I'd imagined becoming a grandmother. Darren's mum was livid when she heard and has rather disowned him, poor lad, so it looks as though I've gained a son along with the baby.... But he's not a bad kid, once you get to know him.'

'Has he got a job?' I asked bluntly.

'Well no, not at the moment, but he's got an interview on Friday – kitchen porter at the Red Lion – and he's pretty hopeful. And Emma's working hard for her GCSE's, so at least she'll have some qualifications to help her find a job later on.'

She reached over and patted my hand. 'Oh come on, Jill, don't look so grim! I know it's not ideal, but there's no point being gloomy. What's happened has happened, and I'm determined to make the best of it. You never know what life's going to throw your way – you just have to smile and get on with it.'

That was Sally all over. Always accepting, never protesting or trying to change things. Sometimes her acquiescence made me want to shake her. Instead I looked at my watch and pretended I needed to be somewhere else.

'I'd better be off,' I said. 'Give my love to Emma, won't you, I'll see you both soon.'

But I didn't see them both soon. Without consciously trying, I managed to avoid having a conversation with either of them for several months. And the longer I left it, the harder it became to make the first move. I waved to Sally from the safety of my car, and twice I shouted hello to Emma over the garden hedge, but that was all, until one morning Sally rang and invited me for supper.

'We don't seem to have seen you for ages,' she said, 'I thought it was time we had a catch-up.' The world would be a sadder place without people like Sally. She knew full well that I was upset about the baby, but she wasn't going to let that ruin what had been up until now a pretty good friendship. She was making the effort and I owed it to her to respond in full.

I had a large glass of sherry before setting out, to fortify myself for the ordeal ahead. Small talk with idiot Darren wasn't going to be easy, but I was determined to do my best.

As it happened, I needn't have worried. Darren had got the job at the Red Lion, and was hard at work doing whatever it was a kitchen porter did. So it was just me and Sally and Emma, sitting in the kitchen eating lasagne and salad. I have to say that Emma was looking quite lovely, almost radiant. She had always been a pretty girl, but pregnancy had given her a new serenity, a calmness, that made her seem older than her sixteen years.

I was relieved that there didn't seem to be any awkwardness after our four month estrangement. I told them about my holiday in Sorrento with the art group, and made them both laugh as I recounted the trials of being stuck in the hotel lift for two hours with George and Wendy. Emma was quietly confident about her impending exams, and nonchalantly declined my noble offer to give her some maths coaching and French practice. Some people just don't appreciate the effort one makes for them. Her only worry seemed to be that the baby might decide to make an early appearance in the middle of her exams and prevent her from finishing them. The actual birth didn't seem to bother her much. 'Mum and Darren will be with me,' she said, 'I'll be fine.' Such a close-knit family they seemed, bonded by genuine affection and joy about the baby, and I was ashamed to realise I felt jealous.

When James was born I was all alone in the cottage hospital, my mother being the last person I would have wanted at my side for support. We didn't have that kind of relationship. And Clive had made it very clear that his duties ended when he handed me over to the nurse. 'Phone me when it's all over,' he had said, with a hearty laugh. Well, that's what men were like back then, none of this touchy-feely stuff. I wouldn't have wanted him there anyhow, I'd only have fretted that he was bored, or disgusted. Ours may not have been the perfect marriage, but at least we had done things properly, and waited a few years until we had saved up enough money to have a baby. Not like the irresponsible young things nowadays, who know that the taxpayer will pick up the tab for their inability to plan or wait. I was getting angry all over again. Emma was saying she'd like a water birth if possible, and I made myself smile and say all the right things, but inside I was seething.

'Goodness, is that the time?' I said as soon as the apple crumble was cleared away. 'I've got an early start tomorrow,' I lied, and I made my escape. I didn't like myself for feeling so cross and resentful and bitter, but I couldn't help it. Call me old-fashioned, but there are ways of doing things, and Emma's situation offended me to the very core of my being. This was clearly the result of poor parenting; Sally should have been more disciplined with Emma, instead of letting her having such a free rein. I firmly believe that it's a mother's job to be a parent, not a friend, but whenever I said this to Sally she just laughed. My parents were extremely strict with me and my sister, and as a result we have both led calm, disciplined lives.

There was of course that brief period of rebellion when I was seventeen, when I found myself a most unsuitable boyfriend, but that was quickly nipped in the bud and quite right too. Just imagine what might have happened had Sam and I been allowed to stay together. He was very charming and rather wild and I often wonder what happened to him... But I can see that my parents only had my best interests at heart when they banned me from seeing him. Locking me in my room for ten days was perhaps a little extreme, but if that's what it took to make me promise never to contact him again, then it had to be done. I remember that I cried myself to sleep for weeks, but after a while I was able to settle back down to my studies and get some excellent A levels and go off to teacher's training college, exactly as planned. If I had carried on with Sam, goodness only knows what might have happened. He had no wish to improve himself, he said - he was perfectly happy tinkering with cars at the local garage, earning enough to pay the rent and drink plenty of beer. He was always telling me to lighten up, to enjoy life more. Enjoying life was not something my parents rated highly – self-discipline, responsibility, hard work, those were their values; and apart from my little wobble way back then, they have always been mine too. Mother knows best, I would tell myself as James was growing up and becoming a little headstrong. He needed me to make decisions for him (joining the scouts, taking violin lessons, choosing Latin rather than woodwork, dropping football) and make them I did, despite the protests and whinging.

And if he had not turned out as I had hoped, at least I could never blame my lax parenting for his failings. They must be due to Clive's genes - I had always found his brother Nigel distinctly peculiar. Of course it would be nice if James phoned me occasionally in response to the messages I left on his answering machine, but I consoled myself that once he'd run through the small legacy that

Clive had left him in his will, he was bound to get in touch with me, if only to ask for more money. A card or a phone call on my birthday would have been lovely, but everyone knows that it is hard for boys to remember these things.

I kept myself busy over the next few months, repainting my kitchen, and planting neat rows of runner beans and cabbages in the vegetable patch. I had, I realised, become somewhat obsessed by The Baby, and although I tried to drown out my thoughts with Radio 4, they snuck into my head at intervals throughout the day, and with a vengeance at night when I was trying to get to sleep. I kept remembering all the things Emma had been planning to do with her life - the travelling, the jobs in the fashion world, the opportunities that being young and unencumbered could provide. All that destroyed because of a thoughtless fumble with a stupid boy who couldn't be bothered to wear a condom. But surely she was on the pill? Maybe she'd forgotten to take it, which actually made her the idiot...No, I preferred the first version, I was rather fond of Emma.

She had been five when I had moved from London into Buttercup Cottage, and she and I had spent a lot of time together in those early days. Clive's life insurance and pension were such that there was no need for me to return to the teaching I had given up in order to nurse Clive after his stroke, and once I'd sorted my new home, my days were long and empty. After three long and frankly unrewarding years of caring for my pompous, dull and extremely heavy bed-ridden husband, I was finding it hard to adjust to life as an unemployed widow, with only myself to consider. I thought I would relish the freedom when it finally came, but I didn't. I was delighted to be able to offer my services to my new neighbour, who was sweet and friendly but quite frankly, rather hopeless as a mother. Sally often worked late at the hospice, and I was happy to look after Emma, making her nutritional meals and reading her sensible stories, even having her overnight sometimes. I had done my best to make up for Sally's shortcomings as a mother by being firm with the child and not letting her get away with any nonsense. I quite enjoyed her company, but for some reason her visits tailed off round about the age of eight, and I saw her much less often after that. I did wonder whether it was because Sally had become a little jealous of our special relationship. But I didn't let that bother me, and made sure that I invited myself to birthday tea parties and Christmas gatherings, so that I could give Emma proper educational presents to compensate for the Barbie dolls and other such rubbish that poor Sally saw fit to buy her.

    I have to admit that I was a little hurt that Emma hadn't told me her baby news herself, but I expect she was nervous of my reaction. She probably felt she had disappointed me, after all the trouble I had taken with her.

    I was nevertheless determined to do all I could to help her, and when I saw her sitting by herself in the village playground a few weeks before the baby was due, I hurried over. There were no children there, just Emma and her very large bump, slumped forlornly on a bench.

    'Are you alright, dear?' I enquired, sitting down next to her. Her only reply was to shake her head and blow her nose, so I sat patiently and waited. Finally she gave me a watery smile and then, with some coaxing, the whole sorry tale emerged. Darren, it seemed, had got cold feet as the birth date drew near. The scan that told them the baby was a boy had terrified him with the reality of it all, and he'd told Emma that, on second thoughts, he didn't think he was ready to be a dad, and that he was going to live in Scotland with a friend who could find him work up there.

    'Oh dear,' I said, thinking this might well be the best thing to have happened. Perhaps now she would realise that the sensible thing would be to give the baby up for adoption. But when I suggested this, Emma shrieked with horror. 'He's mine!' she exclaimed, clutching her belly possessively. 'I'm not giving him to anyone else, how could you even think that?' Then followed a torrent of tears and I grew a little anxious that all this emotion might bring on the baby. 'There, there,' I soothed, stroking her hair, 'It's alright, don't cry. Tell me what else Darren said.'

Not a lot, apparently. He would keep in touch, he had generously offered, and he would send her some money when he could, but essentially she was on her own.

'But you're not on your own!' I consoled her, grasping her hand between mine. 'You've got your mum – and of course you've got me! I've got lots of free time, I'll look after the baby when you need a break, it'll be fine, you'll see!' Emma collapsed onto me then and as I hugged her it suddenly hit me that I was the only person in the world able to give her some proper help. The sort of help that was based on practical common sense, not sloppy sentimentality.

I lay awake most of that night, thinking and planning. There was no doubt in my mind that this baby would ruin Emma's life. She was far too young to take on the responsibility, and Sally would only repeat the same mistakes with her grandson as she had with her daughter, with correspondingly disastrous results. And I knew only too well what misery a boy could cause, despite the best of upbringings. After all, no one could have been more conscientious or dedicated a mother to James than I had been, following Dr Spock to the letter and exerting exactly the right amount of discipline at every stage of his development. Yet I had received not one ounce of gratitude in return. James had found himself a menial job and left home as soon as he'd done his 'A' levels, rejecting all my helpful advice. The last time he had spoken to me was on January 12th four years ago, when he must have picked up the phone without checking the caller ID and was so cold and unfriendly that I would have wept, had I been that sort of woman. I wouldn't wish that pain on anyone, let alone poor unsuspecting Emma. It was now far too late for an abortion and she had ruled out adoption, so there remained only one way out of this mess. It's not always easy to do the right thing, but sometimes you have to be cruel to be kind.

    Baby Liam made his appearance two weeks later, and Sally reported that Emma had been very brave. I called round to see them a few hours after they arrived home, and the baby was small, spotty and very noisy. Emma, though, was besotted with him and kept exclaiming with wonder at his tiny fingernails. Sally was beside herself with excitement, skittering about, and wanting to hold the baby at every opportunity. Mindful of the momentous task I had set myself, I acted every inch the doting auntie, cooing and smiling and generally behaving like a perfect fool.

    The next few weeks were torture for me. I knew that every minute that went by was bonding Emma closer to her baby, but she refused to let him out of her sight. Finally, after days of watching and waiting, I got my chance. Sally had to be at work, Emma had been invited to a party just around the corner, could I mind Liam for a couple of hours? Of course I could, I would be delighted.

    He was brought round to my cottage in his little Moses basket, and Emma and I settled him on my bed. He was fast asleep. I would be in the kitchen, I said, just down the passage, and I would pop in and check on him every twenty minutes or so. If he cried I would cuddle him back to sleep. He wouldn't be hungry, as he had just been fed. Nothing could possibly go wrong, I assured her, she should go off to her party and have a bit of fun, she deserved a treat.

After a final adoring gaze at the baby, Emma was gone, promising to be no longer than two hours. It didn't give me long, but it was now or never. If I shirked my responsibility, I might not get such an opportunity again for a long time.

I had read up about cot death on the internet, and knew that about three hundred babies died of it each year, that the peak age was two months, and that boys were fifty percent more at risk. Liam was six weeks old, so the timing was perfect. There would be a post-mortem of course, to ascertain the cause of death, but apparently usually no cause is ever found. Babies sometimes just stop breathing, no one knows why. Emma would be distraught for a while, and would need lots of comforting and support through her grieving period – but then we could gently start talking about her future, and revive all those plans that had been put on hold, and in time she would appreciate what a lucky escape she had had.

I thought about having a drink to calm myself, but decided against it. I needed all my faculties sharply in focus for this task. I had worked out exactly how to do it, now I just had to get on with it. I glanced at the kitchen clock and saw that fifteen minutes had already passed since Emma's departure. I went into my bedroom and looked down on the sleeping baby. The bedside light cast a soft glow over the Moses basket and I had to admit that Liam looked rather sweet, lying there with his tiny fists up on either side of his face as if to say, ' I surrender, do what you must, it's alright.' Emma had placed a soft fleecy baby blanket over him, and all I had to do was pull it up and lay it over his face, covering his mouth and nose. I wasn't sure if he would struggle a bit in an effort to breathe, but if so, I could just hold down the blanket until he stopped.

I very slowly started to move the blanket up, over the top of his chest and onto his face. I had reached his chin when suddenly the phone in the hallway rang, and I froze. Liam gave a little whimper but didn't open his eyes. I let go of the blanket and raced to the phone, anxious that it wouldn't wake him up. I wasn't sure that I could do what I had to do if his eyes were open.

I lifted the receiver.

'Hello,' I whispered.

'Hello Auntie Jill,' said Emma, 'I just had to check that Liam is alright – is he still asleep?'

My mouth was completely dry. 'Yes dear, he's fast asleep,' I said, hoping that my voice didn't sound strange. I swallowed. 'You mustn't worry. How's the party?'

'Oh it's ok, but I don't want to be here – it all seems a bit silly, you know, just people mucking about and talking rubbish – all I want to do is get back to Liam. I'm going to leave in a minute.'

My plan was crumbling. 'Oh no, don't do that,' I said. 'There's really no need to hurry back, why don't you stay and enjoy yourself?'

'That's just it, I can't enjoy myself away from him! I never realised it would feel like this, having a baby, every second away from him I feel terrible! I never knew that love could be so strong, isn't it amazing? Everything else seems so unimportant when you love somebody this much!'

In the background I could hear the thumping of music and someone near Emma let out a shriek of laughter. I didn't know what to say.

'So anyway,' she said, 'I'll just say hello and goodbye to a few people and then I'll be back to pick him up – see you in about twenty minutes, bye.'

I replaced the receiver and just stood there for a minute, staring at it. I felt so humbled by that phone call. Had I ever, in my entire life, experienced anything close to that kind of love? Not for Clive, that went without saying, but had I ever felt like that about my own baby? I knew that I hadn't. I'd done my duty by James, but that was all - we both knew that, which was why we now had no relationship at all, and would never be able to have one. I hated myself, and no wonder. I would die a lonely unloved old woman, because where my heart should have been was a dried-up husk. Emma and Sally, with their generous, loving natures, were worth so much more than me. Their love, for each other and for the baby, was completely unconditional, and I realised, with a shudder of shame, that this was an alien concept to me. All my life I had been nothing but a bossy, conceited control freak, judging people and trying to make them conform to my ideas. All my life I had thought I knew best, but now I realised I'd actually been completely ignorant about the only thing that mattered.

I walked very slowly back into the bedroom, back to the tiny defenceless infant I'd had the breathtakingly arrogant stupidity to consider smothering. I couldn't bear to think how close it had been. I looked down at little Liam, who would never know that this night had nearly been his last. I gently pulled the fleecy blanket down from his chin, and I reached in to stroke his head. He stirred a bit, and made a little kissing noise. It was as if he were forgiving me.

'I'm so sorry, little man,' I whispered to him. I carried on stroking his soft little head very gently with my finger. 'I'll make it up to you, I promise. We'll have such fun, you and I. I won't boss you about, I'll let you be just who you want to be....'

Back in the kitchen I poured myself a large glass of Merlot and collapsed onto a chair. My knees were shaking

and so was my hand, and a splash of wine landed on my notebook, where I had been writing a list of jobs to do. I love writing lists, I feel so productive and in control of my life as I draw a line through each completed task. I stared down at my instructions to myself for the following day:
- Water conservatory
- Pay gas bill
- Change sheets
- Hem new trousers
- Book car in for MOT

It all seemed so sterile, boring, selfish. I picked up the pen and wrote:
- Buy camera for taking pictures of Liam

That made me smile with anticipation. I had so few pictures of James, partly because Clive always said it was a silly extravagance, but partly, if I'm honest, because I too could never see the point. But now I could. Poor James. I added another job to my list.
- Write to James. Tell him you're sorry.

I had so much to apologise for that I hardly knew where to begin. Perhaps I should start by taking back the things I had said about his girlfriend, that last time we argued. For all I knew, she could be his wife now! Perhaps I had missed my own son's wedding through sheer stupidity and pig-headedness.

Emma arrived, breathless and full of gratitude to me for having looked after the baby, and shame trickled down my back like cold sweat. Then they were gone, and suddenly I couldn't wait to get started on my letter.

'Dear James,' I wrote, and my pen flew across the pages as I confessed and retracted and criticised myself. After forty years of being convinced I was right all the time, it felt so liberating, so purifying, so breathtakingly honest, to finally admit that I had been wrong. About everything. I even found myself telling him about long-ago Sam, and I said that perhaps it was having to close the door on that happiness that had stunted the loving part of me, had turned me into someone cold. I said that I intended to open the door now and let the love flood in. I said that I hoped he could forgive me, so that we could try again.

It was nearly two o'clock when I finally ran out of things to apologise for and explain, and I had just enough energy left to crawl into bed, light-headed with tiredness and relief. I felt vulnerable and yet strong at the same time; the suit of armour that had cloaked and choked me all my adult life was gone, and the freedom was exhilarating. I could still feel the softness of that tiny velvety head beneath my fingers.

'Good night little Liam,' I said into the darkness, and I do believe that I fell asleep smiling.

Something Wild

It was Dad's remark that got me thinking. It was Sunday night, our regular film slot, and we had just watched 'Thelma and Louise' on the telly. We were sprawled in our armchairs trying to get our heads round the wonderful, terrible ending, when he said wistfully, 'I can't imagine what it would be like to have that much fun.' He meant, of course, the 'to hell with it all' high spirits that blazed out of the women when they were bombing along the highway, drinking whisky and yelling along to the music on the car stereo. They were in serious trouble with the law, seeing as how Louise had killed a man and Thelma had committed armed robbery, but despite their problems, they were obviously having the time of their lives.

My dear old dad, an 83-year-old widower, has always been very calm and sensible, as far as I know. He was a postman all his life, up at the crack of dawn and in bed by 9 o'clock, so not much scope for fun there. In his spare time he collected stamps and went to steam engine rallies, but now he's old he hardly does anything at all. It was obviously too late now for him to have some wild fun, but it was not too late for me. Though it would be, pretty soon. The question was, how was I going to find it? I couldn't just sit around waiting for it to happen, I had to *make* it happen with some decisive action. Wild fun meant men, I thought, or at least one man, and it was high time I tried looking for one.

So you can see that I was in a wholly receptive frame of mind when I saw the ad on the noticeboard of the local shop the following Thursday. I always have a quick look at the notices to see if anyone in the village has anything interesting for sale, and there at the bottom, next to Debbie's flier offering gardening services, was a yellow card that certainly hadn't been there the last time I'd looked. It leapt off the board and hit me between the eyes, and I scrabbled in my bag for a pen and bit of paper so I could copy it down. As soon as I got back home I sat myself down at the kitchen table and studied the advertisement that might be going to change my life for ever:

Looking for love and fun? Farmer, handsome, 6 ft, young 50's, look no further! Phone John on 07700900496

He sounded so confident, so full of life and so ready for someone. Maybe that someone could be me? Or was I too late, had lots of other women seen the yellow card and already contacted him? Women who were younger, prettier, more appealing than me?

I went into the bathroom and made myself take a good hard look in the mirror over the basin. It's not something I do very often, but really, it wasn't so bad. You could see that I spend a lot of time outdoors, but a farmer wouldn't mind that. He would probably be ruddy-cheeked himself, and we would want to match, complexion-wise. At least I look healthy – not like some of those scrawny stick-creatures you see wafting around, just waiting for a gust of wind to blow them over. Sturdy, that's what I am, and there's nothing wrong with that. Nice straight teeth, a bit yellow it's true, but if I don't open my mouth too wide he won't notice. What I have been lucky is with my hair – plenty of it, and curly, so that I've never had to bother with rollers and such like. I just wash it and leave it and occasionally give it a trim with the kitchen scissors. A touch of grey here and there, but that only shows character, I think. Like the wrinkles. After all, if you didn't have those, your face would look all bland and boring. And wrinkles round the eyes show you smile a lot, have a good sense of humour. I read that once in a magazine and it cheered me up no end.

I went back to check the ad. 'Handsome', he says. Well, I could say 'attractive', on a good day. 'Young 50's' he says. Now that's interesting. If he were under 55 he'd surely say 'early 50's'. So 'young 50's' probably means he *feels* young, but is actually nearer 60. That's okay, I wouldn't want him younger than me. I certainly don't feel 56; some days I feel more like 12, when the sun's shining and I get an overwhelming urge to roll all the way down Pinder Hill as I did as a girl and land in a giggling heap at the bottom. I don't, of course, but I want to, and that's what I mean about needing a man to do something wild with. Something wild in a field. I expect he's got lots of fields we could do something wild in.

I decided to phone the number in the ad right away, before I chickened out. Dad was having his weekly pensioners' lunch at the village hall, so the coast was clear. The phone call went like this:
- Brrrring, brrrring
- Hello? (the voice was mature male, casual, confident.)
- Yes, hello, is that John?
- Speaking.
- Er, my name's Shirley, and I'm phoning in response to the ad on the shop noticeboard.
- What ad would that be? I didn't think I'd put an ad there lately. Was it for a cattle drinker?
- No, it was headed 'Looking for love'....

- (long pause) 'Looking for love? What, you mean like Lonely Hearts?
- Yes.
- (another pause) Really? Can you tell me what it said?
- (horribly embarrassed) Well, it goes, 'Looking for love and fun? Farmer, handsome, 6 ft, young 50's, look no further! Phone John.' And then it gives your number.
- (guffawing) Hee, hee, hee!
- That's not you then?
- Hah, hah, hah! I'll get him for this! Hee, hee, hee!
- (cough)
- Oh, sorry love,(chortle, chortle), it's my crazy son's idea of a joke. He always does something good for April Fool's Day, I've been waiting to see what he came up with this year, he's surpassed himself this time! Hah, hah! Wait till I get my hands on him! Young 50's indeed!
- You're not in your 50's then?
- I was 67 last time I looked! (More laughter, cut short) Sorry, love, but I'll have to turn you down. The missus wouldn't be too pleased, you see.
- Yes, of course, sorry to have bothered you. Goodbye.

After I'd hung up I went for a walk. It was a blustery kind of day, with little flurries of rain starting up from nowhere and dying away just as quickly. The trees were dancing about in the wind and they seemed to be teasing me, laughing at me and my stupid hopes and dreams. I strode along very fast, head down, trying at first not to cry and then thinking, 'Oh go on then, it doesn't matter if you howl your head off, there's no one to see.' Before long I emerged at the top of Pinder Hill, and as I gazed out over the valley I could see a rainbow. I love rainbows. And I cried a bit more then, looking at all the beautiful nature, and letting go of the idea that I could ever do something wild with someone who loved me.

I lay down on my back and looked up at the sky and at the wispy clouds scurrying along. The wind died down, and the sunshine played on my face and comforted me. And I thought, 'I don't need to have fun with someone else. I can do something wild with just me, right now.'

I guess rolling down a hill isn't everyone's idea of an exciting time, but believe me, it can be very exhilarating if you do it right. You have to get up enough speed, and keep your arms and legs springy, and push off with your elbow at just the right time at every roll. There's quite a knack to it, and I hadn't forgotten. When I got to the bottom, I lay there for a while, getting my breath back and grinning with pride. I even giggled a bit.

And then I went home, a little stiff and sore after my adventure, but also much happier. I had a long soak in the bath and then searched about in the video cupboard for a good film to watch with Dad on Sunday. I found 'Goodbye Mr Chips' and put it ready by the telly. We haven't watched it for ages, and it would be just the thing to get us back on an even keel. Nice and soothing, with no surprises and an entirely to-be-expected ending. Not a bit like 'Thelma and Louise', which was probably too unsettling for Dad. I'll make sure we stick to gentle films from now on; it's not good for him to get churned up about things at his time of life.

After all, when I feel like a bit of excitement I can always roll down Pinder Hill.

Alice Bridger: my statement

Friday February 26th

Mr Nutshall says it may help my defence and the outcome of the trial if I write down everything that has happened. I don't really want to do it, but the hours are very long in here and it's not as if I have anything else to do. It's good that I'm allowed to stay in my room most of the time, because on the few occasions I've made it to the dayroom I absolutely hated it, the stares, the questions, the roughness of those dreadful women with their tattoos and bleached hair. I would much rather be left alone in here.

But I have always been such an active bustly sort of person, I think I'll go mad if I don't do something with all this time I suddenly have, so I'll give it a go. Start at the beginning, says Mr Nutshall, explain what your life was like when you met Dave, and carry on from there. Take it slowly, he says, just say how you were feeling. Perhaps putting it all down calmly and logically will go some way to explaining why I behaved the way I did. Perhaps it will all make sense.

I haven't written anything more than a thank-you letter to Aunt Nora since I left school, so this isn't going to be easy. I don't like the idea of strangers reading what I've written and judging me, feeling sorry for me, not understanding. So what I've decided to do is pretend that I'm writing this, not for Mr Nutshall, but for some nice sweet motherly lady who would be kind and sympathetic and maybe even understand. Mary, I'll call you. This is for you, Mary.

I've just walked around the room a bit and sat down again. I'm feeling ridiculously nervous about this. I don't want to write about me, as though I'm at all important. I know perfectly well that I'm not, I'm an absolute nobody. I've always been a timid sort of person, staying in the shadows, happy to look on from the side lines and not be noticed. Before I did what I did to Dave, if you had asked me to name something adventurous that I'd done, I'd have been really stumped. Would shoplifting a toothbrush from Boots count? In my defence, the queue was a mile long and my time was nearly up in the car park. And the toothbrush was very cheap....Even now, years later, I can feel my cheeks burning with the shame. I felt so guilty every time I used the wretched thing that in the end I threw it away and bought another much more expensive one. From the same shop of course, to make amends.

I'm waffling a bit, stalling for time, like I used to in history essays at school when I didn't have enough material to answer the question. But I do know enough this time. I must be disciplined and just get on with it. I'll start at the beginning.

I was born in Reading, an only child, and lived on the outskirts of the town with my parents. My father was a successful accountant, and my mum took in ironing. She didn't need to, we had plenty of money, but she loved ironing and was very good at it. I should say at this point that she suffered from agoraphobia, and this job was something she could do without leaving the house; people would drop off their ironing and come and collect it, and she hardly had to speak to them at all. She liked the idea of being useful, I think, but she didn't want to talk to her clients. As well as being agoraphobic she was extremely shy and found it really hard to talk to people. I often wondered how she and my dad, also very quiet, ever managed to get together. Their courtship must have been monosyllabic. Mum liked cooking and housework and was, now I come to think of it, rather a boring woman. Just like me. She was a good cook though, we always had a nice tea to look forward to every evening. Dad and I used to do the shopping together, which I quite enjoyed, it was our bit of together time and we often rewarded ourselves with a cup of tea in the cafe before heading on home. Those shopping trips stopped when the local supermarket started doing online ordering. Dad was delighted - he thought supermarket shopping was woman's work and rather demeaning for an important chap like him.

I had no friends at all at school, and was rather bullied because I was plump back then and a bit of a swot. I never got invited to anyone's house after school, or to parties; I pretended not to notice all the fun things that were going on around me, but it hurt a lot to be so left out. I dived into my books instead and worked really hard, and especially enjoyed maths. I got my 'A' levels, and thought maybe I'd train to be an accountant like Dad. But before I had a chance to do anything, Mum burnt the house down by setting fire to the kitchen curtains with the chip pan. She was very traumatised by this event, well we all were, but Mum was inconsolable. We moved to a far nicer house near Calcot, to make a fresh start, but her agoraphobia grew much worse. Dad thought the beautiful garden might encourage her to get out of the house, but as it turned out, she rarely left her bedroom, and most days she didn't even want to get out of bed. So I had to stay home and look after her and take over the cooking and housework and gardening. The thing is, I didn't really mind, it meant that I had a good excuse not to do anything more challenging.

So for the next 8 years I looked after my mum, but I guess I wasn't much good at it because she grew worse and worse and then one day she just gave up and died. I went in with her lunch on a tray, scrambled eggs on toast it was, and she was lying there with her mouth open, as if she had at last thought of something interesting to say, only there was no one there to hear it.

The next bombshell was that Dad had a heart attack. According to the doctor he'd had angina for years but he hadn't liked to say anything because Mum was so bad. He died 6 weeks after her, while watching some golf tournament on the telly. I'd been in the garden all afternoon, pruning the hydrangeas, and I went into the kitchen to make us both a cup of tea. Only when I took his in to him I could see at once he wouldn't be needing it. I sat with him quietly for a while before I phoned the ambulance.

I sat there and talked to him gently and drank both cups of tea to keep my strength up.

So there I was, an orphan at 26, with no career but with 2 lots of generous life assurance, savings in the bank, a trust fund and a lovely house with no mortgage. I bought an annuity to give me a monthly income and I had enough money not to have to work at all, but I thought I ought to do something. Like Mum, I wasn't confident about mixing with people, so I did an online accountancy course which I found dead easy, and then advertised in the local paper for small businesses to get me to do their tax returns for them. I hardly left the house and garden except when I had to go shopping or change my library books. I was pretty happy, actually, leading my boring little life. I had no friends but that didn't bother me. My clients would just drop the paperwork off and disappear, supremely grateful that someone else was trawling through the figures for them. It's fortunate that what some people hate to do, others love; personally, I found it deeply satisfying to produce a neat column of figures from piles of receipts. I was in my element when the kitchen table was covered in orderly monthly piles, just waiting for the stapler to keep them firmly in place for ever. I felt so in control, with everything just as it should be.

That was before I met Dave.

I think I'll stop for today. I'm actually quite pleased with what I've managed, perhaps this isn't going to be as hard as I thought.

Saturday February 27ᵗ

The accountancy business was supposed to be a little sideline, but word got round that I was cheap and efficient, and it wasn't long before I was turning people away. I was earning far more than I needed to live on, and hadn't even touched my trust fund. I couldn't seem to find anything to spend money on. Other people had holidays and ate in restaurants and bought big tv's and had their hair done, but I wasn't interested in any of that. One of the best things about having Dave in my life was that suddenly there was a reason for being well-off. Dave was awfully good at spending money.

It was on a rainy October afternoon that I met him. I had spent the afternoon in the library, one of my favourite places – it's so calm and quiet and always exactly the same. There was a really nice lady who worked there, Lesley her name was, and she looked out the latest romances for me and put them to one side. I suppose she was the nearest thing I had to a friend. I had a favourite chair in the reference section, and I enjoyed browsing through the art books. Pre-Raphaelite painters it was that day, lovely stuff.

So I came out of the library and was walking back to the car park, just pootling along minding my own business, still thinking about those beautiful paintings. As I approached the car, I could see that there was a man peering in at the driver's window, which was a bit odd. I hung back a bit, to see if he'd go away, but he didn't, he moved round to the back and seemed to be stroking the bodywork. This was terrible, I thought. It was beginning to grow dark, it was drizzling and I wanted to go home. Surely if I moved towards the car, he'd be embarrassed and move away....

I soon learnt that absolutely nothing embarrassed Dave.

'Well hello there!' he boomed at me as I approached. I was pretending to be looking in my bag for my keys so that I could act as though I was surprised to see him.

He didn't wait for me to answer but kept right on, telling me what a gorgeous car I had and asking me all sorts of questions about it that I couldn't answer. How many miles to the gallon, what was the engine size, that sort of thing. Of course, I had no idea. The Jag was my dad's car, his pride and joy, and when he died I did the easiest thing which was to register it in my name and carry on driving it. Otherwise I would have had to sell it and buy another car, both of which seemed daunting prospects, and unnecessary ones at that, when I had a perfectly nice car at my disposal. I have to admit I enjoyed the polished walnut dashboard and the beautiful leather seats and the satisfying thud it made when I shut the door. Poor old dad had nothing much to spend his money on, since his wife wouldn't leave the house, let alone go on holiday. So his one extravagance was to give the garage down the road loads of money every year to maintain his cherry red Jaguar E type. One of his little rituals was polishing the dashboard and rubbing hide food into the burgundy leather, while listening to the football or cricket on the car radio. I think he was at his happiest then.

Dave told me later, much later, that he'd seen me drive into the car park that afternoon. It was the car he noticed of course, but he was interested to see a youngish woman getting out. After I'd gone he'd looked to see when my ticket ran out and made sure he was there waiting for me on my return. It was my car he fancied, not me.

Though, to give him his due, he did a very good job of hiding that fact. He soon realised that I wasn't very interested in the car, so he switched his conversation over to talking about me. I think the reason I fell for him so helplessly and completely is that no one had ever taken the trouble to talk to me about me before and I was entranced by the way it made me feel. For the very first time in my life I felt interesting and unusual and important. I felt as though I had just as much right to be on this earth as the next person and believe me, that was an extraordinary thing for me to feel.

Because it was drizzling, and because we still – apparently, amazingly – had so much to say to each other, it seemed only sensible that we should sit in the car to carry on with our conversation. At one point, when I was telling him about my dad dying, he reached over and squeezed my hand sympathetically, and I was so overwhelmed that I couldn't carry on talking. He could though, he was a great talker, my Dave. He told me all about himself (and I discovered later that some of it was even true) and he made me laugh, and after about half an hour it seemed perfectly natural that we should decide to carry on the evening in a cosy little Pizzeria he knew on the other side of town.

I had never been to a restaurant with anyone but my dad and my aunt Nora, and this was a whole new experience. The waiters seemed to know Dave well, and there was lots of joking and back slapping. We sat at a candlelit table and drank Chianti and ate delicious pizza and tiramisu and it was the best evening by a thousand miles that I had ever spent. He was so lovely to look at, with his laughing eyes and his messy hair and his grin. When I looked at his mouth, I felt weak with longing, and I kept wanting to touch his hand, his arm, any bit of him that was within reach. Because I had drunk too much wine, Dave drove me home in my car and helped me unlock the front door and kissed me on the cheek to say goodnight. I stumbled into bed, shocked and ecstatic and trembling and passed out immediately. In the morning I thought I must have dreamt it all, but when I looked out of the window, there was the Jag in the drive, not in the garage where I always put it, so I knew my magical evening had happened.

Of course I couldn't concentrate on my accounts that day. I kept getting up to look out of the window and to check that the phone wasn't off the hook and finally at 7.30 he rang. He said he hadn't been able to stop thinking about me all day and when could he see me again. Now, I said, come now.

That was a Friday, and he ended up staying all weekend. It was all so new to me, I didn't stop to think that maybe he would think more of me if I waited a bit. It seemed to me that I had waited far too long already.

I was a virgin of course, and a ridiculously ignorant one at that. I had always found the whole business of sex deeply embarrassing, and as it seemed very unlikely that I would ever need to have anything to do with it, I had managed to block the whole subject from my mind. If ever a lovey dovey scene came on the telly, I would decide it was time to make a cup of tea, so I hope you can see, Mary, why I was so bowled over by Dave and the novelty of sex. Maybe as a woman you will understand, maybe you were a late starter too....

I won't go into details, but I expect you can imagine the roller coaster of feelings I experienced that weekend. There were parts of my body that I didn't even know I had, and Dave brought them to life and made me cry, often, with the extraordinary depths of feeling that he awakened in me. I think (I hope) that my naivety made it fulfilling for him too. I know I wasn't much to look at, but I was so willing to learn and eager to please, and so responsive, in a way that perhaps a more sophisticated woman, who had done it all before, wouldn't have been. The weekend passed in a whirlwind of bed and wine and more bed and shared baths, and massages (of course I hadn't known there was such a thing as a massage) and lots and lots of talking, and by Sunday night I knew, with a ferocity that rather frightened me because I wasn't accustomed to feeling strongly about anything, that I didn't want Dave to go.

As it happened, he didn't need to leave on Monday morning because he was, as he put it, in between jobs. But I did have some accounts I needed to finish for a client who was collecting them at lunchtime, so I left him snoozing while I hurriedly checked the figures for the tax return, not much caring if they were right or not. Suddenly all that was unimportant.

It seemed so obviously the right thing to do. There was I, rattling round in this big house on my own, with far too much money and no one to talk to or share things with – and there was Dave, brimful of ideas and creativity and so much ENERGY, just needing someone to take care of the practical things like providing a home and paying the bills, so that he could do wonderful things with his life. It may seem to you, Mary, that we rushed into marriage, but I had never felt more certain about anything, ever. I know we had only known each other for 4 weeks, but I was never happier than that day in the registry office, with Lesley from the library, and Nora (Mum's younger sister) acting as witnesses. I remember that Nora did her best to persuade me to wait a bit when I phoned to invite her to the wedding, but I was so obviously happy and determined that she had to give way. She did insist on arriving the day before so that she could meet Dave, and he was so lovely that day, so charming, so loving towards me, that she melted and stopped protesting. She could see how it was.

Dave didn't invite anyone to the wedding, which I thought was a bit sad. But like me he was an orphan and an only child, and he said his friends were all busy that weekend, we hadn't given them enough notice. I hadn't actually met any of his friends at that point, there never seemed to be enough time as we were so wrapped up in each other, but he promised lots of exciting things like dinner parties and pub lunches and cinema outings with them. I couldn't wait for this wonderful-sounding social life.

We honeymooned in Las Vegas, Dave's idea. Frankly, I didn't care where we went as long as we were together, and it was quite fun, in a crazy sort of way. He adored the casinos and especially the roulette wheel, and I found I became quite addicted to a game called 'Coin Pusher' where you insert coins in the slot and try to position them so they push coins off the ledge. It is strangely mesmerising and you have to keep going because it's impossible to believe you're not just about to win lots and lots of coins. I didn't of course, but the game kept me happy while Dave did his more serious stuff at the roulette wheel. The fact is I'm not good at spending money, it makes me feel uncomfortable, even though I have plenty. So I was fine with my $10 worth of coins, that pile would keep me going all evening. But Dave, being the adventurous and courageous man that he was, preferred to play for much larger stakes. One evening he did really well, and was $3000 up when I went to bed. Unfortunately, he confessed over breakfast next morning that he hadn't been able to stop there, and had ended up losing it all. Well I could understand that, it was just like Coin Pusher, only a bit more expensive. And he looked so sweet as he confessed to me that we had already spent the

$5000 worth of Travellers Cheques and could he please have some more. Dave was very hard to say no to, back in those early days. I was so happy, I would have given him anything he wanted. Actually, I did give him anything he wanted. After all, as I kept telling myself, it was only money and I had plenty.

For the very first time it has occurred to me that being left all that money actually did me no favours at all.

Sunday, February 28th

After Dave and I got married, the money didn't stretch so far because there were two of us, and also it cost quite a lot to set up Dave's business. He had been out of work for a while when I met him, but it seemed obvious to me that with his energy and talents, he was bound to make a success of the furniture-making business he had always dreamed of. So we had a beautiful workshop built at the bottom of the garden and filled it with high quality tools and benches and so forth, and last month Dave finally finished the gorgeous coffee table he had made for the conservatory. He explained to me that making furniture is an art form; you can't just do it day after day like my dreary old accounts, you have to be in the mood. That's why, on days when he wasn't in the mood, perhaps because he had too much energy, he had to take himself off on an adventure. After 6 months he still hadn't actually earned anything from his business, but it was early days.... And I had enough for both of us ,so it was absolutely no problem. Dave said early on that he hated having to ask me for money, so we set up a separate account for him that I paid into each month. He said he was planning to branch out into drawing and painting, and art materials were so expensive . As soon as his business was up and running he would start to pay me back, but really I wasn't bothered. It was rather nice to be needed and to be able to help, and after all my life was so much richer with Dave than it was before I met him. It was love that mattered, not money, I told myself.

Dave and I couldn't have been more different, but I thought that only explained why we worked so well. Unlike him, I have to force myself to do anything outside my comfort zone. I think he liked the steady normality of me, which meant that his shirts were ironed, the bills were paid, there was always petrol in the car and beer in the fridge. That left him free to be the mad one, free to abseil down a cliff on a Saturday afternoon, or take a few days off work and go windsurfing instead. Sometimes he would take himself off on what he said was an all-night bike ride, whereas I was usually tucked up in bed with my book and cocoa at 10pm. He had so much pent-up energy that he needed to work off, whereas my preferred leisure activity was pottering around my garden doing a bit of gentle pruning, or going for a stroll along our pretty leafy lanes. In fact, he was away so much, that after a few months we decided to get a second car, and it made sense for him to have the Jag, which he loved, while I had a little Ford Fiesta, so much easier to park.

The sex tailed off pretty quickly. I was a bit sad about that, but not surprised, because of course Dave had all his other interests, taking up his time and his energy. I still felt so incredibly lucky. For boring old me to have found someone so exciting felt rather miraculous, and I thanked my lucky stars every day that my husband was the kind of man who constantly surprised me with his antics and adventures. Imagine if I had married someone like me, I used to say to myself, what a nondescript life we would be leading, doing the same old things day after day. I needed Dave ,I thought, for so many reasons, the main one being that he filled my life with vicarious excitement – I never knew what he was going to say as he burst in the door, and I could enjoy all the thrills without having to actually find them or experience them, which suited me down to the ground. Frankly, I couldn't imagine anything more ghastly than abseiling down a cliff face, but of course I didn't tell him that.

I would worry though, sometimes, sitting alone in my kitchen wondering what he was doing. When he had been gone for more than a couple of days I would grow a little despondent, and fret that my unadventurousness made me dull and predictable. Would he prefer to be with someone more like him? When I said this to him, he always laughed and said he liked me just the way I was, but still I couldn't stop the uneasiness niggling at me. I wished he'd say 'love', not 'like'. I would make myself sit down every day with the paper and note all the interesting stories so that I could tell Dave about them when he came home. He, of course, never had time to read the paper.

I would practice my lines before he came home. 'They've caught the man who robbed the Post Office,' I would tell him, injecting lots of bright intelligence into my normally rather flat voice. 'Apparently he had only just got out of prison, what a prize idiot!' I found 'From our own Correspondent' on Radio 4 a great source of interesting information. 'Did you know that in Azerbajan they drink tea through a sugar lump?!' Usually he just grunted in response. I wasn't being interesting enough, I thought, I had to try harder.

I was such a fool.

Wednesday March 3rd

I got a bit depressed after the last lot of writing and have been putting off continuing the sorry saga of my disastrous life, the heroine being the stupidest woman who has ever lived.... But Mr Nutshall was kind enough to say this morning that what I had written so far was 'enormously helpful', so I shall grit my teeth and keep going.

One of the things Dave used to do regularly (apparently), was have a night out with 'the boys' . I wished he would bring one or two of them back home so I could get to meet them, but I knew they wouldn't want to spend an evening with me when they could be down the pub doing whatever it is men do in pubs. So of course I never even suggested it, instead bravely declaring that I had something riveting to watch on the television.

It would probably have helped if there had been a girlfriend or two I could have called on for company on those many occasions when Dave was absent. It was funny how much lonelier I felt after meeting Dave than I had been previously. Before Dave, I had spent every evening on my own perfectly happily, but afterwards, I used to wish he was with me and wonder what he was doing instead.

'Perhaps a child would have filled the gap?' I can hear you asking, Mary. But I've never felt that urge to have children that I gather drives most women, and although I adored him, even I could see that Dave was far too irresponsible and selfish to be a good father, so that was a conversation we never bothered to have. I went to the doctor and put myself on the pill and that was that. Although sex was so infrequent after the first few weeks that I probably needn't have bothered.

I was happy enough, I thought. Probably not as consistently happy as I had been before I met Dave, but I told myself that the occasional highs from being with him compensated for the lows when I wasn't. 'I'm so lucky he's in my life,' I would say to myself as I washed and ironed his clothes. I would get a little thrill of pleasure each and every time I folded his underpants and laid them carefully in his drawer. I absolutely adored his body. ' How lucky I am to have someone to love,' I would say as I scrubbed his collars. You'll notice, Mary, that I didn't say 'someone who loves me.' I was stupid, there's no denying that, but not quite that stupid.

So I plodded on, making sure my days were full, with my garden, my accounts, and planning and cooking interesting meals for Dave. I had begun to take an interest in food, now that I had him to cook for, and I would spend hours looking at recipes and planning menus. I even started a dinner party file, with ideas for beautifully balanced 3 course meals, ready for that momentous occasion when Dave would invite some of his friends over. And of course, there was always the telly. I especially loved those programmes when people go house hunting, fortunately there are lots of those.

Also, I walked a lot. I wasn't at all sporty like Dave, but I've always loved walking. We have some delightful little lanes all round our house, and every day when it wasn't raining, and sometimes even when it was, I would take myself off for a lengthy stroll. One of my favourite walks took me past a handsome farmhouse, set back from the road and surrounded by a beautifully stocked garden. In the spring the azaleas and rhododendrons were simply breathtaking, and I always lingered to drink in the sight and the scent. The woman who used to live here drove a large 4 x 4 in a most aggressive manner; she always made me reverse for her if I was unfortunate enough to meet her in our narrow lane, and she never once smiled a thank you.

So I was delighted when I saw the 'For Sale' sign go up in October, and even more so when the 'Sale Agreed' board took its place only 3 weeks later. I kept walking past the house in the hope of catching a glimpse of the new owners. That's how lonely I was. Pathetic really.

Thursday March 4th

I remember very clearly the day I met Harry, because it was my 1st wedding anniversary, the 10th November. I had woken early, all excited and full of plans for the day. In my bedside drawer was the beautifully wrapped Rolex watch I had bought for my darling husband. But his side of the bed was empty. Lying on his pillow was a scrawled note. 'Morning sleepy head!' it said. 'Didn't want to wake you. Have gone off to join my walking group for a stomp around the Lake District, will do some painting too, back on Friday. Can you take my suit to the cleaners, ta xxx

I am used to disappointment. After all, most of my life has been one long disappointment. But that morning it took me quite some time to pull myself together. Fresh air would make me feel better I thought, so I took myself off for a walk, past the nice farmhouse. Perhaps the new people would have arrived.

As I rounded the bend in the road, I could see a tall, dark haired man, late 50's perhaps, in the process of screwing a stylish new letter box to the gate post. The name 'Willowgate Farmhouse' was painted in white against the black metal. I slowed my steps and hoped he would turn round. He must have heard me, because turn round he did, and my heart did a little flip at the sight of his smile. I guess I wasn't used to people greeting me with such friendliness. Dave had been rather off-hand for months, almost as if he resented spending any time with me at all. And of course my heart was still feeling bruised from earlier.

''Hello there!,' the man said. 'You must be one of my new neighbours! I'm Harry, Harry Richardson, I just moved in yesterday.' He offered me his hand to shake, and as I placed my hand in his it instantly felt small and safe and at home. I know that sounds ridiculous, but that's exactly how it was. I have never really felt safe with anyone, not with my parents, both of whom were weird and detached in their different ways, and certainly not with Dave, who was not at all the nurturing type and who I've always thought could take off and leave me any minute. As indeed he just had. I let my hand stay in Harry's for a little longer than I should because it felt so happy there.

I told him I was Alice Bridger and that I lived up in the lane in the little white cottage by the stream. I didn't mention Dave; I was still so upset with him and needed to punish him by treating him as irrelevant. It wasn't that Harry was particularly handsome, he was nothing out of the ordinary to look at, but the way he made me feel safe was so overwhelming after months of feeling insecure with Dave that I struggled to keep my wits about me. What I really wanted to do was laugh with relief at having found a friend.

All the tension that living with Dave had stored up in me was dissolving away.

I felt a bit dazed and stupid and didn't want him to think me a complete idiot, so I muttered something about having to get back and started off up the lane. But suddenly I was miserable because I had left too soon, so I did something so unlike me that I still can't quite believe it. I waited until I was just around the bend and then I gave a shriek and threw myself onto the ground. Sure enough, Harry was by my side in an instant.

'Are you okay? What happened?' His voice was full of concern and sympathy and I lapped it up. Dave hated it when I was feeling poorly and always made himself even scarcer than usual, but I could imagine Harry being a wonderful person to have at my bedside. To have at my side full stop. As he was right then.

I explained, in a rather wobbly voice, that I had slipped on some wet leaves and hurt my knee (actually that last bit was true), and he insisted that I should go in to his house and have a cup of tea. Perfect.

His big kitchen was full of boxes labelled 'Crockery', 'Food', 'Glasses', and I sat down at the huge farmhouse table the previous owners had sold to Henry at what he called an absurdly high price. He said that he hadn't liked the woman either, and that the husband, whom I had never knowingly seen, was a poor hen-pecked shadow of a man. I had a good look round that beautiful kitchen and I thought to myself, 'This is exactly the kind of kitchen I would like to have.' Because I have never had any friends, Harry's was the very first kitchen apart from Aunt Nora's that I had ever set foot in. I had, though, seen lots of kitchens on my property programmes and had formed a pretty clear opinion about my ideal kitchen, and Harry's was it. The previous owner may have been a ghastly woman but she certainly had beautiful taste, right down to the slate floor and the granite worktop. And of course there was the all-important island. Just lovely, all of it. I wanted to move in at once.

'Are you married?' I heard myself say, and was amazed at my boldness. I took a gulp of tea to hide my confusion and burnt my tongue.

'Not any more,' Harry replied cheerfully. 'We've parted company, very amicably, after 25 good years. Sheila's gone to live in France, so I bought this place which is too big for me really, so that there'd be somewhere for the kids to come to for weekends. I've got 4, 2 of each. What about you, any children?'

I told him no. This was surely the moment to mention Dave, but still I didn't. Instead, I asked him about his work (recently retired as a solicitor for big firm in London) and his hobbies (gardening, wine tasting, golf) and we sat there, chatting away quite as if we were old friends, as the early evening sky outside slowly darkened and I wanted to stay forever and never go home.

But then I caught him glancing at his watch and realised with horror that I had long outstayed my welcome. Harry was so obviously a gentleman that I wasn't surprised when he insisted on driving me the very short distance to my front door because of my knee, and when he had turned the car round and disappeared up the road I collapsed into an armchair in my sitting room and cried like a baby.

It felt good to cry, even though I wasn't at all sure what I was crying for. My wasted life probably. To think that if I'd tried a bit harder I might have met a man like Harry, had children with him, done something with my time instead of just letting it pass me by. I cried because I at last admitted to myself what I have of course known deep down all along, that Dave had only married me for my money and didn't love me at all. There, I've gone and said it, Mary, the great truth that I expect you realised straight away.

Where was Dave supposed to be right at that moment? Oh yes, climbing the Lakeland Fells with his walking group, none of whom I had ever met, and who almost certainly didn't exist. It's far more likely that he was with some woman, spending my money on taking her out, the pair of them laughing at my stupidity. And on our wedding anniversary! How could he be so mean and hurtful and selfish and uncaring.....

Suddenly I was sick and tired of pretending to myself that everything was alright. It was so demeaning and draining. I decided to get angry instead. Meeting Harry had given me courage. I wasn't the complete drip Dave and his lady friends took me for, I had a mind of my own and it was high time I used it.

Dave was due home the next day, and he would be expecting me to be waiting for him, dinner in the oven. Well, I decided I'd surprise him by being out. I'd go and stay with Aunt Nora for a few days and sort out in my head exactly what I was going to say and do, and then I'd go home, and say and do it.

Aunt Nora is lovely. She's my only relative, so it's just as well. She's much softer and kinder than my mother ever was, and though I don't suppose they ever really got on, I appreciate the fact that Nora has never once said anything bad to me about her sister. She lives 2 hours' drive away, in a rather horrid retirement flat, with a grumpy warden on call, a view from her window of a row of garages and no one nearby she can call a friend. But she never complains, she just isn't the type, and I always enjoy visiting her; she makes me recognise that my life could be worse – it could be like hers.

We have a little routine, Nora and me. That is, we used to have before I met Dave, because since then I haven't seen her except for when she came to the wedding. I used to visit every few months and stay for 2 nights in her tiny spare room. In the morning we would go for a drive in my car and stop for lunch in a pub. Nora would have a large glass of wine with her lunch and fall asleep in the car on the way home. We would have a light supper in front of the DVD I'd brought with me if there was nothing on the telly. It was fun and gentle and I'm sure I enjoyed it every bit as much as she did. It was wrong of me to have discontinued my visits, and I felt bad about it.

So that's what I would do, I'd go and see Nora, make it up to her and sort everything out in my head. After that first meeting when Dave was so charming, they hadn't met again, but I think she'd formed her own opinion over the months. Whenever we spoke on the phone, he always seemed to be away on one of his adventures, and although she never said anything I could tell that she thought he was neglecting me. I see now that I should have taken more notice of her opinion, but I was so blinded by amazement that anyone as interesting as Dave would want to be with me that I blocked any negativity.... I'd take her a huge bunch of flowers to say sorry for abandoning her, and for not paying more attention to her feelings.

Before I left home I put a note for Dave on the kitchen table explaining where I'd gone and when I'd be back. As I wrote 'Friday afternoon', it occurred to me that my resolve would be strengthened if I could have some actual proof of his worthlessness, so I crumpled up that piece of paper and wrote the note again, saying Nora had some hospital appointments so I'd be back Saturday lunchtime. I could appear unexpectedly on the Friday and see what it was that he got up to when he thought I was safely out of the way. It would be rather fun to find out, now that I no longer cared. Not now I had Harry. Whenever I found myself wobbling a bit about a future without Dave I would make myself think of Harry, so close by and so dependable. His being a solicitor would be very useful, as he would be able to help me with the divorce and money and all that side of things. And with selling, or perhaps letting, my house when I moved in with him.

Mary, I know what you're thinking. And I can see now that I let my imagination run away with me. I had always been a great reader of romantic novels, you see, and I made the leap from meeting a man to sharing my life with him rather too effortlessly. But after all, it was exactly the way it had happened with Dave, and he was the only male experience I had to base my ideas on. I had far too much time on my hands in which to day dream a rosier future for myself, and on the long drive to and from Nora's I concocted a delightful life around me and Harry, based entirely, I'm embarrassed to admit, on one shared cup of tea and a kind face.

My visit to Nora didn't go as well as usual. I found it hard to listen to her rambling stories and she soon noticed that I wasn't my normal attentive self. 'Is everything alright dear?' she kept asking and I had to work hard at not getting irritated. Poor old stick, it wasn't her fault that I was distracted with thoughts of Harry (how strong his arm supporting me felt, how lovely his laugh was), and of Dave (exactly how much money had I given him so far?) But we muddled through and I made a quick escape after breakfast on the Friday. Next time, I told myself, I'd stay longer and be a proper dutiful niece….

Friday March 5th

Honestly Mary, I didn't know what was going to happen. I thought Dave and I would have a talk, a little heated perhaps, but not out of control, because after all there was no passion in our relationship, not any more... I thought we'd be able to sort things out and we could both move on, as they say. But it didn't turn out that way...

I pulled into my drive at lunchtime, and was not a bit surprised to see another car tucked in beside the Jag. Of course it could all be perfectly innocent, but I made sure that my car was blocking Dave in, so there would be no quick exit for him. She could go running off if she wanted to, I had no interest in her. I let myself quietly into the house and walked through the sitting room to the kitchen. The remains of a rather messy breakfast were spread all over the worktop, and there were 2 empty bottles of my favourite Medoc in the recycling bin. One of the wine glasses had a red lipstick imprint on the side and my pulse quickened.

I stood in the hall and listened, but there was no sound from upstairs. Suppose they were both fast asleep in my bed, had I really got the nerve to just walk in on them?

'Dave!' I called, in a brave attempt at casual friendliness. 'Are you upstairs?' Still nothing, so I climbed the stairs and walked into the bedroom, resisting the urge to knock. There had been a half-hearted attempt to make the bed, but it certainly wasn't as I had left it. For a start, there was another empty bottle on a pillow, this time the champagne I had bought to celebrate our anniversary. Now that really annoyed me, and I turned on my heel and stomped down the stairs. There was only one other place they could be.

The state of the art workshop that was supposed to inspire all sorts of creativity from my good-for-nothing husband lay at the end of a winding path at the very bottom of the garden, well away from prying eyes. There was of course no sound of a saw or drill as I approached, but what I could hear was a feminine squeal of delight, followed by a low guttural laugh. I stopped, feeling rather sick, all of sudden, and I had to resist the urge to creep back the way I had come. I made myself think of Harry, of the lovely life I was going to have with him, and I pressed on. I had no desire to embarrass myself by catching them at it, so I called out as I approached the door, 'Hello, it's only me!' and gave them a minute before I opened the door.

The woman was behind the sofa with her back to me, yanking on her jeans. Dave at least had the decency to look a bit sheepish as he walked towards me. His big hairy feet were bare. I've always disliked his feet and the sight of them gave me courage. I told the hussy to leave us, and she slinked off without a word to Dave and without looking back. I stood there and looked at my husband. A good long hard look, while he grinned at me and tried to charm and lie his way out of his mess. I have to give him full marks for inventiveness. He claimed that he'd decided to take up life drawing, and that Melanie had offered to model for him.

I asked to see the drawings, and then was when he got angry. How dared I come stomping into his studio, disturbing him while he was working... I cut him off in mid-flow. 'Actually,' I said,' It's my studio, my house, my tools, my paints, my everything, since you haven't contributed a single penny towards any of it. I'd like you to go now, just take what's yours, which is hardly anything, and go. Our marriage is over.'

He laughed then, and the sound was quite scary. He was so confident, so sure of himself. 'Oh I think you'll find it's not as simple as that!' he smirked at me. 'Why do you think I married you, you stupid cow? I'm entitled to 50% of everything, including the house, and I'm not going anywhere until I've had my share.'

'That can't be right,' I said to myself, 'we've only been married a year! No, that can't be right. Harry will know.' Harry! The thought of him filled me with hope and strength. Harry would make everything alright. I marched out of the studio without saying another word to my detestable husband, and jumped into my car. I was in too much of a hurry to walk. When I got to Harry's house I ran up to the front door, and rang and rang at the doorbell and pounded on the door. I tried to open it but it was locked.

'Where is he?' I was screaming in my head, 'Come on Harry, I need you right now!'

After what seemed ages the door opened and I can remember gasping in surprise at the sight of a tall elegant blond woman in jeans and a t shirt, a coffee cup in her hand.

'Who are you?' I demanded, 'Where's Harry? 'I expect I sounded rather rude, and a bit mad.

'I'm Jenny,' she said calmly. 'Harry's in the shower right now, he'll be down in a minute, would you like to come in?'

I followed her into the kitchen, my mind a whirling panic as the pieces tried to reassemble themselves. I grasped at a long shot. 'Are you one of his daughters?' I said, although I knew she was too old.

'Bless you dear, 'she said with a laugh, 'no, I'm a friend of Harry's. And you are...?'

I couldn't answer. 'A friend of Harry's'. That meant, of course, a girlfriend. That meant, of course ,that Harry wouldn't want me. This woman was gorgeous and confident and everything I wasn't and wouldn't ever be. I was a boring nobody . Harry wouldn't want me, just as Dave didn't want me, I had been the most complete and utter idiot to have pinned my hopes on a man I had met once.

That moment, I think, was when I lost the plot completely. I felt so wretched and embarrassed, but stamping out all my other seething emotions was the absolute fury I felt at Dave for having treated me so badly. Why hadn't he left me alone to continue my contented little life? Why had he swanned into my world and stirred me up and made me so miserable? I wished I'd never been born, but more than that, I wished he'd never been born.

Harry's beautiful lady friend was looking at me. She was amused I think, but also growing a bit impatient. 'I'll just give Harry a shout,' she said.

'Darling!' she called from the foot of the stairs. 'There's someone here to see you!'

But actually there wasn't. That 'Darling' was enough of a spur to send me hurtling back out of the front door and into my car. I tore up the lane and arrived in a cascade of pebbles back at my house.

I headed down the path to the workshop. I remember that everything seemed very loud in my head — I could hear twigs cracking beneath my feet, and a tractor engine in the nearby field, and my heart thumping. I had lived my life up until that moment in a fairly drippy state of passivity, just letting things happen to me, trying not to get too emotional about anything — but suddenly it was as if the elastic bands holding me together had loosened. I was free to do exactly what I wanted, I had right on my side and nothing was going to stop me. And what I wanted was to remove Dave completely and immediately from my life.

The door to the workshop was open and the Rat was inside, stretched out on the red leather sofa with his feet up on the arm, listening to jazz on the CD player. That sofa had cost me a ridiculous amount, but Dave had insisted that he needed something comfortable in case he was on one of his all-night creative sessions and needed to take an occasional power nap. I snorted at the memory, and at the sound he raised an arm and sort of waved it at me. 'Back so soon?' he said? 'Calmed down a bit have we?' Nonchalant, that's what he was. I think that had he made even the slightest effort to apologise, pretend to be sorry, anything….. but no, he just lay there as if he hadn't a care in the world, and it was more than I could bear.

The tools in that workshop were all of the very best quality, Dave had insisted on that. On the end of the workbench was the hammer that had been the very first tool I ever brought him, back in the days when I had such confidence in him and in us. It was a heavy, solidly built claw hammer, top of the range, none of your cheap Chinese rubbish for Dave. He was lying there, his stupid hairy foot jigging up and down to the music, and he couldn't even be bothered to look round at me. Big mistake. I had the advantage of taking him completely by surprise, so that he didn't even have time to bring up his hands to defend his head. I held that hammer by its moulded handle and brought it crashing down on Dave's head with all the hatred that was coursing through me, and I know I probably shouldn't say this Mary, but it felt utterly wonderful. He made a strange whimpering noise and then fell silent, his eyes staring up at me in amazement, and his mouth open. There was a hole where his forehead had been, and a lot of blood.

I didn't want to look at his face so I put a cushion over it.

And then I didn't really know what to do, so I did what you're supposed to do when you've had a shock, which is to make a cup of tea. I went up to the house, and I made some tea, and I tidied up the kitchen and the bedroom so as to remove all traces of that tart. I changed the sheets and put the washing machine on, and then I phoned Nora to tell her I'd arrived home safely. No one listening to that phone call would suspect for a second that I had just murdered my husband. I was very proud of myself for my ability to keep calm and act normal.

As well as property hunting programmes I also watch a lot of police thrillers on the telly. I knew that I had to get rid of Dave's body and destroy the evidence. The answer leapt into my brain straight away. All I had to do was start a fire in the workshop and go out. I knew at first hand how much damage a fire could do. There had been nothing left of our house in Reading, the fire took hold so quickly and mercilessly, and by the time the firemen had got it under control our home was nothing but a heap of ashes. I longed for Dave's beastly body, and especially his horrible hairy feet, to be a heap of ashes.

I could go shopping. It would be wonderful to do some carefree food shopping, buying all my favourite snacks, without having to think about interestingly varied meals for the Rat. I would treat myself to a large box of chocolates and I would be able to eat all the toffees without feeling I should save some for him. By the time I got back, the workshop would have burnt to the ground and Dave would be gone. He was always lighting candles and joss-sticks, I would tell them, shaking my head sadly. I warned him, again and again... With the insurance money I would put up a pretty summer house instead.

I poured the two cans of lawnmower petrol all over Dave and the cushion. I wiped the hammer clean and replaced it on its hook on the wall. I had a last look round that beautiful workshop which had been such a waste of money and hope, and then I struck a match and dropped it on the floor by the sofa. I waited to make sure the flames took, and then I shut the door and went shopping

I really enjoyed that saunter up and down the aisles at Tesco's. I felt light and carefree and kept smiling at total strangers. I took as long as I could over choosing my chocolates and cheese straws and honey roasted peanuts and then I went to the library to change my books. Lesley had 2 new romances ready for me and I also found a gardening book with lots of summer house ideas, and a biography of Dickens. And then I went home.

Sunday March 7th

As soon as I turned down my lane I realised that my plan had failed. I was supposed to be the one who called the fire brigade, once the fire had destroyed everything – but here they were already, 2 of them, and an ambulance, and lots of people in uniform milling about.

Harry was there too, and he came running up to meet me. He had been the one who raised the alarm apparently, and it was all my fault. If I hadn't gone to see him in such a state, he wouldn't have come to check that I was alright..... he guessed it was me who had called from Jenny's description, and came round to the house and smelt the smoke. At first he thought I was having a bonfire, but then he saw the flames coming from the workshop and phoned the fire brigade.

'You need to prepare yourself, Alice,' he said, as he helped me out of the car. 'I'm afraid there was someone in the workshop, they've got him in the ambulance now...'

I nodded and said nothing. I am so useless at everything that it came as no great surprise to me that I'd bungled this as well.

A paramedic came over and put her arm round me. 'Are you Alice?' she said. 'We've got your husband in the ambulance, he's had a severe blow to the head and is badly burnt, you'll need to be brave. Would you like to ride with us to the hospital?'

I didn't know what else to do so I said yes. I sat in that ambulance and I held Dave's hand and I told them his date of birth and doctor's name. Everyone was far too nice to me in the hospital, especially when they took me into a little room to tell me he was dead, and I was relieved when after a while the police came and took me away. It meant I didn't have to pretend any more.

Monday March 8th

So there it is Mr Nutshall. Do you still think we have a chance with temporary insanity? Or maybe just insanity full stop.

I'd like to thank you for encouraging me to write this down. I don't expect it will help to reduce my sentence, but you never know. And it's been an interesting exercise.

I hope you got to the end Mary, and that my story didn't shock you too much. He took my virginity and my vulnerability you see, he took the precious part of me and tossed it aside and that was unbearable. Dave had to be punished, I hope you can see that. And now I have to be punished too.

Actually I'm in no hurry to get out, life outside is fraught with danger it seems to me, best to stay locked up and safe. I'll soon think of some ways to keep busy, I expect. Perhaps I'll take up jigsaw puzzles, I'm sure it's hard to think about anything else when you're trying to choose the exact piece of sky from forty pale blue pieces. It must feel lovely when all the pieces are squidged down in their correct places; you can look at the finished puzzle and smile triumphantly, and then break it up and start all over again.

Calypso Red

The hospital room was depressingly characterless and cramped and smelt of disinfectant, but at least we were alone in it. This would be so much worse if there were other patients in other beds, distracting me from the only person who mattered to me right now. I got up from the vinyl padded chair and glanced out of the window at the vast car park below. So many cars, so many people, scurrying about in the late afternoon sun. So many worries and problems, fears and forebodings. Then I caught sight of a young man heading towards the maternity wing with a baby's car seat swinging jauntily from his hand anI amended my catalogue of gloom. Although I couldn't see his face I knew it would be lit up with excitement and pride. Life goes on, after all.

A slight whimper made me turn and move quickly back to the bed. Carrie was lying on her back, her dark curly hair spread out on the pillow and her skin waxy pale. I have always thought my sister was pretty, but at this moment, when she was on the verge of leaving me, she was positively beautiful.

'Carrie?' I whispered, leaning right over her and noticing how one eyelid flickered whenever she breathed out one of her tiny shallow breaths. 'Can I do anything for you?'

There was no answer. The worst thing about a deathbed vigil is your powerlessness. There is nothing to do but wait. 'It might be a few hours, or she might linger on until tomorrow,' the consultant had said, and when he patted my shoulder gently I almost lost it. It is surprising how the smallest of physical gestures can mean so much.

Remembering that, I took hold of Carrie's hand and stroked it, and I'm sure that her fingers curled, just a little, in response. It was as though she were saying, 'Don't go Jess, I know you're here.' This was easily the most wretched I had ever been. I felt so alone in my misery, and so selfish for wanting someone to share it with me. I longed for Matt's strong arm around me, his practical capable help - but how could I be thinking about my wants at a time like this? What about Carrie's wants? She deserved so much more than just me with her. Her husband should be here by her bedside, her mother, her father, her son. The only family she had left in the world was me and I felt sure I was failing her. No one tells you the right thing to do in these situations. Should I be talking to her? Could she even hear me?

I moved the chair as close to the bed as it would go, then I sat down and took her hand in mine again. It felt so small and frail as I traced the delicate blue veins, and my eyes welled up again. A strange business this crying – so many tears from a seemingly bottomless pit of sorrow, and what was the point of them? As I rummaged through the assorted rubbish that had collected in my large and pocketless bag in search of some tissues, my fingers closed around something round. I drew out a dumpy little bottle of bright red nail polish and held it up to the window. It was so bold a colour, so alive, and I couldn't help smiling. It was saying, 'Look at me! Life is fun! Be happy!'

I found the pack of tissues and blew my nose noisily. Then I picked up the nail polish again. 'Calypso Red', the label said, and I had bought it a week ago for the name alone, thinking that anything called Calypso had to be gorgeous. It was strange to think that in all the flurry of the last few days, the frantic phone calls, the planning, the talking, the crying, the frustratingly long hours of travelling, all this time the cheery little bottle of Calypso Red had lain buried at the bottom of my bag waiting to be rediscovered. Carrie had always loved bright colours. As far as I knew, she didn't possess a single black item of clothing, and she lit up the room as she entered, in her peacock blues and vibrant greens and fire-engine reds. She was the only person I had ever known who looked great in yellow. She would have adored this nail polish.

Her hand was still in mine. I gently spread her fingers out on top of the sheet and studied them. She had long, slim fingers, with beautifully shaped nails which she had never bitten or chewed, unlike me. Slowly I unscrewed the lid of the polish and then, my tongue sticking out with the effort of doing this important task as carefully as I could, I applied two coats of Calypso Red, blowing on each nail in turn between coats.

I replaced my sister's hand on the sheet and nodded with satisfaction. This was not the hand of a dying woman. This was the hand of a woman who had spent her 36 years living and laughing and, most of all, loving. A woman who had been strong enough and brave enough to pick herself up after the car crash that had robbed her so brutally of her husband and child and carry on giving. She would be noticed now, I thought, as I moved round to the other side of the bed. The doctors and nurses and porters and - I swallowed hard and kept going – the people in the mortuary and the funeral parlour and the crematorium, all these people would notice my darling Carrie now because of the Calypso Red, and maybe they would take special care of her.

I ignored the big plastic thing sticking out of the back of her left hand and set to with the nail polish.

'Goodness!' said the fat nurse who came bustling in to check Carrie's pulse and to write something on her notes.

'Those nails do look pretty!' Either she had a cold or else she needed her adenoids removed. She lowered her voice. 'I don't think it will be long now, dear.'

I glared at her back as she left the room, wondering how much longer the seams of her navy top would hold out against the strain of her bulging flesh.

I pinched my nose between my fingers. 'It won't be long now dear!' I repeated to Carrie, who had always enjoyed my impersonations. I didn't know whether to be angry or upset so I was both.

Now, I don't expect anyone to believe me, but what happened next was too extraordinary to make up. My feisty, fun-loving sister, who was inches away from death, wriggled her toes at me! There was a cardboard tray lying on the foot of the bed and I definitely saw it shift a little as Carrie moved her toes beneath it.

In a second I had the sheets untucked and the horrid tight sock off Carrie's right foot. Her toenails were not as delicious as her fingernails, of course, but still I poured my love and admiration into every one of those strokes of the brush.

When the nails on both feet were dry, I let the sheet settle back gently around Carrie, but I didn't tuck it in. The room was very warm and in any case, both of us had always loathed being tucked in tight. 'We need to float free!' we would say as we yanked the sheet out from under the mattress. This was a nightly refrain when we stayed with our Gran, who was a stickler for tight hospital corners. She refused to entertain the idea of duvets, 'those nasty foreign things', insisting that sheets and blankets were much more hygienic. She made no secret of the fact that she considered her daughter-in-law to be an inadequate mother, always 'gallivanting' off to the other side of the world to write her travel articles, and dumping us on Gran at a moment's notice. We didn't mind a bit, we loved going to Gran's; in wonderful contrast to our cramped flat and empty fridge we had the run of an old vicarage and its rambling garden and, best of all, we were given three generous meals a day. Mother often forgot to feed us, and would wave us away with a distracted air when we came whining for food, saying, 'I'm sure there are some beans in the cupboard.' There usually weren't.

    Gran made a big thing about the ritual of bedtime, believing that a set pattern paved the way to a good night's sleep. So every night, after our baths, we would climb into the big brass bed we shared, and wait for the clip-clop of her heels along the polished floor of the landing. Gran would sit herself down in the armchair and open the current bedtime book at where we had left off the night before. She read beautifully, and her special forte was accents. 'Little Women' was one of our favourites, and 'Huckleberry Finn' and best of all, 'The Secret Garden'. After a chapter or two, she would position the embroidered bookmark that she had made as a girl, close the book with a thwack, and then tuck us in firmly with a kiss on our foreheads and the words, 'Goodnight my angels, enjoy your sleeping.' We adored our Gran, but were also a little nervous of her, so we would wait until we thought she was safely out of earshot before we noisily released ourselves from the tight bedclothes with our refrain of 'We need to float free!' Now I come to think of it, she must have heard us, but she would have enjoyed adding this touch to the bedtime ritual.

    I grew quite misty-eyed, sitting there thinking about Gran and those lovely bedtimes. Then it occurred to me that what I could do for Carrie was to read to her like Gran did. A tiny copy of Keats' poems lived in my handbag, and who better to send her on her way? I gave the sheet a gentle flap and pulled it up a little so that the beautiful toenails were in full view. I found my leather-bound book of poems and felt a little surge of rightness. This felt good. 'You float free, my darling,' I said to Carrie as I sat back down on the chair. 'I'll be here by your side, and I'll read you 'The Eve of St Agnes and 'Isabella' and your favourite, 'Ode to a Nightingale', and I won't stop reading until you've floated away to where the sun will shine forever on your Calypso Red nails.'

And that's what I did. I concentrated on pouring my love into those wonderful soul-stretching words, and they meant more to me than they ever had before. How did a man who died at 25 know how to say such things so exquisitely? After a while I had to get up and put the light on because the print in my little book is very small, and I noticed then that Carrie's eyelid had stopped flickering. I leant over her to check that she was still breathing, just as I used to do when the children were babies. When I heard that tiny breath, I sat back down and returned to the odes. The one to the nightingale I knew almost by heart. When I got to:

'Now more than ever seems it rich to die,
To cease upon the midnight with no pain,'

I heard Carrie give a funny little noise. I made myself keep going to the end of the poem because I knew but I didn't want to know, not yet. I sat there, holding her hand, and then when I was ready I stood up and kissed her on her forehead, and I could see that she wasn't breathing, not even a little. She looked perfectly calm, lying there, and not a bit afraid.

'Goodnight my angel, enjoy your sleeping,' I said, and then I turned off the light, sat back in the chair and waited for the nurse to come.

Film Night

I hurried along the pavement, anxious not to miss the start of the film, cross with myself for leaving it so late. It had been a last minute decision, no time even to grab a sandwich. I hoped my stomach wasn't going to rumble. The arty cinema has a large window onto the street and I glanced in as I passed and then skidded to a halt.

There they were at the ticket counter. There was no mistaking her hideous mop of frizzy red hair. He was wearing his favourite green sports jacket, the one whose elbows I've twice patched with leather. I considered my options, but only for a second. My battered sense of pride struggled to life and I decided that I wasn't going to let them prevent me from seeing a good film. But I could loiter for a few minutes until they had taken their seats. Or I could just brazen it out. After all, I was completely okay now about us splitting up, wasn't I? Of course I was. My legs were moving by themselves and suddenly I was there in the queue, with three people between us. My heart was banging about so violently that I had to clutch my coat around me to keep it under control.

I had time, while I stood there, to study the two of them together, something I'd never done before. Oddly enough, it wasn't jealousy I felt, but indignation on his behalf. She didn't need to explain that they would have to sit on the end of the row because he couldn't clamber over people's legs. And while she belittled him he just stood there. 'You're paying,' she told him, and he meekly got out his wallet. I felt my face grow hot at the indignity of it all.

'Stop it!' I wanted to shout at her. 'He can't help having bad knees!' But of course I said nothing.

At last they were finished, and turned away from the counter. They hadn't seen me, and I could have just let them go on their way. But something made me reach out a hand and touch him on the arm.

'Hello David,' I said, and from somewhere I produced a smile. It was probably a slightly manic smile but at least it was a smile.

He looked startled, and for a minute it seemed that he was trying to remember who I was.

'Oh hello,' he said, 'Nice to see you!' He looked past me to see who my companion might be, and when I followed his eyes I was delighted to see that the man behind me, who of course I'd never seen before, was about 25 and very good looking. David might think I'd come with my toy boy. Excellent.

I made myself look at her then and say hello, and that used up my entire stock of social skills. I wasn't even able to register whether or not she replied; it was as much as I could do to scuttle back in line while they moved on out the door.

'Can you remember where the woman with the frizzy hair is sitting?' I asked the ticket man. I was gratified that he knew who I meant by that description. 'Only I don't want to be next to them.'

I took my seat, which was a few rows behind them. I watched as The Frizz fussed about with her coat and her bag, and I was ready with my mobile pretending to read messages if either of them had glanced behind to see where I was sitting. But they didn't.

Then the lights dimmed and the film started. There are often no ads at the arty cinema, which is a shame because I like cinema ads. We launched straight into the film and I would be lying if I said I gave it my full attention. I did try, but the trouble was the story line had certain uncanny similarities to my marriage, which was very distracting, as I kept wondering whether David was thinking that too. The heroine was married to a much older man and she fell in love with someone her own age who was way more fun. Actually the story of my marriage had rather more twists and turns in it than that and would probably have made a much more interesting film. The dull Husband was lovely and blameless and behaved beautifully, unlike mine. The Wife's Lover was charming and shallow and bound to dump her, and by the time he did I was pretty fed up with her too. She did a lot of sitting about moping and had quite the ugliest knees I've ever seen. If I'd been that actress I'd have asked them to find a knee double for me. I'd have paid for her myself rather than have the whole world know about my knees.

The Husband was my favourite character, not that there was much competition, and he had the best lines. 'After a while the anger has gone and you are only left with regret', he said sadly, and of course I wondered whether David was registering the truth of that. If I'd been sitting next to him I'd have nudged him. I had always made sure that he never missed a good line when we went to the cinema together.

It seemed a very long film, with the added complication of leaping backwards and forwards in time. When we finally got to the end, I was more than ready to leave. As soon as the credits started to roll I was up on my feet and heading for the exit. I didn't want them to see that I had been sitting on my own like Jenny No-mates.

I felt the chill of loneliness settle over me as I drove home. David would be discussing the film with The Frizz. I felt sure he would have hated it as much as I had, but perhaps he would be pretending to have liked it to keep her happy. Was he trying harder in this new exciting relationship? I shook my head, cross with my train of thought. Move on, I instructed myself, think about something else. Think about what you'll do when you get home, where you are in the enviable position of having no one to please but yourself.

And what I did was just lovely. I toasted a bagel and smothered it in cream cheese studded with sundried tomatoes. Delicious. I ran a deep foamy bath, and lit all the candles in the bathroom. I put Supertramp on the CD player and grinned in delight as the music came out of the new speaker I'd had installed above the loo. I opened a bottle of Chianti and found a glass. I got undressed , lowered myself into the bubbles and took a long appreciative drink of my favourite wine.

There. Life suddenly felt good again. I didn't have to pretend to anyone that I'd enjoyed the film. I didn't in fact have to do anything I didn't want to do. I reached for the sponge and gently squeezed some foam over my knees. I thought they were looking particularly pretty in the candlelight.

Talking to Laura

It had been an awful day. Work was frenetic and frustrating, the rain relentless all afternoon and the traffic on the journey home a nightmare. The office had been unbelievably stressful these last few weeks, and I couldn't believe it was still only Wednesday. I wished Phil was at home, but it was probably just as well he wasn't, given the mood I was in. I pulled into my driveway and made a dash for the front door. The briefcase held over my head did little to keep out the rain and I cursed loudly as several large drops ran down my neck.

As soon as I got inside, I poured myself a glass of red wine and went to find Laura. Normally she's slumped in front of the telly and I have to nag her to get on with her homework, but today the sitting room was empty, and the house was unnaturally quiet.

'Laura?' I called. 'Are you in your room?' Still no answer, so I headed up the stairs. I knocked at her bedroom door and pushed it open without waiting an answer.

My lovely, infuriating 15 year old daughter was on her bed, propped up on her pillows and doing, as far as I could see, nothing at all. I rather envy her the ability to do nothing. I'm not sure I ever possessed it and it looks so relaxing. I can't sit still without doing something, it seems such a waste of time. I can't watch telly unless I'm doing the ironing, and knitting has proved invaluable when I'm forced to sit and have a conversation. Last week I knitted half a sleeve while Mother told me what had happened at the supermarket.

'Darling?' I said. 'What's the matter? Don't you feel well?'

She looked up at me then and her beautiful brown eyes were swimming with tears. My Laura can have hysterics like the best of them, but this silent crying was most unusual. Alarming in fact.

I put my glass down on her desk and sat on the bed, my mind busy with possibilities. A fall out with her best friend Nicky? A telling-off from her beloved Spanish teacher? A boy? Was there at last a boy?

'Come on darling,' I crooned, squeezing her arm 'Tell me what's happened. It can't be that bad, surely?'

She pulled away, reached under her pillow, and drew out a white plastic stick.

'Yes it can,' she said, as she handed it to me.

My brain went numb as I stared down at the little screen. In my day you had to search for a blue line, but they've made it much easier for you now. *pregnant* it said, in crisp little non-committal letters. It might be the best news in the world, or an absolute calamity, these letters didn't care. They were just stating the fact.

But I couldn't believe it. Not my Laura. Not after the up-bringing she'd had. Not after all the talking and explaining, it just wasn't possible. Her friend Nicky, now that I could believe - she hadn't had the parenting and her mother Janice was, let's face it, something of a tart herself. Hardly a good example for a daughter. But I had done it all properly, I had been so careful to make sure Laura understood how things should be. This just didn't happen to people like us.

My second reaction was fury. At this unknown boy, for taking advantage of her. Who was he? Did he know she was underage? Did he care? Had he been gentle?

And finally, while she looked at me with those eyes, trying to be brave, but showing the terror underneath, overwhelming sadness. For the pain this pregnancy would cause, whatever the outcome. For the loss of her childhood, for the loss of my little girl. I hadn't even known she'd been having sex, surely I should have known?

I couldn't help it. I knew it was the wrong thing to do – immature, selfish and completely unhelpful. I burst into tears, grabbed a pillow, buried my face in it and howled.

'Mum?' Laura was bending over me, sobbing too, poor lamb, and my maternal instincts came back to me in an instant. This was, after all, not about me.

I managed to get myself together and pulled Laura in close to me for a cuddle. For a long time we said nothing. We just sat there, rocking slightly from side to side while we sniffed away our tears, and I tried to think of the right way to deal with this.

'Abortion!' was the word screaming inside my head. The obvious, sensible solution. But I knew my Laura well enough to know that I couldn't just tell her what to do. I had to find out what she wanted first. Only then could I lead her there gently.

'So,' I said, stroking her head. She has beautiful hair, long and blond and silky. I badly wanted to reach for my glass of wine, but I resisted. The clearest of heads was needed for this task. 'When do you think it happened?' I was amazed at how calm I sounded.

She didn't reply, but kept her face buried against my chest.

'It's been more than once then?' I said, trying not to let myself imagine anything at all.

Laura grunted, and then shook her head violently. That was something, I supposed. I could be excused for not knowing if it had only been the once. But what rotten luck. I thought you only got pregnant first time in Hardy novels.

'And who is he?'

'I don't know.'

For a minute I was paralysed. She didn't know? Had she been raped?

'You mean, you don't know his name?'

'I don't think he ever told me.'

Okay, so now we had reached the land of the unimaginably terrible. Not only had my little girl had sex, but she had had sex with someone she didn't even know. My beautiful angelic little girl was in fact a slut.

'I don't understand,' I croaked. 'How can you not know his name?''

'Well he may have mentioned it I suppose. Only I was drunk, so I don't remember.'

I shut my eyes. This wasn't happening. This child cuddled in my arms was actually a total stranger. I carried on stroking her hair, but what I really wanted to do was go downstairs and start cooking some sausages, just as if this was any old school night. I wanted Laura to be sitting at the table in the kitchen chewing her pen as she tried to do her maths homework. I wanted Phil to be coming in the back door saying 'That smells good!' and kissing my neck and reaching for a cold beer. I longed for Phil. I couldn't do this on my own, it was simply too huge. Of all the stupid times to be away on a business trip! He should be right here at my side, helping me to present a powerful, united and utterly adult front. I shouldn't have to be doing this on my own. But I was, and I would just have to get on with it.

'Do you often get drunk?' I asked politely.

'No, just the once really.' There was a pause. 'Sometimes Nicky and I have a bit of vodka and coke when we're at her's but I don't usually get drunk.'

'I see.' It was no good, I had to get at my wine. I stood up a little unsteadily, reached for my glass and took a gulp. There. That was better.

'So this particular time, when you had sex with this boy, was it at a party?'

'Yes, it was at Steph's, Nicky's friend in Luton. You remember, you said I could stay over afterwards and come back with Nicky the next day. You and Dad went to that wedding and didn't get back till the Sunday afternoon.'

I remembered, and my heart gave a sideways lurch. That weekend in May, when Phil and I had gone to Margate for Maggie's wedding and Phil hadn't wanted to go and we drove the whole way in frosty silence. As it turned out, it was every bit as bad as he had predicted, but I was annoyed that he didn't even try to disguise his boredom. The hotel was horrid and the car wouldn't start in the morning and we had to wait ages for the AA, so in fact the entire weekend had been ghastly. When we eventually got home all I wanted to do was dive into the bath and I hardly spoke to Laura, except to comment that she was looking tired - which I put down to her sleepover party. Any clues she may have given me that something momentous had happened would have completely passed me by.

'But why didn't you tell me?' I wailed, although I already knew the answer.

'I wanted to, but you weren't in the mood to listen when you got home!' Ouch. 'And I knew you'd get upset and I felt so awful about it all and I just wanted it to go away...'

She dissolved into tears again, and I hugged her to me saying, 'It's ok darling, I understand,' although of course it wasn't and I didn't.

'And I might have told you the next day or the day after, but somehow it never seemed the right time and you were so stressed at work and I knew you'd be disappointed in me , 'cos you always told me how I should look on sex as something special and precious and I'd gone and ruined it all by getting drunk...

So she had been listening! This provided me with a crumb of comfort, but I needed another one.

'So this was the first and only time then, this time at the party?'

'Yes, of course it was, and it was probably horrible but I can't remember!'

Some weird part of me suddenly wanted to giggle but I managed not to. You never forget your first time, they always say. Unless you're my daughter and get drunk and have it off with a total stranger and can't remember anything about it.

'Did he hurt you?' I suddenly remembered to say. What was the matter with me? I was doing this all wrong.

'Not really,' she said, 'I think it helped that I was too drunk to resist.'

I nodded, astounded and appalled at how mature she suddenly sounded. Who had she been talking to? Oh god, how many people knew about this? Was it all round school? Were they sniggering behind her back? Would we have to move, start again where no one knew us?

'Apart from Nicky,' I began cautiously, 'and, obviously, the boy who did it, who else knows?'

'No one! Steph doesn't know, and Nicky wouldn't tell anyone, I'm sure she wouldn't...' I relaxed just a little. Perhaps we wouldn't need to leave town after all.

'And Susie, of course. Nicky thought I should see this counsellor at school, and she's been really kind. You can tell her anything and she's not shocked or surprised and she's been talking me through my options.'

There she went again, sounding like a teacher.

'And did one of these options include telling your mother?' I asked, my voice hard with jealousy and outrage. How dare this Susie hear things from my daughter that she couldn't bring herself to tell me?

'Yes, of course, and she'll be really glad I'm finally telling you. She got me the pregnancy kit 'cos I was 2 weeks overdue and we did it together in the lunch hour and she said that now it would be very helpful if I told you.'

Thank you very much Susie, I thought. Remind me to send you a bunch of flowers, for swanning in and taking over my role so effectively. I mustn't be angry, stay focussed, she's opening up, I must keep her talking.

'There were two tests in the packet,' Laura said, her voice wobbling. 'I so hoped it might be wrong, and I did it again when I got in from school, but it says the same thing.'

Her pretty little face was pinched and drawn, and I felt another stab of fury – at the boy, at life, at the injustice of it all. I hugged her to me again, trying to imagine what it must be like to face such a crisis at so young an age. She was little more than a baby, for goodness' sake, still into boy bands, still cuddling a teddy. She hadn't let me take her Barbies to the charity shop last month, saying she needed to hang on to them a little while longer – not to play with, she said, just to know they were there.

I gave a heavy sigh, and Laura pulled back a little to look at me. 'I'm so sorry, Mum,' she said, and I didn't know what to reply. 'But,' she went on, 'there is a bit of good news I can give you!'

There was? What on earth could be good about any of this?

'Susie took me to a clinic to get tested for STD's and they've told me I'm clear, I didn't catch anything horrible! That's good isn't it?!'

I was rapidly revising my opinion of Susie. How long would it have taken me to think of taking her for tests? I felt completely out of my depth, but it seemed that Susie had thought of everything.

'Yes darling,' I said, 'That's fantastic!' It occurred to me that I would have used exactly the same word if she had told me that her history essay had been given an A. Suddenly history essays seemed so unimportant.

I was trying to marshal my thoughts into some sort of order. I needed Phil, with his calm logical brain. Though of course even he would have trouble being calm about this. I shook the image of Phil's anguished angry face from my thoughts and tried to concentrate. It seemed that Laura had emerged relatively unscathed physically, but what about the emotional trauma? How was she coping with the fact that her poor little body had been assaulted by some drunken boy? Would she be put off sex forever? Would this ruin her chances of having a normal relationship?

Laura reached for a tissue and blew her nose. 'I don't think he'll have told anyone, Mum, and anyway he doesn't know my name. He was pretty stoned, he probably doesn't even remember...' I was torn between fuming at the idea of him not remembering and wanting him to have forgotten. I pushed the reference to drugs away from me, I hadn't got room to think about that as well. Laura was pinching her neck now, a habit from babyhood that always recurred in times of stress. She'd been doing it a lot recently, and I'd put it down to exam nerves. Another clue I'd missed.

I got angry again, to deflect the guilt. 'If Nicky was there, why on earth didn't she do something? How could she just let this happen?' I didn't know Nicky very well, but she was certainly large enough and loud enough to create a scene.

'She didn't see, Mum, she only found out afterwards. I was down in the basement and she came to find me when everyone was going home, and I was throwing up in the loo, over and over, and I told her what had happened but I begged her not to say anything to anyone, not even Steph. I'm sure no one else knows, it was a very drunk sort of party. Everyone was really out of it. Nicky rang her mum and said I wasn't feeling well and Brian came as fast as he could to get us, and he was really nice about it. He just thought I'd got pissed and he made me drink lots of water and he wasn't even annoyed that I'd got him out of bed.'

More shifting of opinions in my bewildered brain. Brian was Janice's latest squeeze and I'd dismissed him as a beer-swigging, football watching lay-about. But he'd driven all the way to Luton to rescue my daughter in the middle of the night, and looked after her when I was miles away, and he and Janice had never even mentioned it.

'And the boy? I said. 'Who was he?' I wanted to kill him.

'I don't even know!' A wail tore through her slender frame and she reached out and clutched my hands. 'Steph was sharing the party with her older brother and there were loads of his friends there... I was feeling really shy and then this one guy started talking to me and he was really good looking and everyone else was pulling and I'd had loads to drink 'cos I was so nervous and he seemed really nice at first and we were kissing and that, and I was so thrilled 'cos I was finally doing what everyone else has been doing for ages and there wasn't anything wrong with me after all ....And when he said, 'Let's go downstairs,' I didn't understand what he wanted and I went with him down to the basement and we were mucking about and he pulled me on to the floor. Then realised what he was doing and I said I didn't want to, but he just laughed and the next thing I knew he was ... you know... on top of me and inside me, and I couldn't do anything, I just couldn't do anything Mum, he was so much bigger than me and I couldn't move....'

I rocked her backwards and forwards, saying all the soothing things I could think of, and all the while my brain was boiling with anger.

'And then what happened?' I asked.

'Well, then suddenly he was finished and he rolled off me and said he was going to get another drink and did I want one and I said no thanks. And he went upstairs and I lay there for a bit and then I started to feel really sick and I stumbled to the loo and that's where Nicky found me. She was really great Mum, I think you should like her now, she was so sensible even though she was nearly as pissed as I was!'

'Hmm,' was what I managed to come up with. I felt numb with too many emotions.

'So what do we now?' I asked her. It felt as if I were the child.

'Well, even before we did the pregnancy test, Susie and I talked about what I would do if it was positive.' Another stab of jealousy but I just nodded. 'I should have taken a morning after pill but I didn't know about them and by the time I spoke to Susie it was too late for that.' She sighed heavily and blew her noise again. 'If I had got pregnant from a boy I loved it would have been different, but this was SO not like that, Mum, I don't want to have this baby, I want to get rid of it. I know there are childless couples out there longing for a baby, but I can't do it Mum, please don't make me!'

'Oh darling, of course I won't make you!' I cried, relief coursing through me. 'And from now on I want you to tell me everything. I'll make the appointment for you and I'll come with you to the clinic and I'll be beside you all the time, I promise.' Even as I said the words I was beginning to panic. How would I find the right clinic? It wasn't like asking a friend to recommend a hairdresser. Susie, I needed Susie!' 'What I'll do,' I continued more slowly, 'is come with you tomorrow to meet Susie and thank her and we'll sort it all out with her help.'

'But what about work?' Laura asked 'Can you take the time off?' Her eyes were huge and hopeful.

'Of course I can,' I said, thinking it shouldn't have taken a crisis to get my priorities right. 'Don't you worry my darling, we'll get through this together.' I stroked her hair, wondering how Phil was going to react. 'I must phone Dad in a minute,' I said, 'He needs to know what's happening, he'll want to help.'

Laura jerked away from me. 'No!' she shouted, 'I really, really don't want Dad to know, not yet, not till I've done it. He'll be so upset, Mum, I can't bear that on top of everything else. Please don't tell him, please!'

This threw me. I had been counting on Phil coming home tomorrow, to be with us at this dreadful time. I needed him, and more than that, I had no right to keep this from him. Phil would be distraught of course, but he'd be even more upset if he found out later that I hadn't told him. I rocked Laura in my arms, my mind racing. She was my priority, I mustn't cause her more upset, but I simply couldn't be so unfair to Phil.... Think, what would Susie do? I was on the point of asking Laura for her number when the answer came to me. I would tell Phil, but he mustn't come home early or let on that he knew until Laura was ready to tell him herself. It would be hard, but he would do that for her.

'Alright,' I said. 'I don't like keeping things from Dad, but perhaps it would be best to leave it for now.'

Laura gave a groan of relief. 'And the other thing you should know is that I don't want anything done about that boy,' she announced. Once again, she was miles ahead of me. 'By the time I told Susie, I had washed away all the evidence and I absolutely refused to let her take me to be checked by a doctor. I couldn't stand to have to say what happened over and over again and be asked all those questions. I know what he did was appalling, but I should never have let myself get so drunk, and if I had to go to court and give evidence and all that sort of thing it would be a huge part of my life for ages and I don't want that – I want to put it all behind me, and learn from it and move on. I refuse to let a stupid drunk boy, who I'll never see again, turn me into a victim!'

She was sitting bolt upright on the bed, her eyes flashing with indignation, and I felt a huge surge of pride. How much of this was Susie talking I had no idea, but it sounded exactly right to me. There would be plenty of wobbles ahead, I knew that, but Laura had taken the first brave steps and together we would get through it. I held out my arms and she threw herself into them.

'It's such a relief to have told you,' she murmured. 'I can't tell you how much better I feel.'

This was of course music to my ears. I squeezed her tight to me, trying to put my hurt little girl back together again. I decided that from this moment on, I was going to be a perfect mother. I pulled myself back a little, and gently stroked a lock of hair away from her eyes.

'How about a bacon and banana sarni?' I said, and was rewarded with a tiny smile. 'Curled up on the sofa in front of a double bill of 'Friends'?'

Move over Susie. I'm on board now and we're going to do this together.

Deirdre

While I was in the library today, I found out that there's a word for the fear I had. Some people are afraid of spiders, that's arachnophobia, some of flying, that's aviaphobia, but me – I was scared of growing old, and that's called gerontophobia. At least, I was scared of growing old on my own. It was alright when I had Geoff, because we were a team, united against the world. When I was with him I wasn't scared of anything and I looked forward to every single day.

But when he died it all changed. Without Geoff to look after and love and need, I couldn't seem to see the point of being alive, and I would sit and shake with fear at the prospect of the years stretching out ahead of me. I would get up every day, try to think of things to do with myself for hours and hours, and then go back to bed. I felt I was a waste of space, taking up room on an overcrowded planet. I wanted to do my bit for the environment and rid it of me. I had cluttered it up for 64 years and that felt like quite long enough.

I was falling apart, an expression that suddenly made sense. I had to make a conscious effort to gather myself together at the start of each new empty day. It surprised me that grief felt so physical, that the ache of loneliness actually hurt. I even went to the doctor, thinking I must have a blockage somewhere, and she listened and let me cry and run way past our allotted time span of seven minutes, and eventually she patted me on the arm and said, 'It'll get easier, you know. Give it time.'

Well I gave it time, and it got worse instead of better. All the things I used to do so effortlessly – cooking, cleaning, shopping - became a huge horrible chore and I was so very tired. That's why I made up my mind to call it a day. Stop the world, I thought, I want to get off.

I became completely absorbed in thinking about how I was going to kill myself. It's not as easy as you might think, because I'm a terrible coward. I couldn't possibly cut my wrists in the bath, or tie a plastic bag over my head, or drive a car into a brick wall. My options were rather limited. What I really wanted was for someone to come into my bedroom when I was fast asleep and point a gun at my head and pull the trigger. That would have been perfect.

Geoff was never a great talker, but he was an attentive listener and such a companiable man. It was his love I missed. The sight of his smile when I walked through the door, the way he would hold my hand when we sat and watched the telly. He even liked to hear about my dreams. Twenty six years, and not one cross word. The only troubled bit was early on, when I was trying so hard for a baby, and month after month it didn't happen. I was just too old I expect. But one day Geoff said, 'Does it matter so much darling? Aren't I enough for you?' and I looked into his anxious face and I realized that he was, of course he was, and I relaxed then into the delicious twoness of us. Now I wonder whether a son or a daughter would be a huge comfort to me, though what the point of wondering that is, I can't imagine.

It wouldn't have been so bad if I'd still had work to go to, but I had taken early retirement so as to be able to spend all of every day with Geoff. With him gone, I couldn't bear prowling round my empty house, talking to the walls, so most days I would go out in the morning and wander around the streets, trying to get so tired that I would sleep through the night. One day I walked further than usual and came to a halt by a newsagent. They had one of those boards there where people can stick their advertisements for a week and I studied those ads, thinking about the sort of people who have a nearly new sofabed for sale, or an unwanted juice extractor.

Then I sat down on the low wall for a rest. I was wriggling my toes in my shoes to encourage them to embark on the long walk home, when the newsagent came out of the shop with a tall gentleman. I was sure I'd never seen him before – I would have remembered, because he was very elegant, in a shabby sort of way. He looked as if he had once had money. His raincoat had seen better days but still looked pretty stylish, so much better than those awful anoraks everyone seems to wear these days.

'If you could put it in for two weeks I'd be most grateful,' he was saying to the newsagent. He sounded very posh.

'That'll be three quid then,' came the reply. 'There you go, nice and central.'

When they'd gone I got up to have a look at the shiny new card in the middle of the board. 'Philip Rashleigh', it announced in an elegant typeface, 'I have the answer to your problem. No job too small or too difficult.' And then a mobile phone number.

I'm not normally a drinker, but I was feeling more peculiar than usual the day I first saw Philip, and after carefully writing his number down in my diary, I went into a supermarket and bought a bottle of milk and a bottle of whisky. Hedging my bets, you see. I could go for cocoa or a nightcap, depending on my mood.

And later that evening, when I had drunk three little glasses of neat whisky and was feeling floaty and not really like me at all, I picked up the phone and dialed his number.

'It's a little hard to explain over the phone,' I told him. 'Could we perhaps meet to discuss matters?'

****

The following evening at 8 pm I walked through the door of the King's Head. I was dolled up in my smartest dress and a pair of high-heeled shoes, which were supposed to give me confidence, but actually only made me feel self-conscious. I had never been in this pub before, but Philip had suggested it, on the grounds that it was nice and quiet, a good place to talk. I went up to the bar and asked for tonic water with ice and lemon; it would look like a gin and tonic but I needed to keep a clear head. It occurred to me that on this day, when I was hoping to arrange to die, I was feeling more alive than I had for months.

I took a sip and turned to survey the other customers. A group of young people were slouched round a big table in front of the window, two men were on stools at the bar with pints of beer, but there was no Philip. I felt a twinge of panic. What if he didn't come? I was pinning my hopes on him. I walked over to a table in the corner and sat in the chair facing the door. I arranged my features into those of a sensible, serious woman. He would discover soon enough how peculiar I was, no need to scare him off too soon.

I had nearly finished my tonic water when I saw him come in. It must have started raining since I arrived, because his hair was plastered to his head and his raincoat was dripping. He removed it, gave it a little shake and draped it over his arm before hastening across the room towards me.

'You must be Deirdre,' he said, 'I simply can't apologise enough for keeping you waiting.' I felt a little thrill of excitement run through me at the elegance of these words.

'That's quite alright,' I replied. 'I've only just got here myself.'

'Allow me to freshen your drink.'

'Thank you. Just a tonic water please.'

He returned with our drinks and sat down. My heart was hammering away and I wondered if he could hear it. Could I really go through with this?

He was studying me. 'You look very sad,' he said. 'Can you tell me why?'

I could, and I did. I looked into his gentle, weary face, and the words came easily. He nodded at intervals and smiled his sad smile and seemed genuinely interested in me and my miserable little life. He didn't seem to think it at all strange that I should want to die.

'You are very lucky, you know, to have experienced such love,' he said quietly, and we sat for a moment in silence while I felt comforting warmth spread through me. I hadn't looked at it in that way before, but of course he was right.

Philip cleared his throat. 'So,' he said,' You would like my help to engage someone to speed you on your way. Someone to put you out of your misery, as you would a dog that was suffering. Someone, moreover, who would do it quickly and cleanly, preferably while you were sleeping.'

He was making it sound a perfectly normal request, almost like booking my car in for an MOT. 'Yes,' I breathed, not able to look at him now, 'Would it be easy to arrange?'

'No problem at all,' he said smoothly. 'The going rate is £350, does that sound acceptable?'

I took a gulp of my drink. I couldn't believe this was happening.

'Yes,' I replied. 'Yes, that would be fine. Very reasonable, in fact.' He wrote something down in a small black notebook and then leant forward and gave my hand a little squeeze.

'Are you sure you're that unhappy?' he asked, I nodded emphatically. He was silent for a moment, and then he said, 'I think another drink is called for.' I offered to buy this round, but he refused, saying he was old-fashioned that way.

'My life is in this man's hands,' I thought, 'and I don't know anything at all about him.' Suddenly I wanted to giggle at the melodrama of it all. I looked over at Philip, who was counting out the coins from a pile of change he had laid on the bar. He looked so tired and care-worn, and that helped me to take matters more seriously. After all, this was an extraordinary thing that he was doing for me, a total stranger. I wondered how often he had organised this particular job before, and how much of the fee he got to keep for himself. Not for one second did I imagine that he would be the one to do it – he was far too much of a gentleman.

He placed my glass in front of me and gave me an encouraging smile as I took a long drink.

'Here's what we do,' he announced, his voice firm and authoritative. 'You spend a week doing the things you have always wanted to do. Not to make you change your mind, you understand, but just to ensure you go out on a high. If, after a week of fun, you still want it done, then I'll arrange it. How does that sound?'

It occurred to me that there might have been vodka as well as tonic in the drinks he had bought me. I was feeling pleasantly fuzzy, soft around the edges, in a bit of a daydream. Philip's voice brought me out of my reverie.

'Well? Are we agreed?'

I wanted to ask him how he would arrange it, where he would find the gunman, but the tense expression on his face told me to shut up. What did it matter anyway, as long as it was done? So I said, 'Agreed!' with a bright smile, and held out my hand to shake on the deal.

'Good. Now, how are you going to spend your last few days?'

That stumped me. It was ridiculous, but I honestly couldn't think of anything I had a burning desire to do. I looked at him helplessly.
'Give me some ideas,' I said, 'My mind's gone blank.' He had a lovely smile, so kind and gentle. He didn't seem to despise my lack of imagination.
'Isn't there somewhere you'd like to visit? Or someone?'

I tried desperately to think of something, and then glumly shook my head. What an incredibly dreary person I was. The truth of the matter was, I was nobody without Geoff at my side. He had always been enough for me, so that just being with him had been all I ever wanted. That, I now realized, had been a mistake. That was why I had no real friends to comfort me and was now so alone. My earlier euphoria had seeped away and I was wishing I hadn't agreed to a week's delay. It would have been better to get it over with quickly.

'Well then - tell me, what was the best holiday you ever had?'

He reminded me of my old English teacher Mr Parsons, who had tried so hard to see if there was anyone interesting inside me. I racked my brains. I had always loathed family holidays, with Mum and Dad pretending it was so jolly, when really all that any of us wanted was to be back home and in separate rooms again. Geoff and I hadn't taken a holiday after our rain-drenched honeymoon week in Skegness, where we had holed up in a shabby little hotel on the seafront, and tried not to think how much more comfortable we would have been in his flat. Had there been children of course, we would have made the effort, but on our own there never seemed to be any point. We were perfectly happy at home, saving our money for restaurants and cinemas and music.

We hadn't felt able to refuse though, when his sister invited us to her son's wedding in France five years ago. That wasn't a holiday, though, it was a family duty. 'Please come,' Brenda had wailed down the phone, 'It'll be all her French friends and family and poor Sam needs all the support I can muster.' We had dutifully applied for passports and caught the Eurostar and then a train to Rouen, and the weekend had passed in a confused blur of eating and drinking and not understanding much at all, and then there was the overwhelming relief of being back home again. I guess some people are just not cut out to be adventurous. And yet here I was, having to dream up a holiday for one.

I shook my head helplessly at Philip, and to my relief he laughed.

'Heavens,' he said, 'You are in a bad way! I can see I'm going to have to do this for you. Let's meet at the travel agent's in the High Street tomorrow morning, and we'll sort you out a holiday then. Bring your credit card!'

I made my way slowly home, my feet aching in the silly high heels. I ran a lovely deep bath, and poured into it an extravagant amount of bubbles. No point in saving them now.

****

Philip was studying the placards in the travel agent's window when I arrived just after 10.

"You choose,' I said. 'I really don't care - I'll pretend I've won the holiday in a competition!'

And that was how I ended up in a 4 star hotel in Paris, in the Latin Quarter. It was such an ordeal. I'd forgotten what little schoolgirl French I ever possessed, and I dreaded having to speak to anyone. There was an unseasonal heat wave, I had taken all the wrong clothes and I was far too nervous to attempt to buy anything cooler.

The only bit I liked was looking at the paintings in the Musée d'Orsay, which I discovered on the third day, so I spent the rest of the week there. It was an easy walk from the hotel and they had proper tea in the beautiful tearoom. I especially loved looking at Van Gogh's work, I spent hours simply gazing into the canvases and losing myself in the colours. When I looked at 'Starry Night over the Rhône' something seemed to shift inside me, and start to unfurl, like a small flower. So that was an unexpected bonus.

I had 6 nights in Paris and then flew back to Birmingham and arrived home in plenty of time to meet Philip at the King's Head that evening. He went straight to the point. 'Do you still want to go ahead?' he asked. I said I did and gave him all the information he asked for. My bedroom, I told him, was on the first floor, second door on the left. The first door was the bathroom. 'In case he wants to wash his hands,' I said and then blushed at the foolishness of this remark. Philip snapped shut his notebook.

'Right, then. It'll be soon after 11 tomorrow evening. He'll let himself in through the back door - be sure to leave it unlocked. Go to bed early, and remember to take some pills to make you sleep. That way you won't know a thing. The police will receive an anonymous tip-off the following day, so you needn't worry that you'll be left undiscovered.' It hadn't occurred to me to worry about that. Philip was wonderfully considerate.

He coughed politely. "There's just the small matter of his fee, and then I'll be on my way.' I had the cash all ready for him, in a pretty pale blue envelope.

'Goodbye, Deirdre,' he said, and he raised my hand to his lips, which no one had ever done before. I thought it was nice to have a novel experience right at the end of my life.

I was up all night, putting the house to rights. Silly, wasn't it, but I didn't want the police thinking I was a slut. I had to smile at the thought of how puzzled they would be at this motiveless murder. The thought that I would be forever an unsolved case gave me great satisfaction. I cleaned and dusted every inch of the house, and I put fresh sheets on the bed. By the time morning came there was nothing left to do, so I got out the 1000-piece jigsaw of Monet's garden and managed a fair chunk of the sky. I always do the tricky bits first. It was the longest day of my life, but eventually it started to get dark, and I took three sleeping pills and went to bed. I didn't think I would sleep, but off I went, dead to the world.

****

It was the dustmen banging about under my window next morning that woke me. It took a while for the mistiness in my brain to clear, for me to remember what was meant to have happened, and to understand that it hadn't. I lay there, letting the realisation that I was still alive seep into me, and I didn't know whether to laugh or cry, so I did both. What a fool. A brainless, gullible and fantastically lucky fool.

It was a beautiful day. I stayed there, lying between my lovely clean sheets in my best nightie, looking out at the cloudless sky, and a calmness settled within me. A newness, a freshness, a lightness of heart. The heavy weight of misery that I had been carrying around with me for so long that it had become a part of me, seemed to have floated away during what was supposed to have been my last night. I felt, for the first time since Geoff had died, content. Life wasn't perfect, of course it wasn't, but Philip had given me a second chance to make the best of it, and, having gone right to the edge of the cliff and not fallen over, I felt I owed it to myself to have a go. And to Geoff. He wouldn't have wanted me to be a quitter.

I would make a start on my new life straight away. I would go to the library and see if they had a book on Van Gogh or Cezanne. I could do an art appreciation class, maybe I could even have a go at painting myself. It wasn't too late to try something new. It wasn't too late at all.

There was one thing I had to do though, before embarking on my new life, and that was to call Philip. I was smiling as dialed but the telephone lady said, 'The number you have called is not recognized.' He must have changed his number already in case I tried to get a refund. I thought that was such a shame, because of course I didn't want to do that, I wanted to thank him. £350 seemed to me a very small price for getting my life back.

****

I keep looking for him, when I'm out and about, but I've never seen him again, and his card has disappeared from the shop. I like to think he is travelling around the country helping people like me. My friends from the painting class are used to my funny ways now, and sometimes they join in when I raise my glass in the pub and toast him. I did that tonight when we finished making the final arrangements for our trip to Florence next week. We're going to look at the paintings in the Uffizi and I can't remember ever having been so excited. 'Here's to Philip!' I said, and everyone smiled. They just think he's a friend of mine who got me into painting, and in a way, I suppose, they're right.

The Man He Used to Be

I loathe my brother-in-law, but I've always tried not to let that spoil my relationship with my sister Martha. So when she phoned last night, sounding unusually despondent, I offered to accompany her when she visited Vincent at the nursing home today. Apparently he's not expected to hang on much longer; a third stroke is anticipated any day now and that will be that. A rotten way to end up of course, but there's a large part of me that can't help feeling it serves him right.

Martha picked me up after lunch in her little Peugeot and I kept her entertained during the ten-mile journey by telling her all about Keith's promotion.
'It'll mean even more travelling for him, of course, but neither of us have ever minded that. It's good to have space in a marriage, don't you think?'

Martha grunted, and I didn't press the point. She and Vincent have hardly spent a day apart in the last thirty years, which must have been perfectly ghastly for her, poor thing. At least she's getting a bit of a break from him now. I moved on to giving the latest news of the twins. I noticed that she didn't ask as many questions as usual, but I expect she was concentrating on her driving.

We parked the car and went to find Vincent. Martha was walking so fast that I had to break into a trot now and then to catch her up. Vincent's room was small and dark and unoccupied, so we made our way along the narrow corridor to the residents' lounge. This time our progress was much slower, because an enormous lady on a zimmer frame was inching her way forward in front of us. I thought about offering to help, but decided against it. Health and safety and all that. In any case, I was in no hurry, Vincent wasn't going anywhere. Martha had brightened up a bit now and was looking almost pretty. Her new haircut had taken years off her, and when I told her this, she gave me a nervous little smile.

'Vincent always liked me to wear it long,' she said. 'But they had a new girl at the salon yesterday, very bright and bubbly, and before I knew what was happening I'd agreed to try it shorter. I was scared stiff while she was cutting, but when she'd finished I really loved it! I only hope it doesn't upset Vincent – he does so hate anything to change.'

With any luck, I thought grimly, she won't have to worry about precious Vincent's feelings for much longer. We reached the door of the lounge, and I had quite a job manoeuvring myself in between the large lady and the door so that I could open it. I received a nasty blow on the ankle from the zimmer frame, which I bore most stoically, and eventually all three of us made it inside.

The residents' lounge was a long narrow room, with three harsh strip lights and maroon vinyl armchairs. The walls were blancmange pink, and dotted about with dreary flower prints in plastic frames. The full-length curtains at the big window overlooking the car park were the colour of putty. I smiled with satisfaction at the décor, which I knew would be sure to fill Vincent with disgust. He had a thing about good taste and elegance – an obsession, really - and poor Martha had never been allowed to indulge those natural feminine urges to prettify her austerely decorated home. I know for a fact that he once made her return four scatter cushions because he claimed they made the sofa look untidy.

I wrinkled my nose. There was an unmistakable odour of incontinence in the room, and an attempt to mask it with cheap air freshener hadn't helped much. Poor Vincent. He suffered from a keen sense of smell, and one of Martha's household tasks was to keep the house aired and free of all whiffs. He liked onions in his food, but couldn't bear to smell them cooking, so Martha had to juggle with doors and extractor fans in an attempt to keep the kitchen aromas away from Vincent's small, sharp, twitching nose.

'Excuse me, but there seems to be a horrid smell in your kitchen,' he informed my mother the day we first met him, and I have never forgiven him for embarrassing her so. Martha had brought him home for tea and cake, and was fluttering about in a state of high excitement. Being so shy, it had taken her ages to procure a boyfriend, and we were all curious to meet him. But I was also harbouring a lot of resentment, because up until then I'd assumed I'd have my big sister's undivided attention just as long as I wanted it. I was vexed at the thought of her doing something that didn't include me.

And so the minute Vincent made that remark to my sweet flustered mum -whose only crime had been to leave an open tin of cat food on the counter- I knew I was always going to hate him. He and Martha married with indecent haste, a mere three months after they met. 'What's the hurry?' I remember wailing to Martha and she just laughed. Such a confident laugh. After the wedding I stayed out of Vincent's way as much as I could, only ever visiting Martha at home when he was out. We were forced to meet at family parties and Christmases and such like, but that was all. I think he's only set foot in my house half a dozen times, though of course Martha comes over often. She has always been such a devoted auntie to my girls, and they love seeing her. They say they like Vincent too, though of course they don't know him like I do.

  Martha must have known how I felt about Vincent – it's not in my nature to be good at pretending - but it didn't appear to bother her. Her loyalty and adoration were as unwavering as they were baffling. I simply couldn't see why she thought he was so wonderful. As far as I was concerned, he was a stuck-up pompous prig, who made no effort to join in. Having no family of his own, you'd think he'd delight in being able to share in our fun. But he'd often wander away during a family gathering and find somewhere to read a book. Inexcusable rudeness, I called it. He evidently thought himself far too superior for us. He didn't even take an interest in my girls, who were just adorable, especially when they were toddlers. I shall never forget the time my Sally tried to clamber up onto his knee, and he looked at her as though she were a large lizard. 'Martha!' he called, his voice low and urgent, and she stopped in the middle of the duet we were playing on the piano and rushed over to him. She took Sally off him and gave her to me, and spent the rest of the afternoon glued to his side. Hateful man.

  'There he is!' Martha hastened to the far end of the room where Vincent was slumped in a wheelchair. His head seemed stuck on at an awkward angle, and he was glaring as Martha leaned forward to kiss his cheek. Perhaps he didn't approve of the new haircut. We fussed about for a bit, propping him up into a better position with the aid of some gratifyingly hideous patchwork cushions, and then we pulled up a couple of chairs and tried to think of things to say to him.

  At least I tried. Martha didn't seem to feel the need to say anything, and just sat there gazing at him lovingly with those big brown eyes of hers, and stroking his bony hand. Over by the window a tiny woman with a mass of unkempt hair was crooning loudly to herself as she wound and unwound a ball of wool. The large lady on the zimmer frame was still on the move, lurching up and down the room and knocking into the furniture. The other residents were mostly dozing in their chairs or gazing at the large screen of the television on the wall. It was showing a housebuying programme but fortunately the sound was turned right down.

I reached the end of my animated description of Keith's new job, and lapsed into silence. I made myself take a proper look at him, this detested brother-in-law. As always, he was dressed very smartly, in grey flannels and navy blazer. He wasn't wearing his usual cravat though; probably that was too much effort for the time-pressed staff. The resultant bareness at his neck gave him a new vulnerability. I wrenched my gaze from his freckled throat and looked at his face. He was still glaring, and I decided that this was now his default expression, the only way he could show his disgust at his current situation. Even when he had been in full control of his life he had been a glarer, with hard, piercing eyes that I always felt were trying to bore a hole – two holes - into me when I did or said something he considered foolish. And as I usually only spoke to him when I'd had a few drinks and was ready to taunt him, I was quite familiar with his glare.

Martha, on the other hand, was probably not so used to it. She had spent most of her married life, as far as I could gather, ensuring that she didn't annoy Vincent, so that when he looked at her his eyes tended to be approving. On many levels their marriage had worked well, although I never understood how she could be so humble and self-effacing. For some unaccountable reason she had adored him from the start, deciding that he was so far above her that it was nothing short of a miracle that he had noticed her at all. He was a lecturer at the University and had published several important papers on quantum physics, or some such gobbledygook. Hardly a riveting source of conversation for poor Martha over the dinner table.

Her role had been to see to Vincent's every need, and to allow him complete freedom to carry out his lofty work. Not only did she look after the house and garden, and provide him with his favourite dishes, but she also did all the boring jobs like paying the bills, finding a plumber, buying his socks, even carrying out the rubbish. The great scientist didn't have to do anything at all except devote himself to his physics.

Whether or not he realised how much he relied on her, I'm sure Martha that knew, and that it was a source of great satisfaction to her. If they had produced a child, things might have been very different, because Vincent would have been ejected from his position at centre stage. I don't know why they were childless, but I do know that it didn't bother Martha at all. She would just smile serenely when I brought up the subject, and after a while I gave up asking . She didn't have her own kids, but she was more than happy to share mine, and that suited me very well, as she was the perfect babysitter, available at any time and for free. And in any case I didn't want to hear if there were any problems in the bedroom, because I found the image of her and Vincent in bed just too bizarre and, frankly, embarrassing, to contemplate. The only picture I could ever frame was of her kneeling abjectly before him, performing some menial task like cutting his toe nails. Perhaps that was as far as they ever got.

'There's something wrong,' Martha said to me. 'He's looking frightened.'

I took another look at the glaring eyes. 'He's not frightened,' I said, 'he's just cross!' I managed to refrain from adding, 'as usual.'

'Oh no, that's not crossness. That's Vincent being unsure and nervous. Lots of people make that mistake; it's why they always think he's being arrogant when really he's just terrified.'

Suddenly she was on her knees in front of him. I watched, astonished, as she gently pushed his legs apart and planted herself between them, wrapping her arms around his back and resting her head on his chest. It was an astonishingly intimate gesture and I felt myself blushing for her. What an extraordinary way to behave, in front of everyone. I don't believe Keith and I have held hands in public for years.

'I'm here again, Vincent,' she said softly. 'It's alright, I'm right here with you.'

The effect was immediate. His face relaxed and his mouth gave a little twitch on the left hand side, as though he were trying to smile. The glare was gone, and his eyes were gentle now. I was struggling to take in what I had just heard. Vincent terrified? I threw my memory back to times when I had been the subject of that glare. Could I really have got it so wrong? That first Christmas when he refused so curtly to join in a game of charades – could he have been petrified, not contemptuous? Keith was always telling me I was too quick to judge people. Could his subsequent offer to play Scrabble with me possibly have been an act of brave conciliation, rather than an attempt to show off his cleverness? I had refused, of course, just to show him how offensive such rebuttals could be. He had never asked again and neither had I. Rather a shame, now I come to think of it. I love a good game of Scrabble. He would probably have been a challenging opponent.

Martha was still murmuring, and I leaned forward to hear better. 'You'll be fine, my darling,' she was saying, 'You'll see, it'll be alright. No one will hurt you. Don't be scared.'

I realised that my mouth was hanging open and I clamped it shut. This was too weird. Vincent, that supercilious elitist, that fussy, bad-tempered, unsociable control-freak, had suddenly been re-invented as a frightened little boy. My thoughts were skittering about all over the place and I felt most peculiar. I like things to be clear and orderly. I like people to stay in their boxes.

'Who'd like a nice cup of tea then?' The trolley rattled up beside us, and Martha and I were given our tea in flowery mugs by a cheery care assistant. 'Can you manage Vincent's, my love?' she said to Martha, who put her tea down and reached out for a lidded plastic beaker with a straw. 'We'll be fine, Linda, thank you,' she said. I always admired the way Martha knew people's names.

She sat back on her chair now, and gently slid the straw between Vincent's lips. As he drank, his eyes swivelled slowly away from Martha and came to rest for the first time on me. We both stiffened, and he stopped sucking. I forced a smile.

'Hello, Vincent,' I said. 'It's good to see you.' His eyes widened a little, and I realised that this was probably the first pleasant thing I'd ever said to him. I had decided to hate him on day one, and had never tried to get to know him. I should have tried, for Martha's sake, to get to know the man who made her so happy.
I should have tried to understand why it was she loved him so. I should have paid more attention to the clues – like that time I came across her typing up one of his lengthy theses in his study. This was yet another of the menial tasks she performed for him, but not out of subservience or even a

sense of duty, I now realised, but simply because she adored him and wanted to please him. The way I had wanted to please Keith when we were first married. How long had that lasted?

Martha hadn't heard me come into the house that day, and I stood there at the door of Vincent's study, watching her fingers fly over the keys and the bright smile hovering on her lips. She was completely engrossed in her task, which I found extraordinary, seeing as how she surely couldn't have understood one word of it. After a while I gave a cough and she looked up, still smiling. 'Oh hello!' she said. 'You know, it's so wonderful to be married to a genius.' At the time I stored the absurd line away to laugh at with Keith later, but for some reason I never got round to telling him.

I finished my tea, and twisted the mug around in my hands. I could hardly bear to look at him now, but I made myself. I studied those dark, sensitive, really rather beautiful eyes, and I understood then that they had no more glared at me than a rabbit glared at the lamplight. They had been scared, that's all.

He seemed to be waiting for me to say something.

'I'm sorry,' I said. His mouth twitched again, and suddenly I couldn't bear it. I didn't want him to forgive me, because I wasn't ready to forgive myself.

'I'll see you back at the car,' I said to Martha, not looking at her, and I grabbed my handbag and hurried out of the lounge, down the corridor, out into the fresh air.

****

I had finished crying by the time Martha came out to the car, but she knew, and hugged me to her for a long time. 'It's alright, please don't worry,' she said. 'He understood. We both did.'

We didn't speak at all on the drive home. When we pulled up outside my house, I put my hand over Martha's and squeezed it hard. You can say a lot with hands. Which was lucky, because I had so much to say.

'Can we do this again next Friday?' I asked. I had a lot of making up to do, to both of them.

'Thank you,' said Martha, 'Vincent would like that, and so would I.'

Death Wish

Hardly a day has gone by during the last three years without me killing him off one way or another. It has been my favourite day-dream. Sometimes it was a commonplace death, in his sleep perhaps, or with a quick heart attack; but usually it was something more sensational, more violent, more vengeful. Yesterday afternoon, for instance, I had him ramming his BMW into a concrete wall, a scene so real and so final that when, a few minutes later, I heard his car in the drive, I felt a jolt of surprise.

'You're home early!' I said brightly as I took him his customary gin and tonic, but I noticed my hand was shaking. I wonder if he ever had an inkling of just how much I loathed him?

You're probably wondering why I didn't just leave him, if I hated him so. But there was no way that I was going to hand over that wonderful house, that glorious garden, the fruit of years of my devoted labour, so that he could enjoy them with his tarts. Of course if I divorced him for easily provable adultery, the boys and I would get to stay in the family home, at least until they finished their education. But that wasn't long enough.... and in any case, it wasn't as simple as that. Guilt makes a man exceedingly generous, and even a generous divorce settlement would be unable to match the unlimited access to his bank accounts and credit cards that I currently held in my position of wronged but useful wife.

And despite hating him, I didn't really want Neville to leave, because then he would be able to romp about with his floosies without a qualm. That would have made his life far too easy. I rather enjoyed the way he had to creep about, nervous of being discovered, ineptly covering his tracks and making ridiculously flamboyant gestures of guilt-ridden affection. And then there was the matter of my social standing in the town. I was enormously proud of the way I had risen from nobody to the poised and confident wife of the managing director, and while I know divorce is common enough these days, there is still a stigma attached, an unsavoury whiff of failure. I didn't want to be the wife whose marriage had failed, whatever the reason,, I wanted to continue to hold my head high as a bravely coping widow.

So I hope you can you see, why there was nothing for it but to continue to co-habit in a murky state of mutual dependence., until I could pull off the perfect murder.

I now find it hard to believe that there was a time when I didn't hate him, although I suppose that I must have quite liked him once, before I learnt about the other women. His serial infidelity killed any residual fondness, stone dead.

What I can remember, extraordinarily vividly, is the moment when I finally admitted to myself that I found him physically repugnant. It was exactly one week before our wedding and I was standing at the sitting room window of my parents' house, looking out onto the garden and thinking, 'This time next week...' My mind was a dreamy whirl of bridesmaids' dresses and marquee flowers and the beautiful pearl tiara I was to wear in my hair, when suddenly I felt a clammy hand on my bare arm. I started in horror, for I hadn't heard him approach, and instead of apologizing for creeping up on me, Neville laughed coarsely and slapped me on my behind. I can recall shuddering with disgust at his vulgar display of proprietorial affection, and then panicking wildly. Why hadn't I realised earlier how distasteful I found him? How could I marry a man whose very touch made my skin crawl?

The answer was, that at this late stage, I had no choice. I simply hadn't the nerve to back down, not with all the wedding preparations made, the baby on the way and my parents prouder of me than they had ever dreamt of being. I had always been the plodder of the family: dull, hard-working, predictable, nothing much to look at, and for the first time ever I had managed to surprise them. They had been first stunned and then delirious with joy when I told them that my wealthy boss had proposed to me; what they didn't know, of course, was that I had fallen pregnant after a drunken office party fumble, that I craftily threatened suicide when he offered to pay for an abortion, and that he was, albeit reluctantly, doing the decent thing. Quite good of him really.

The wedding was arranged, out of necessity, with the utmost speed, so that we hardly had time to get to know one another. The intervening weeks happened to coincide with a flurry of new orders, so that both he and I were far too busy to do anything but work inside the office, and too exhausted to spend much time together outside it. I was a highly efficient secretary, hard-working and dedicated, with just the right amount of initiative, so I suppose he resigned himself to the prospect of marrying me with the thought I would be equally competent in my role as wife. And after the initial shock, he was much more excited than I was about the baby; he loved the idea of having a son. As for me, I had learned enough about him in the six months I had worked for him to discover exactly how much he earned, and how much more he was likely to earn in the coming years. That knowledge was a great help in overcoming my qualms.

So you can see why backing out at that late stage was never really an option; the shame and the embarrassment would have been excruciating. It was impossible, far more impossible than just gritting my teeth and getting on with it. And that's what I did, firmly closing my mind to the bed part of our marriage, about which I had no illusions, and focusing instead on the large house, the walk-in wardrobe that I would fill with designer clothes, the garden, the two cars, the exotic foreign holidays and best of all, Neville's frequent business trips abroad. I forced myself to believe that his money, his amiability and his generosity would be enough. I remember smiling brightly throughout the reception, concentrating hard on the admiring and envious looks of those of my friends who were still single. He was, in their eyes at least, 'quite a catch', and even now, seventeen years later, I hate to think of anyone else getting their hooks into him.

As it turned out, the sex side of things wasn't too much of a problem. After the initial encounter, of which neither of us had more than the haziest of recollections, I held him at arm's length for weeks, hoping that my lack of passion would be viewed by Neville as endearing modesty. When I finally succumbed (seduced, it has to be said, by a beautiful diamond bracelet), it was every bit as horrid as I was expecting – he was rough and clumsy, and fell into a snore-ridden sleep as soon as he had rolled off me. But it had the distinct advantage of being all over in three minutes. And this pattern never changed. It seemed to be the way he operated, and I soon decided that three minutes every now and then (and after a while it became much more then than now, which suited me fine), was a small price to pay for everything I got in return. Not that I didn't work hard at fulfilling my role as Neville's wife – being dutifully witty and charming at those interminable corporate events, organizing his designer home, his social diary and his holidays, presenting him with a spotless shirt and a neatly pressed suit each morning, and a delicious dinner most evenings.... not to mention providing him with two sons to carry on the family name.

In fact we would probably have muddled along contentedly enough - me busy with the house and garden and spending his money, he absorbed in his work, his beloved sons and his golf - if that sluttish secretary Emma hadn't propelled him into a mid-life crisis three years ago. He discovered for the first time in his life that sex could be exhilarating if you knew what you were doing, and were doing it with someone equally enthusiastic, and he went a bit loopy. One of my many duties as the perfect wife was to turn out his pockets before a visit to the dry cleaners, and I discovered what was going on with Emma almost immediately. Neville was away on a business trip for three days, and so I had time to work out what I was going to do about it. I was in a turmoil of emotions. Although *I* didn't want him, I found I hated the idea that someone else was exciting him. I ricocheted between feeling horribly jealous, frightened that he would leave me, angry, self-righteous, and finally, by the time he returned on the Friday night, I had settled into a cool and steely hatred. No one was going to treat me so cavalierly and get away with it. After all that I had done for him! I decided to say nothing, but to watch and wait until I could get my revenge.

It was easy enough to get Emma sacked – all I had to do was claim she had negelected to pass on my non-existent messages, and feed her some extremely poor advice about the best way to do her job, so that poor Neville had no choice but to end their affair and sack her. However by the time this happened she had introduced him to a whole new world of the flesh, and it had become his latest hobby. Some men take up fly-fishing; Neville took up philandering.

Hatred can be very empowering. I kept an eagle eye on the proceedings, and with the passing of the months and each new slut my loathing grew stronger and I felt more in control of my situation. I was quite certain that I was capable of killing him – all I needed to do was perfect my plan. Most of my waking and dreaming thoughts during that period concerned The Murder of Neville. And when I wasn't actually planning it, I was galloping through murder mysteries in search of inspiration. At one stage I was even making notes, in shorthand of course, but I soon decided that was too risky, and destroyed them. There had to be no clues. By the end of last week, with the help of some lads from the nearby comprehensive, I had rejected the various murder options in favour of the most practical one, which was also, of course, the most simple. I was feeling pretty cheerful at having got the thing sorted at long last - it was a bit like finishing off a protracted school project.

At the back of our house, accessed by a gate in our garden wall, is a lane which is used as a short cut by school children, and is much frequented by dog walkers. On the other side of the lane is a steep ravine, which the council makes sporadic attempts to fence off, but which the kids dearly love to muck about in. Their latest game is to push each other off the path at the very steepest bit, which is right behind our house. The victim shrieks with fear and delight as he careers down the slope, often losing his footing and rolling the last few yards. I was watching them from our bedroom window last Thursday afternoon, and was just about to yell at them for making so much noise, when I realized that they had provided me with the answer.

As soon as they had gone, I hurried down to inspect the murder site, and it turned out to be perfect in every way.

Not only was the fence already broken, but there was a clump of boulders at the bottom of the ravine, on which someone could easily bash their brains out. All I had to do was entice Neville out there (when drunk, as he's most malleable then), at night (no onlookers), hit him on the head with a stone, and then push him down the slope. Then I would follow him down to ensure that he was dead, bash him again if necessary until he was, place the stone with his blood on it next to him, go into the house and hysterically dial 999. I would need to be wearing suitable slope-scrambling shoes and disposable gloves, and there would have to be a stone placed in readiness at the side of the path – but that was all. Talk about simple! And then that very evening Clare rang, to invite us to dinner today, so that everything fell beautifully into place. I had the venue, the method and now the date.

Every few months we get invited to dinner by Charles and Clare Brooker, a rather dreary couple who live down the lane, and who have absolutely nothing to recommend them except for the fact that she is a superb cook. I'm fairly certain that it is all she ever does, which means that hours and hours of preparation would be spent on our beautifully balanced and presented gourmet meal. They never invite any one else to their dinners and after the meal I usually engineer a game of bridge, to spare us all the effort of making further small talk. I can't imagine why they keep inviting us – we never return the favour – and can only assume that they find each other as boring as we do, and have no one else to ask. And we do genuinely appreciate the food – it is every bit as good as the best restaurant we know, and it is lovely not to have to drive. Or pay. Irritatingly, Clare seems to think there is some sort of intimacy between us women, simply because we have been neighbours and sporadic dinner companions for years; she punctuates her inane remarks with statements like, 'Well, you know me, Sarah!', when actually I don't know her at all, and have no desire to.

It was while Clare was wittering on about the menu she was planning for us, that I suddenly realized that this was it, this was the opportunity I was looking for. To carry out my beautifully simple plan, I needed Neville to be drunk and walking past the ravine at the back of our house, and I needed witnesses to the fact that we were a devoted married couple, so that no one would think that I had pushed him. Neville always drank too much at Clare's dinners, out of boredom, and I could easily play the part of the enamoured wife for one evening.

Even without the Brookers' evidence, I was very confident that no one would ever suspect me. My detailed knowledge of police procedure, thanks to my exhaustive study of TV crime dramas and who-dunnits from the library, led me to cover my tracks long before there was anything to cover. During the last few months I had even taken to writing little messages of affection to Neville, such as, 'Thank you Neville darling for last night – you were wonderful xxxx', and squirreling them away in various drawers ready for the police to pounce on if they came searching for clues. Neville stumbled across one of them last week when he was looking for some batteries, and was very puzzled. I watched him out of the corner of my eye and had trouble controlling my mirth, as he read the note, glanced quickly over at me, and then carefully replaced it in its hiding place. He didn't mention it of course, but he was unusually attentive to me that evening, which I found very tiresome. I had to go and have an early and lengthy bath.

Neville looked distinctly put out when I told him about our dinner engagement, so I guessed that he had been planning some extra- curricular activity - probably involving the new blonde behind the bar at the King's Head - and that I had scuppered that arrangement. How very gratifying. He's boring when he's in a sulk though, so to cheer him up, I reminded him about the divine lamb cutlets Clare gave us last time, and that mollified him. He does so love his food.

I was sitting at my dressing table doing my eyes, when he emerged from the en-suite bathroom. Lobster-red from an excessively hot shower, his hair tousled up into silly tufts, his over-fed belly protruding over the top of the towel fastened at his waist: it was not a pretty sight. And yet he seems to have no trouble at all persuading his trollops to jump into bed with him. I don't think it's just his money they're attracted by, it's his unquenchable confidence that he's an attractive desirable man. I wonder why it is that confidence alone is not enough in a woman, that she feels she has to work so hard at maintaining a lovely face and body as well? I pressed my lips firmly together, to prevent anything that could be construed as a caustic remark from escaping them. After all, I could afford to be generous on this, our very last evening together.

A couple of fortifying whiskies later, we set out cheerfully enough to walk the 500 yards to Clare and Charles' house. It was me who suggested going the road way, as we were running a bit late. We could come back via the back lane, I told him, as I gave him the bag containing my gardening shoes (for the return journey) and the bottle of his favourite Bordeaux, thoughtfully chosen for his last night. It was raining, and I held my umbrella close down over my head to give maximum protection to my hair, expensively coiffed only that morning so that I could be looking my best for the police.

There was no pavement on that very narrow stretch of the road, and I was walking in front, around the bend.

There was usually very little traffic, but if a car did come, you had to flatten yourself up against the hedge to get out of its way. When it happened, I'm sure it must have happened very fast, but at the time events seemed to follow each other oh so slowly and with crystal clarity. While lying here I have been able to go over them again and again, and there can be no doubt about what happened. No doubt at all.

I was so sure that he needed me, you see. Not love, of course, I wasn't as foolish as that – but I thought that he relied on me completely as his organizer, his enabler, his partner, and that he would leap to attention if ever I were in trouble. When I slipped suddenly in my ridiculous high-heeled sandals, and fell with an undignified sprawl onto the road, my concern at first was for my hair, because I had dropped the umbrella. It was only when I heard the car that I realised that I had to get out of its way, and fast - but the ankle I attempted to scramble onto gave way immediately with an agonising spasm, and I fell back down, my arm reaching out to Neville for help.

'Neville!' I shrieked, 'There's a car coming!' Even now I find it hard to believe what he did next. Or rather, what he didn't do. He had a weird gleam in his eyes and he looked at me with his head a little on one side, as if he were pondering the answer to a tricky crossword clue. That was when I realized that he was considering whether or not to help me.

'Neville!' I shrieked again. Perhaps I sounded shrill and bossy, instead of pathetic and loveable; whatever the reason, he continued to stand there looking at me, pressed up against the hedge out of harm's way with his arms hanging by his sides. Of course I now see that I should have rolled myself into the hedge, but instead I made another desperate attempt to get up, and slipped again – so that I was lying in the road as the 4x4, with cocky young Simon

Hendry at the wheel, came hurtling round the bend. He always did drive too fast. There was no way he could have stopped in time.

I must have blacked out when he hit me, because the next thing I knew I was lying here on this hospital bed, in what must be the intensive care ward. I can't feel a thing, which I guess is just as well. And I can't move, or open my eyes. I can hear though, and I have heard enough to understand that I haven't got much longer. An hour or two at the most. Apparently there isn't any point in operating, as the internal injuries are too extensive. Neville is here, of course, I can hear him murmuring soothingly to Sam, our youngest. Ben, it seems, is at an all-night party somewhere and can't be reached. Typical. He always was a selfish little sod, and now he can't even make it to his mother's deathbed.

I can see the funny side, even now. As I lie here listening to the machines bleeping and feeling the life force ebbing slowly from my body, I feel that if only I had the energy, I would laugh. All that planning, scheming, dreaming – all of it come to nothing. Neville has won the battle, and he didn't even know we were at war.

Making It Better

Judith was so nervous that her mouth had dried up. When she tried to wet her lips there was no saliva to lick with. Her hands, though, were clammy on the steering wheel and she had to keep wiping them on her skirt.

She missed her exit off the roundabout and crawled round again, her face tense with apprehension. She should have worn her black bra. White always looked a little grey after a while, no matter how clean it was. But perhaps she wouldn't have to undress. Couldn't he just massage her shoulder through her jumper? This was worse, far worse, than going to the dentist.

She pulled into the driveway of an unassuming bungalow called 'Sunnyside' and switched off the engine. Her heart was hammering. She told herself to stop being so ridiculous. If she really wanted to do something about her frozen shoulder, then a private physiotherapist was the only answer. Her neighbour Heather, who was always injuring herself, said she simply didn't know what she'd do without Alan Simms. Judith locked the car and marched up the drive, trying to look braver than she felt.

A sign directed her to the waiting room at the side of the house. It also told her to beware of the Alsatian. Judith gave a little moan. There was no reply to her knock on the door, so she inched it open and walked in. The waiting room was just a hallway, with three chairs lined against the wall and some women's magazines on a shelf. A smart suede jacket was dangling from a coat hook, a wispy scarf trailing from its pocket. Judith sat down and studied the impressive display of framed certificates lining the wall opposite her. Alan Simms was very well-qualified in all sorts of areas – apparently he'd even passed his advanced driving test, though quite what that had to do with easing muscular pain Judith wasn't sure. One certificate had his photo on it, and she got up to have a closer look. She gasped. The man glaring back at her was bald with beady, bulging eyes.

Judith glanced about her. No one had seen her arrive, so perhaps she could just slip away.... but it was too late. She could hear voices, and the door at the end of the room opened. A woman was chuckling.

'Well, I'll do my best,' she said. Judith froze. She knew that voice.

'But you know me, Al, I'm a bit lazy!' declared Isabel Spencer, self-appointed First Lady of the Bridge Club, as she emerged through the door. Her wide smile vanished when she saw Judith.

'Judith!' she exclaimed, her face suddenly very pink.

'Hello, Isabel,' said Judith evenly. Of all the women she knew, Isabel was the one Judith found the most intimidating. Many a time had she felt herself reduced to a quivering heap of insecurity by Isabel's withering reprimand for playing the wrong card at the bridge table. Isabel was always so sharp, so quick, so self-assured. Judith had never once seen her lose her steely composure, and she couldn't imagine why being encountered at the physiotherapist's should embarrass her so. She looked past Isabel at the possible cause.

Alan Simms in the flesh was an improvement on his photo, but not enough of one to put Judith at her ease. He was short and stocky, and his white tunic was stretched tightly over his belly. His trousers and trainers were white too. He looked like a nurse in a mental hospital, ready to put any wayward patient into an armlock. His jolly grin wasn't at all reassuring.

He planted a kiss on Isabel's cheek, and she broke away to grab the suede jacket. 'Must dash!' she trilled, not looking at Judith. 'Bye!' She was gone.

'Hello, Judith,' said Alan. 'Come on in, and let's see what we can do for you.'

Judith took a deep breath. She only had to do this once. It would be okay. After all, Isabel had just done it. But then Isabel – clever, elegant, confidant Isabel - was a very different sort of woman from Judith.

The treatment room felt very warm after the unheated waiting area. Judith was pleased to see that the sheet covering the couch was clean and wrinkle-free. She removed her coat and sat down on the chair facing Alan's desk. He pulled out some forms from his filing cabinet, and smiled at her. 'So you know Izzy, do you? She's one of my regulars – been coming for years! I'll just fill these in – won't take a minute.'

Judith tried to swallow.

'Um – do you think I could have a glass of water?' It came out in a jumbled rush.

'Course you can, love,' he said. He reached behind him to the bottle on the filing cabinet and poured some water into a glass. For a moment Judith thought the buttons on his jacket would give way under the strain, but they held. She managed to turn her nervous giggle into a cough.

Alan began with the medical stuff – where was the pain, how long had she had it? He grunted with sympathy as she told him about slipping down the attic stairs in her socks, and landing heavily on her shoulder. Any heart problems, operations, medication? Then he moved on to more personal things, but in such a gentle, interested way that she soon lost her stiffness.

'My husband Geoff died six years ago. He was only 56, we'd had such plans for his retirement... Yes, two children, but living in London and Scotland. I keep myself busy with the garden, and I read a lot, and play bridge. I used to go swimming regularly, but not since I hurt my shoulder.'

She wished her life sounded more interesting. As she was struggling to come up with something unusual to tell him, he said, 'Right then, let's take a look at this shoulder. Stand up and show me how far you can raise your arm.'

Judith managed to reach shoulder height before grimacing with pain, and Alan jotted something down. 'That's fine,' he said. 'If you could just strip down to your bra please – you can leave the bottom half on – and then lie on your tummy on the couch.' He said all this so nonchalantly, as if it were the most natural thing in the world for her to take off her clothes in front of a strange man. At least in the hospital where she'd gone for her x-ray, they'd given her a little cubicle to undress in and provided her with a robe.

Judith could feel the blood rushing to her cheeks as she stood up and jerked her jumper over her head, and then unbuttoned her blouse. She was acutely conscious of the post-Christmas bulge that protruded above the waistband of her skirt. It didn't matter. He'd seen it all before. Hundreds of times. She just had to blank her mind and get on with it.

She slipped off her shoes and clambered onto the couch, positioning her face on a cushion with a hole in its centre. It felt surprisingly comfortable. She studied the black squiggles on the lino below and tried not to panic. Now what was he doing? She could hear him rubbing his hands together and then suddenly he was right over her saying, 'Just relax. I'll undo your bra so I can get at your shoulder.'

Judith stiffened. This was ghastly. But there was no way out. She bared her teeth at the squiggles and then gasped as Alan's slippery hands came down on her back and started to knead her flesh. For a second her mind went numb with horror, and then, to her amazement, she began to realise that it was beginning to feel quite good. She let herself sink further into the vinyl-covered foam. Actually, it felt completely wonderful. No one had ever massaged her back before, and no one, not even Geoff, had ever touched her in this way. It was as though these hands loved her, and more than that, knew her – knew her better than she knew herself. She felt small and cherished and melting and she didn't want this feeling to end. She was smiling euphorically through the hole in her cushion.

'That feel alright?' asked Alan, and Judith groaned happily.. 'You're carrying a lot of tension in your back, you know – I'll just ease out some of these knots.' The pain was exquisite; how could something hurt and feel delicious at one and the same time? Now he was concentrating on her damaged shoulder, getting right in at the source of the pain and at one point making her yelp. 'Sorry, love,' he chuckled, evidently not sorry at all. 'Now I can see exactly where the problem is.' He asked her to stretch out her arm and he gently manipulated it as far as it would go, and then helped it go a bit further. It hurt, but she found that she trusted this man completely, and when he praised her for gaining another inch, she felt absurdly proud of herself.

Alan was doing up her bra. She desperately didn't want that to be all. 'Right, now I need you to roll onto your back,' he said, 'and I'll work on it from the other side.'

Judith's self-consciousness flooded back as she turned over, sucking in her stomach. She squeezed her eyes tight shut. She heard the squelch of oil being reapplied to Alan's hands and then they came down, firm but kind, on her neck. She lifted her chin to give him more room. At one point he paused to move her hair away from her neck and the gesture felt astonishingly intimate. She could pretend he was Geoff. But no, that didn't work – Geoff would never have done this. George Clooney then. That was better.

Alan's fingertips were rubbing under her armpits now, his fingers strong and confident as they drew little circles on her skin. Then he moved to the top of her chest and his thumbs joined in as the circles became larger. Judith felt battered with conflicting emotions. It was squirmingly embarrassing, but at the same time utterly blissful. 'The muscles run along here to your shoulder,' Alan explained, but she didn't need a reason. Just as long as he kept doing it. 'Now push against my hand,' he instructed, and push she did, with her eyes still tight shut.

'Well done, you've worked hard today,' he told her. 'You lie here and relax while I write up your notes.' He gently placed a large warm towel over her – was there no end to the pleasurable sensations this man could dream up? Judith drifted away, reliving the entire experience. She could still feel the touch of his fingers. She thought about Isabel, tight, controlled, bossy Isabel, stripped to her undies, turning into someone called Izzy and dissolving away under Alan's hands. She understood now why she had blushed. She understood completely.

The towel was lifted off her and reluctantly Judith opened her eyes. Alan told her to sit on the edge of the couch and raise her arm as high as she could, which was a good 9" higher than before. 'By the time I've finished with you, we'll have that arm up by your ear, good as new,' he promised.

'Will it take long?' Judith asked anxiously.

'Oh no, a couple of months I should think - as long as you do the exercises. Come over to the door and I'll show you what to do.'

Obediently, she slid off the couch and padded over to the door, and Alan showed her how to walk her fingertips up it. He pushed down hard on her bad shoulder, and then he put his hands around her waist and straightened her spine. Judith was all confusion and had trouble taking in what he was saying.

She felt light-headed as she got dressed and handed over her money. It seemed a very small amount for such a momentous experience. 'I'd like to see you once a week,' said Alan, his pen poised over the diary. 'Same time next Wednesday?'

'Oh yes, please!' exclaimed Judith, and then, more calmly, 'That'll be fine.'

Alan held open the door for her. There was no one in the waiting room. Judith paused, wondering if the kiss was meted out to first-timers. Evidently not. 'See you next week then, Judy – and don't forget those exercises!'

She walked slowly to her car. A couple of months. Once a week for a couple of months. It wasn't much. Then she smiled. Of course, there was nothing to stop her having another little accident when her shoulder was better. Perhaps she could pull a muscle in her thigh. After all, Heather said she had been coming to Alan for years....

Friday's Bridge Club would be interesting. She was looking forward now to playing on Isabel's table. 'Two spades!' she would declare with supreme confidence, no longer intimidated in the slightest by Isabel's much-vaunted mastery of the game. She would look her in the eye and give her a conspiratorial smile. Because Judy and Izzy weren't so very different after all.

Sarah's Visit

I awoke this morning feeling troubled and I didn't know why. I lay there for a while, slowly coming to, listening to the birds and to the gentle snoring of the dog.

Something was happening today and I needed to remember what it was.

'Benny,' I called out softly to the spaniel who is even older than I am in dog years. He stopped snoring and opened one eye.

'What's happening today, Benny dog? Can you remember?'

He yawned, roused himself slowly from the floor and padded round to the side of the bed. I fondled his silky ears and then it came to me. Today Sarah was coming, and I had to be alert and fully functioning.

I would start with a shower, and I would seek out something clean and decent to wear. Something that wouldn't make her purse her lips when she looked me over. I glanced at the alarm clock. 8.25. But not just yet. I would doze for a little longer, mustering my strength. I would need every ounce of it to get through the next few days. It was good of her to come, of course it was, but already I was looking forward to her leaving.

****

Seven hours later I pulled up outside the station, praying that the Paris train had been delayed. I was late, having missed the turning and had gone on about five kilometres before it dawned on me that I was on the wrong road. Sometimes I find it hard to remember where I'm supposed to be going. I expect I would be just as absent-minded if I still lived in England, but I like to think that it's the enticing nature of the empty French roads that leads me astray...

She was there of course, sitting on a bench beside the entrance, doing something on her phone. Texting, I think they call it. Probably reporting back home that I'd failed the first test. I opened the car door and she looked up and saw me. Relief and annoyance battled for a moment in her face, and luckily for me, relief won. She has a lovely smile, my Sarah.

'Hi Dad!' She had whizzed her bag on wheels across to the car in the time it took me to extricate myself from the driver's seat. I hesitated, never quite sure whether I'm supposed to hug or kiss or do something else entirely. She gave me a quick peck on the cheek and I managed a pat on her shoulder.

'Sorry I'm late,' I said. Her face seemed to have more wrinkles in it than last time, but she still looked pretty good for her age, I thought. A lot like her mother in fact.

'Only 20 minutes, that's not bad for you!' she replied as she heaved her case onto the back seat. A cheerfully delivered remark, but still it rankled. Surely I'm not late every time?

She drove, of course. Neither of my children will let me drive them, as I'm considered far too dangerous on the roads. It was too much to hope that the dented bumper would go unnoticed, and she immediately began to cross-examine me on it. I tried to keep my replies light and amusing, but she didn't seem to find my slight disagreement with a Volvo in the supermarket car park very funny.

'If you lived in a town you wouldn't need to drive at all!' she declared, quite as if this were a new observation. Sarah has been trying to get me to move for the past five years but so far I've managed to stay put. I don't mind that my house is surrounded by nothing but fields, and that I can go for days without seeing another soul.

'You could walk to the shops!' she continued, and I agreed that this would indeed be the case. I then had the bright idea of enquiring after the grandchildren, whose names had temporarily escaped me. This diversionary tactic worked a treat, and no further mention was made of my faulty lifestyle choices for the rest of the journey.

I was able to let my mind wander a little while she chattered on about schools and ballet lessons. Had I remembered to buy anything for supper? I rather thought not. My problem is that I just don't find certain things, like food, important. Should I suggest that we stop at a shop on the way home? Suddenly it all seemed too much effort. I felt very tired. I was missing my afternoon nap.

I was right about there being nothing much in the fridge for supper. Most of what there was ended up dumped in the bin because it was apparently way past its sell-by date. Fortunately Sarah had brought baked beans and crumpets with her from London, so that's what we had. Very nice they were too. Washed down with several glasses of Cotes de Rhône from my wine box – now there's something I never run out of. By her third glass Sarah had become pretty mellow.

We did the dishes together and then she announced that she was going to bed. "We've got a busy day tomorrow!' she announced ominously. 'You should probably turn in too, Dad.' By way of a mini-rebellion I stayed up till 1 am watching some incomprehensible police thriller. It felt strange, knowing someone else was sleeping in the house, and I couldn't decide whether I liked it or not. I am so used now to living on my own.

****

The next morning I was woken by the sound of the pipes gurgling. It took me a few moments to work out what the strange noise could be, and then I remembered Sarah and realised she must be having a shower.

When I arrived in the kitchen she was already at the table making a list. Her hair was still wet, sleeked back behind her ears in a way that made her look very severe.

'Morning, Dad,' she said, without looking up. Oh dear, something was wrong already.

I said hello and busied myself with letting Benny out.

''The bathroom loo doesn't work,' she went on. 'Why is it that the loos in this house never work? I had to lift the lid off to get it to flush. First thing I'm going to do today is call a plumber.'

I refrained from mentioning that the cistern lid in my shower room was permanently off, I had grown so used to this way of flushing that it didn't bother me in the least. I nodded and shuffled about getting my breakfast. Same thing every morning, Cornflakes, sliced banana and a pot of tea. Usually I have the radio on, and try to pick up some new French phrases to note down in my little book. Today of course I couldn't do that. I kept my head down low over my bowl while Sarah tried to summon a plumber. I was very proud of the fact that I had the calling cards of two I'd used before pinned to my cork board. I knew better than to offer to help, though her French was really not very good. It seemed the second plumber said he'd try and come in a few days' time, and she replaced the receiver none too gently.

'At home,' she announced tersely, 'I have a marvellous plumber, who would not only have come today, but would have sorted those wretched loos for once and for all.' I rather doubted both these statements, but I just smiled apologetically.

I made her some coffee while she rummaged irritably through my cupboards. Several more items were judged unfit for human consumption and binned. An attempt at appeasement was called for.

'Would you like me to come with you to the supermarket?' I offered.

'No, no,' she replied hastily. 'I'll be fine. It'll be an easy shop, because you need absolutely everything.'

****

When she'd gone the house felt very quiet. I stood in the hall watching the sunlight stream through the window on to the faded rug, and it seemed as though the house and I were breathing a sigh of relief at being alone again. It was so good of her to give up several days of her busy life to come and sort me out, but the thing is, I'd really rather she didn't. When my son comes to visit – which isn't often, I have to say – he does absolutely nothing except sit in the sunshine, watch my Sky sports channel and drink all my wine. Oh, and sleep. The amount of sleeping he does when he's here is astonishing. He's a very relaxing guest.

Benny nudged at my legs, and I remembered that in all the excitement I'd forgotten his breakfast. I found him some dog biscuits and then we had a gentle stroll around the garden together.

My garden is a source of enormous pleasure to me, and I spend as much of the day as I can in it. One job I can still do is sit on my ride-on mower and cut the grass once a week. The rest of it I leave to the gardener, who everybody says is costing me too much.

'Why not move to a flat?' they ask. 'Think of all the money you'd save by not paying a gardener.'

'And think of all the pleasure I'd lose by not having a garden,' I say in my head. I've learnt over the years not to argue. It's much simpler to agree and then do nothing.

****

She's back. That was quick! It takes me an hour to buy one bag of groceries, and here she is already, back with half the shop. I helped to bring in the bags, and offered her a glass of wine.

'No thanks, it's a bit early in the day for me,' she said pointedly, which didn't stop me from pouring myself some white from the fridge. White at lunchtime, red in the evening is my pattern.

I sat down on the terrace opposite her. I tried to listen, I really did, but most of it just floated over my head. She showed me some 'ready meals' she'd bought – 'Three minutes in the microwave, that's all!' she enthused and I smiled back at her. Why would I need something that only took three minutes? I, who have all the time in the world? Some evenings it takes me several hours to decide what I want to eat, locate the various ingredients and work out some way of making them edible. Quite fun really, and it has led to some interesting meals...

'Don't forget this, it's better if you do that'..., on and on it went. I fetched myself another glass of wine and tried very hard to look as if I were paying attention.

Soon lunch appeared on the terrace, and for a while we ate in silence.

'This is nice, being able to eat outside in April,' Sarah said, and she tilted her face back to drink in the sun.

I agreed, and got up to make the coffee. As I entered the kitchen the phone started ringing, and I reached for the receiver.

'Grandad?' The voice was a child's and seemed to be tearful. 'Is my mum there?'

I should have known who it was, but I didn't. I wasn't even sure if it was a boy or a girl. Sarah has four children, two of each. I think.

'I'll just get her for you,' I said, and turned to call Sarah. But she was right there beside me. She seemed very different, all of a sudden. She wasn't being bossy or controlling as she murmured down the receiver, just affectionate. Totally absorbed in the task of pouring love and reassurance down the phone.

'Daddy can do that,' she crooned. 'Oh Ben, of course he can! And I'll be home tomorrow night.'

I pricked up my ears. That sounded pleasantly soon. Didn't she normally stay longer?

I plodded out to the terrace with the tray of coffee, and then had to go back for the sugar.

Sarah had replaced the receiver and was sitting there with her head in her hands.

'Sarah?' I said uncertainly. 'Is everything alright?'

She lifted her head up and looked at me and I could see that she was crying. This was very bad. My strong, capable girl, who was always in control. I didn't know what to do, so I gave a little cough and reached for the sugar bowl on the shelf.

'Coffee's ready,' I said. 'Come back into the sunshine, it'll make you feel better.'

She followed me out onto the terrace, sat down and fixed her eyes on her coffee cup. I knew I ought to say something.

'Problems at home?' I ventured.

She drank from her cup, and as she put it down I noticed that her hand was shaking. 'Yes, Dad,' she said. 'Actually, John and I are splitting up. He's met someone else. The usual story.' She gave a bitter little laugh. 'He's trading me in for a newer model. The kids are having trouble coming to terms with it all.'

This was terrible. And completely unexpected. They'd always seemed rock solid, John and Sarah, completely right together. I felt stunned and bewildered and so very sad for my poor girl.

'And how are you holding up?' I asked gently.

'Oh, I'll be alright. You know me, one of life's copers. I've got to be, haven't I? For the kids' sake. They need me to carry on as usual.'

I nodded. For the life of me I couldn't think of anything to say.

'More coffee?' was what I finally came up with.

'No thanks, I think I'm jittery enough after that phone call! Now, I thought that this afternoon we'd tackle the paperwork that I noticed was piling up in your office. We could check that you're on top of the bills, tidy up your desk. How does that sound?'

Perfectly ghastly, I thought. I hate anyone interfering in my office. I had rather hoped that the shut door might have been a signal to her to keep out. It might look a mess to outsiders, but I have my own system. Sort of.

I nodded gamely, thinking that the least I could do was be acquiescent. If sorting through my muddled papers was really what poor Sarah wanted to do, then who was I to stand in her way? I roused myself to make one last effort.

'Is there anything I can do to help?' I said. 'I mean, with the situation at home?'

'Like what, exactly?' The question wasn't harsh, just realistic.

I shrugged. 'Well, I don't know. But if you and the children need a break any time, you know you're always welcome here.'

'Thanks, Dad. I haven't got round to thinking about the summer yet, but we might just take you up on that.'

We lapsed back into silence, and I closed my eyes. This was the worst part of being a parent, watching your children suffering and knowing there's nothing you can do.

Benny chose that moment to give an enormous sigh, which just about summed up the prevailing mood.

Sarah gave a little hoot of laughter, a laugh that reminded me so much of her as a young girl. She had always been full of energy and fun, always playing games and laughing. Until being a working wife and mother had turned her into this careworn woman with wrinkles in her face and tired eyes.

I smiled at her. I'd had an idea. There was something I could do after all, something that would make her forget her problems for half an hour and revert to the bright-eyed child who was still there somewhere inside her. I might be old and doddery and forgetful, but I had managed to remain pretty agile on my feet.

'Tell you what,' I said. 'I've got a much better idea than doing boring old paperwork. Do you fancy a game of ping pong?'

'Oh Dad,' she said. And the look on her face told me that for once, I'd got something right.

First Steps in Kyrenia

It was late afternoon in Sheffield and the weather was grey and miserable. So was Kath. She was walking down the street, heading for the chemist with her prescription. A group of scruffy teenagers was clogging up the pavement. 'Excuse me!' said Kath but they ignored her, and she gritted her teeth with resentment as she pressed up against the travel agent's window in order to squeeze past them. Staring her full in the face was a huge red and yellow poster shouting, 'Last Minute Offer! 5 nights in Northern Cyprus for only £299 ! Leaving tomorrow!'

    Kath didn't usually act on impulse – it was one of the many reasons Clive had cited for wanting a divorce – but for once it felt exactly the right thing to do. Until that moment it hadn't occurred to her that she could go away for half-term. She had imagined that she would spend the week holed up in her now hateful flat, with only the aged cat, depressing reminders of Clive and her bitterness for company. Plus, of course, the mountain of marking she had been staring at for days. But now she entered the shop, pointed back at the poster and, minutes later, handed over her credit card.

    It was only when she got back home that she realised she had forgotten to go to the chemist. A whisper of a smile hovered on her lips as she wedged her gold sandals – bought 3 years before but never worn – into the corner of her case. A week by the sea in sunny Kyrenia instead of in her damp flat on the outskirts of Sheffield seemed like a very good idea indeed. The anti-depressants could wait until she got back.

****

Thank goodness she'd had the sense to wear her padded jacket, although she hadn't imagined she would still be needing it in Cyprus. As she trudged down the airplane steps at Ercan airport, Kath reached into the pockets for her gloves, and pulled the collar up around her neck. A nasty cold wind was whipping at her hair and she could feel a few spots of rain. Average temperature in October: 28º, the travel agent had said. Trust her to manage to arrive during a freak spell of wintry weather.

It was 6 o'clock local time, and just beginning to grow dark. Kath followed the representative of the optimistically named Sunshine Club across the gleaming arrivals hall and onto the waiting minibus. She narrowed her eyes at her fellow holidaymakers who were folding themselves into the cramped seats, shoulders drooping after the tedium of the long day's travelling. Most were late middle-aged couples grumbling about the weather, but there was one young blond woman who seemed genuinely excited to be there, her nose pressed up against the glass so as not to miss anything of her new surroundings. The sight of her made Kath feel old and tired and gloomier than ever.

The travel rep launched into her 'Welcome to Northern Cyprus' spiel as the bus swung out onto the main road, but Kath didn't bother to listen. She was thinking about her cat Alfie and wondering if Tessa was looking after him properly. Would she remember to give him a drop of milk after his tea? Was he missing her? The tears that threatened so often these days sprang into her eyes, and she blew her nose to dispel them. Would that dreadful woman never shut up? Her sing-song nasal voice was beginning to grate on Kath's nerves.

They were on the outskirts of Kyrenia now and her spirits plummeted still lower. This didn't look anything like it was supposed to; even Sheffield was more attractive than this untidy sprawl of shops and factories and signposts clamouring for attention. She looked to see how the young woman was reacting, but she seemed to be fascinated by it all, and not a bit disappointed. She must have sensed Kath's eyes on her, for she turned suddenly and flashed her a cheerful smile, a smile so full of warmth and happiness that Kath caught her breath in a spasm of envy. She managed a tight-lipped grimace in reply.

It's all a question of attitude, she admonished herself in her best schoolmistressy manner. You can be miserable or cheerful – it's entirely up to you. She had said this so often to her grumpy 6th formers, but it never seemed to work for them, and it wasn't working for her. She was as unhappy as she had ever been in her life, and that was that.

But at least the view from her window had improved dramatically, now that they were in the town. This was more like it. This was what she had paid her hard-earned cash to see: a flood-lit white mosque, a laden fruit stall, an ornately carved building with a stone staircase winding up the outside...

The minibus drew up outside an old hotel, and Kath retrieved her suitcase and dragged it up the ramp into the lobby, which was huge, and full of mirrors and pillars and enormous potted palms. The floors and walls were marble and there was even a fountain, adorned with a grinning cherub. Kath found herself grinning back at him, her mood considerably boosted by the unexpectedly lovely décor.

The receptionist was an elderly man with kind brown eyes and near-perfect English. He seemed a little concerned when he ascertained that she was on her own, and his smile was warm and gentle. As she filled in the form he apologised to her for the weather, and assured her that the forecast for the rest of the week was very good. His hand hovered for a second over the key board, before settling on a large key attached to a heavy brass ball.

A couple that she recognised from the bus accompanied her in the lift.

'Will you stop going on about it?' the man hissed at his thin-lipped wife. 'Okay, stupid me, I left it on the kitchen table, big deal. I expect they have shops in Cyprus, don't they?'

The wife glanced in Kath's direction and gave a meaningful cough, her face rigid with disapproval and annoyance. It occurred to Kath that there was most definitely an upside to holidaying alone.

'This is us I think!' declared the man, with a brave attempt at joviality as the door opened on the 2nd floor. His wife was still looking grim as they wheeled their matching cases out of the lift.

Kath got out on the next floor and walked slowly along the corridor in search of number 310. She turned her key in the lock and opened the door of the largest bedroom she had ever seen. There must be some mistake – this couldn't possibly all be for her. There was a vast bed, which would sleep four very comfortably, several armchairs and coffee tables, a writing desk, and a colossal wardrobe. Beyond that, the door to the en-suite bathroom stood open, revealing an ivory bath with claw feet. Kath's mouth dropped open as she took in the French windows leading onto a balcony. She sank into the nearest armchair and took a deep shuddering breath of wonder. This couldn't be right;

someone was bound to come along in a minute and tell her she was in the wrong room. But meanwhile she would just sit here and try to savour the moment...

The trouble was that Clive wouldn't let her. Every time she tried to be calm, and just concentrate on the now, the memory of his hateful words and the image of him and that slut of a girl would flood into her mind and make her feel sick with the shame and the horror of it all. What a terrible mistake it had been, to get jobs at the same school, so that they had been the subject of merciless gossip for months. Probably most of the staff, and a good many of the pupils too, had known about his affair with the P.E. teacher long before she did. And once she had found out – not through any clever deductions of her quick-witted brain, but through Clive having to sit her down one ghastly evening ten days ago and spell it out to her - lots of hitherto puzzling things immediately made perfect sense. The growing awkwardness in the staff room, which had led her to anxiously check her breath and her armpits for malodorous whiffs, the outbreaks of uncontrollable giggles amongst the girls in her tutor group.... Kath groaned aloud at the unbearable embarrassment of it all.

At that moment there came a gentle knock at her door. Here goes, she thought grimly. This is where they tell me to move to a tiny room down the corridor and where I meekly obey, even though if I had a spark of gumption in me I would protest and demand to stay put... She looked about her and her eyes alighted on the wardrobe. The perfect hiding place. They couldn't make her change rooms if they couldn't find her.

The wardrobe smelt, not unpleasantly, of lavender and mothballs. There was a trickle of light coming through the pierced flower design at the top of the door. Kath stood quite still, clutching the door shut with one hand and stopping the coat hangers from jingling with the other. She felt ridiculous, but stoutly defiant. Suddenly she realised a sneeze was coming, one of those sneezes it is impossible to stop. It was quite the noisiest sneeze she had ever produced.

'Hello?' The voice was inside the room now. What a cheek! She hadn't said they could come in. Kath burst out of the wardrobe and glared at the intruder, who was standing just inside the door. It was the girl from the bus, the one who was having a great time. She was young, slim and very pretty, precisely the kind of person Kath wanted to avoid in her current mood. The girl smiled sunnily at Kath, as if she thought hiding in wardrobes was a perfectly natural thing to do.

'Yes?' barked Kath.

'Excuse me,' said the girl, in a strong East European accent. 'I am Margita. I am Polish. Sorry to disturb. I see you on bus, and I see you are only like me, and I think we go to dinner – yes?'

Kath was so surprised that for a minute she couldn't answer.

'Oh,' she said, forcing a smile. 'Yes, that's a good idea.' She hadn't given a thought to dinner, but suddenly realised she was starving.

Margita, uninvited, walked across the room to the French windows and threw them open. 'You see?' she said to Kath, pointing down at the lights of the harbour below. 'Many, many restaurants. We go?'

Well, why not, thought Kath. If Margita turned out to be a terrible bore, she would just have to spend the rest of the week avoiding her. It would give her something to do. 'I was about to have a bath,' she said. 'Could we meet in half an hour? Downstairs?' They had a bit of trouble with 'half an hour' and 'downstairs' but got there eventually. Margita was still giggling as she left.

Clive was always telling her to hurry up. Right now Kath could hear his irritated voice telling her she hadn't time to take a bath, a shower would be much quicker. She poured the hotel bubbles under the hot tap and sank back in the water with a sigh of pleasure, a glass of whisky from the mini-bar by her side. Tonight she would drink red wine with her fish, which Clive thought a vulgar habit, and order something deliciously gooey for dessert. Clive never ordered dessert and always pretended to be surprised when she wanted one. 'Are you sure?' he would say, and that made her feel not sure, but she had to eat it anyway, on principle, and all the time his eyes would be on her, making her feel fat and greedy. Margita wouldn't be like that. She would be an enthusiastic eater of puddings. Kath was smiling as she drained her glass and pulled herself out of the bath.

The whisky had made her feel reckless. 'Well, I am on holiday,' she said aloud as she strapped on her gold sandals. They looked a little odd, worn over tights, but pretty all the same. She pulled her warm jacket on over her cotton dress and cardigan. Not exactly elegant, she thought, but who cares? Clive had this habit of looking her over on the rare occasions they went out together, and then drawing his lips back into a thin line. 'Do I look alright?' Kath would ask, despising herself for needing to know. 'Mmm, fine,' Clive would reply. As if 'fine' was any kind of an answer.

Margita was waiting for her in the lobby, sitting on a leather sofa and studying her guide book. She had changed too, from jeans into a crinkly skirt, and she had a turquoise pashmina draped over her shoulders. She looked up as Kath approached and beamed at her.

'I read of the museum!' she enthused. 'A museum of ships in Kyrenia!'

'That's good,' said Kath. 'Shall we go and eat?'

The wind had died down and it felt much warmer. Kath sniffed appreciatively at the air – fish and spices and an unidentifiable something that made her feel a million miles away from Sheffield. Maybe the sandals had been a mistake – it was a long time since she had worn a pair of heels. She concentrated hard on not going over on her ankles, while Margita kept gasping in delight at the prettiness of the lights of Kyrenia harbour.

'Look!' she exclaimed, pointing at a sign advertising boat trips, 'That is fun, yes?' A group of lads in denim jackets walked past and wolf-whistled. Kath scowled at them but Margita only laughed.

Kath stopped to inspect a menu. 'How about in here?' she asked, aware that she didn't really care what she ate as long as there was lots of it and soon. 'Ok, tak,' said Margita, following her into the small restaurant. The tables looking out at the harbour were all taken, and the waiter led them to one at the back of the room.

'Red or white?' asked Kath.

'Ok,tak,' replied Margita, so Kath ordered a bottle of red wine before learning that Margita didn't drink and wanted a Coke. Their drinks arrived very quickly, with a basket of bread and some olives. Kath took a long swig of wine and then another. She felt warm and mellow now and smiled at Margita, who beamed back at her over the menu.

'I take spaghetti and meatballs – these are little balls of meat, no?'

For some reason Kath found this question inordinately funny. She gave herself up to her giggles, realising that this was the first time she had laughed since The Bombshell. For ten whole days she had crept between school and the flat with her head down, festering and aching and agonising inside, but refusing to talk about anything but work with any of her colleagues. She hadn't even drummed up the courage to tell her mother and sister. Later, she kept saying to herself, later - when I can be sure of doing it without crying.

The giggles had stopped at last. Still smiling, she poured herself some more wine and beckoned to the waiter to come and take their order.

'Is good here, no?' said Margita, apparently not at all put out at being laughed at. Kath agreed. It was good, very good indeed.

'So,' said Kath brightly. 'What brings you to Kyrenia?'

'Is good, no?' answered Margita.

'Well, it seems very nice so far. Have you been before?'

'What is before?'

They were both relieved when the food arrived and they could abandon their attempts at conversation. Kath's red mullet was grilled perfectly, and there were chunky chips and a crisp green salad. Margita hummed happily as she ate her meatballs.

'God, I was hungry!' said Kath, sitting back and wiping the salad dressing from her lips. 'That feels so much better.'

Margita nodded happily.

'I'm sorry you can't help me with this wine,' said Kath. 'It's very nice.' She held up her glass and said 'Cheers!' It came out rather loudly and the woman at the next table turned to look at her.

Kath leaned forward and fixed her eyes on Margita's. 'Clive says I drink too much, you know,' she confided. 'But he's not here, thank God, so I can do what I like!' She poured herself another glass.

'Clive?' asked Margita. 'What is Clive please?'

It was as though a switch had been pressed, a lever pushed to one side, a valve opened. Kath took a deep breath and let it all out. She told Margita exactly what Clive was, and the fact that the poor girl understood not one word didn't bother Kath in the least. It felt wonderful to be able to tell someone at last that Clive was vile, pathetic, the scum of the earth.

'He's a pompous, patronising prig. He's stubborn, selfish and inconsiderate. He expects me to clear up after him and then has the cheek to complain if the flat's a bit untidy! He's lazy, unimaginative and soulless. He never reads a book, unless it's a ghosted biography of some stupid footballer. He's going bald, he's got a beer belly and he snores whenever he's been to the pub, which is most nights.' She paused, reflecting for a moment that most of those evenings 'at the pub' had almost certainly been spent in Miss Fuller's bedroom. Kath cleared her throat and hurried on. 'He's a cheat and a liar and a bore and if he was the last man on earth I wouldn't touch him with a bargepole. Amy Fuller' – she pronounced the name with frosty disdain and suddenly the truth exploded inside her in a shower of stars – 'Amy Fuller is entirely welcome to him!'

Margita had been growing increasingly nervous throughout this speech. Years of addressing the back row of the classroom had given Kath the kind of voice that carried. Most of the other diners were looking at her now, some amused, some frowning. Margita was chewing her lip and scrabbling at her purse.

The waiter materialised at Kath's side.

'I'm just so glad that he's out of my life!' She smiled triumphantly up at him.

'You like dessert?' he said gently. 'There is ice cream, chocolate cake....'

'Of course we want dessert!' declared Kath. But Margita was on her feet, pulling her pashmina round her shoulders.

'I go now,' she said softly, looking at the waiter, not Kath. 'I go to hotel, no? I give this money.' She placed some notes under the salt cellar and slipped away.

Kath felt elated, cleansed, as light as a feather.

'I'll have the chocolate cake please,' she said quietly. 'With some ice cream.' The waiter nodded his approval.

In her haste to be gone, Margita had left her guide book on the table. While she waited for her pudding, Kath pulled it towards her and flicked through the pages on Kyrenia. Her Polish was non-existent, but luckily the book had plenty of pictures. She gave a gasp of delight. It seemed that she had stumbled upon the ideal holiday destination. Kyrenia, St Hilarion, Buffavento.....the place was awash with castles, Kath's favourite thing in all the world.

She stared at the extraordinarily beautiful St Hilarion Castle, its crumbling crenellated walls and towers clinging to a craggy hilltop. There was even a perfectly preserved arched window complete with window seat, and she longed to be sitting there and gazing out over the view. She would go tomorrow, and she would stay there all day, and the next day too if she wanted. She couldn't imagine anything lovelier than being able to explore the castle ruins to her heart's content, on her own – no pupils to supervise, no husband to pacify when he grew bored. She could just please herself. In fact, she could spend the whole of this holiday re-discovering what it was that she loved doing, because for far too long she had let herself be bullied by that skunk of a man.

Kath looked down at the thick wedge of chocolate cake in front of her, a large dollop of vanilla ice cream sliding off it. Just like the misery that was sliding off her shoulders. She smiled. First thing in the morning she would buy a little thank-you-and–sorry present for poor Margita, who would be steering well clear of her from now on. What a delightfully productive first evening this had turned out to be.

She picked up her spoon and plunged in.

Nicola

There was a parking space exactly opposite her front door. I reversed into it, concentrating on performing a perfect manoeuvre, just in case she happened to be looking out the window. I turned off the engine and then I just sat there, staring across at the pretty little terraced house, the home of the woman who had taken one look at me 26 years earlier and said, 'No thanks.'

I had dreamed about this day for 20 years, but now I was fighting the urge to start the car and drive straight back home. I unclenched my hands from the steering wheel and wriggled my stiff fingers. All the while my eyes continued to scan the front of the house, searching for information. She kept the front garden very tidy, and there was a wooden bird table, hung about with mesh cylinders of nuts and seeds. I had an almost identical bird table at home, and my heart lifted, just a little. We had something in common.

My mouth was so dry that I had nothing to lick my lips with and I cursed myself for failing to bring a bottle of water. Also I felt sick with nerves. I tried Radio 3, thinking that classical music might soothe me, but some opera singer was warbling in anguish so I snapped her off. Deep breaths, in and very slowly out. I hadn't come all this way just to sit in the car. Besides, I really needed a loo.

'Hello, you don't know me, but I'm your long-lost daughter and I need a pee.' That would be a great beginning.

I checked my reflection in the rear-view mirror and decided I looked okay. My hair was behaving itself for once, so at least I wouldn't make her shudder. I wondered if I looked at all like her, or if I took after my dad, whoever he might be. My eyes were my best feature, I had always thought; large and brown, with very long lashes. Would she have my eyes, or my nose, or my hair?

I ran through again the three facts in my possession, courtesy of Social Services : her name was Sandra Feldman, she lived at 22 Brownlow Crescent, she would like to hear from me. Hear from me, she had said, not see me. I was supposed to write a letter, or maybe phone, not turn up unannounced on the poor woman's doorstep and give her a heart attack. This was madness, a crazy idea. I should go home and compose a careful little letter suggesting we should meet. Give her time to prepare. Give me time to prepare, come to that. I wasn't ready, I had thought I might be, but I most definitely wasn't.

Suddenly my hands were back on the steering wheel, gripping hard. The door to number 22 was opening, and someone, a woman, was coming out. I couldn't look, I thought I was going to faint, I lowered my head and squeezed my eyes tight shut. I was willing her not to approach me, willing myself to be anywhere in the world except Brownlow Crescent.

There was a dainty little tap on my window, and my brain froze. But the tap came again and I forced myself to look up. She was what they call petite, with well-cut shoulder length brown hair, careful make-up and size 8 trousers. She looked nothing like me. She was so pretty and dainty and I hated her. Why couldn't she have been plump and cuddly and comforting, like a mother is supposed to be? Forcing a smile, I pressed the button to wind down the window.

'Excuse me,' she said, and her voice matched her appearance, all clipped and posh. 'I was wondering if you might be Nicola?'

I couldn't bear to be rejected all over again. Someone as classy as this would be embarrassed to have me as a daughter.

'No, sorry,' I said, turning the key in the ignition, 'I'm not Nicola. I was just leaving.' My voice sounded hard and blunt, after her silvery tinkle. I was, all at once, so angry that it hurt. I wanted to get out of the car and slap her pretty little face. How dare she? What gave her the right to throw me away and then go on to live an easy life, getting all poised and posh and elegant?

I pulled out into the road and sped up to the junction, where I looked in my mirror. She was still there, standing where I had left her, and some of my anger fell away. 'Now you know how it feels,' I shouted to my mother as I turned the corner, and at that moment I had the strange sensation that a hole had appeared where my heart had been.

There was a large supermarket just after the junction, and I pulled into its car park and made my way unsteadily to the ladies'. Once safely inside the cubicle, I let everything go, all the tension and anguish of the last few weeks, and I wept and then sobbed and finally just howled. I didn't care who heard me. I had absolutely no idea what I should do next. I couldn't face the long drive home to an empty house, but obviously I couldn't stay in the toilet all night either. A cup of tea, that's what I needed. Things always seem better after a cup of tea. And a piece of cake.

It was while I was sipping my tea that I thought what I could do. I could phone her, right now, and ask her to join me in the café. It wouldn't be nearly as scary as talking to her in her house. I punched in the number quickly, before I could change my mind.

She picked up on the first ring. 'Hello?' She sounded scared, I thought, maybe almost as scared as I was.

I couldn't speak.

'Nicola, is that you?' she said, and her voice was kind now, asking me to be kind in return.

'Yes,' was all I could manage.

'Where are you? I can come to you, just stay where you are and I'll come.'

That made me start to cry all over again. Just hearing those words, the words I had yearned for all my life. I pulled myself together and croaked, 'Tesco's café.'

'Good,' she said, 'That's good. Don't move, I'll be there in 5 minutes.'

I didn't move. I hardly breathed. I stared out of the window and watched the people scurrying about in the car park. I wondered about their lives and if they were happy and whether they had mothers who loved them.

And then she was there, slipping into the chair opposite me, and I could see she had been crying too. She looked more ordinary now, not nearly so elegant. Her mascara had run a little and I saw with a jolt that she did have my eyes, they were exactly the same. Her mouth was a bit like mine and her nose was shiny and I could almost believe that this woman might be my mum. She was panting, she must have run all the way.

'I knew it was you, outside the house,' she said. 'I'm so glad you came.' She reached across the table with her little hand and I met it with my big one, and they seemed to know each other. They felt right together, and I felt my heart give a little lurch.

'So am I,' I said, as our hands squeezed together. But I couldn't think what to say next, even though I had rehearsed this moment a hundred times. I stared at our clasped hands and willed her to say something.

'Is that carrot cake?' she said. 'It looks lovely, can I have a taste? I would get my own, but I don't want to leave you.'

I took a moment to let those last words settle around me and then I smiled and pushed the plate towards her.

Ready for Rapture

Margaret spotted the Fiat the minute she entered the garage forecourt and she was instantly smitten. The most adorable car in the world was over in the far corner, its banana-yellow paintwork gleaming in the morning sunlight. 'Look at me!' it was calling, 'You could have such fun in me!' The other cars were mostly blue or black and looked so dull and ordinary in comparison.

Margaret was paying no attention at all to Mr Sykes, who was detailing the merits of a dark blue Escort he had been attempting to shift for the past nine months. 'And of course, it has a full service history,' he intoned.

'That one!' Margaret pointed at the yellow Fiat. 'How much is that one?'

Mr Sykes' cheek twitched. Another of those dippy women who couldn't see past the car colour. Could be useful. That and the fact that she was obviously single, with no man in tow to ask awkward practical questions and know the market value.

'I'll have to check,' he said. 'It's just come in. I've only had time to give it a quick once-over, but it's a nice little runner. I'll go and fetch the key.'

Margaret was off, almost sprinting in her desire to reach the car. She looked a little absurd, a short, plump woman in a cardigan and sensible shoes, her glasses on their gold chain bouncing on her bosom, and her face flushed with excitement. She peered through the driver's window and beamed at the polka-dot seat covers. It was the kind of car you couldn't help having fun in, she thought. Wasn't it time she had some fun?

Mr Sykes came up behind her and unlocked the car, his mind fast at work on how best to clinch this deal. He had paid remarkably little for the Fiat the previous day in part-exchange; the Italian lady who had brought it in was strangely desperate to get rid of it, and accepted his first paltry offer. He felt a little uneasy about letting it go out again without a proper check-up, but with this batty woman so keen it would be a shame to let her off the boil. And an extra couple of grand in his pocket would be a great help that afternoon, when he was meeting the bank manager to discuss the overdraft.

'Would you like to drive it?' he suggested brightly. She seemed well-heeled, this one, as well as daft. Maybe he could stretch it to £4000.

Margaret sat in the driver's seat, examining the dashboard buttons. When her very first poke at the radio gave her Vivaldi on Radio 3, she gave a squeal of delight. 'My favourite composer - it must be an omen!' she exclaimed, and Mr Sykes produced an indulgent smile.

She turned the key in the ignition, and manoeuvred her way carefully around the forecourt. 'It's perfect!' she declared. 'I feel so at home in it already. How much did you say it was?' Actually she didn't care about the price. As long as it was under the £5000 the insurance company had paid out for her last car, whatever he said was fine by her. Never in her life had she wanted anything as much as she wanted this car.

Two hours later Mr Sykes stood at his office window clutching a building society cheque for £4,500, as Margaret sailed past in her new car, smiling broadly and giving him a jaunty wave. He had banished his twinge of conscience by giving her six months' warranty and finding her some cheap insurance.

Margaret drove majestically through Littlehampton, feeling inordinately proud of herself and quite the happiest she had been for ages. She couldn't quite believe what she had done – she, who was always so cautious, who agonised over every little decision, had gone out and bought a car. Just like that. She had been on her way to the chemist for some corn plasters, and instead had impulsively walked into the garage and fallen in love with a car. What on earth had come over her? Was it the menopause? So far she had only experienced the odd hot flush, but apparently some women started behaving oddly during 'the change', and maybe she was one of them. Margaret tossed her head defiantly. Well, it was about time too. She was bored of the old Margaret who never did anything exciting. The book currently lying on her bedside table was called 'Ready for Rapture', and that was just how she felt...

Margaret changed into third gear and sighed with contentment. She needn't have worried that the foolish accident that had written off her sensible white Peugeot would stop her driving again. It had taken only a few minutes in the right car, and all her confidence had flooded back. The new car's gear-change was deliciously smooth and easy, and the seat back could have been moulded especially for her. She was humming along to a Verdi aria as she pulled up at the traffic lights by the bank, and that was when she heard the noise. Margaret punched the radio off and listened intently. What on earth could it be? It was coming from behind her, from the back seat of the car, and it sounded like breathing – yes, that's what it was, a man's heavy breathing! She peered cautiously round, but the noise had stopped and she could see nothing. She jumped as the car behind honked at her to move on.

Telling herself not to be so silly, that she was just over-excited and imagining things, Margaret put the radio back on and headed out of town. Since accepting the early retirement package offered her in March after thirty-eight uneventful years in the accounts office of Harvey's Cash and Carry, her days had become increasingly long and empty. There was limit to how many hours she could fill reading romantic novels and pottering in her tiny garden. Right now she had nothing to do and nowhere to go – but she did have half a tank of petrol and a shiny yellow car, and a little spin out in the country seemed the perfect plan.

Soon she was on the open road and sailing along at 50 mph – and then suddenly, she heard a man's voice. It was definitely in the car, somewhere behind her, and it was murmuring something, words that sounded amorous and sexy. Margaret slowed down, and turned the radio off again, and then she heard very distinctly the words 'cara mia' and 'bellissima'.

It just so happened that Margaret was passionate about anything to do with Italy, and had been trying to learn the language for years. She was much too timid to venture to an evening class, but she had a teach-yourself course and an excellent dictionary. Her favourite hobby was poring over Italian holiday brochures, imagining herself wandering over those beautiful little bridges in Venice, or sitting in a café on the Amalfi coast, gazing out over the bay of Naples. So she had no trouble deciphering 'my dear' and 'most beautiful'. But who in the world could be saying such things?

She decided to pull in at the next lay-by and have a proper search in the back of the car, although she didn't know what she was looking for. A tape recorder perhaps, or a CD player? The car had only two doors, and it was when she had pulled the front seat forward and was spread-eagled across the back seat, fumbling on the floor, that she heard the throaty chuckle. Margaret froze. She looked ridiculous, she thought, and this person was laughing at her. He chuckled again, and in spite of herself and her strange predicament, Margaret couldn't help smiling. There was, after all, no malice in the laugh, just affection, and she found that she didn't mind it at all. In fact, she quite liked it, but she simply had to find out where it was coming from. She clambered out of the car and planted her feet firmly on the tarmac, trying to think calmly and logically, while she looked about her.

There was nothing to see. She was quite alone, standing next to her beautiful yellow car in a country lay-by. There were fields, but no trees, no hedges, nowhere anyone could be hiding. Except behind the car? Margaret inched her way around the car, and then darted back the way she had come, like in those thrilling games of chase she had played as a child. But there was no one there.

The funny thing was that she felt excited, not scared. This was quite the most interesting thing that had happened to her in years. Could she be losing her marbles? If so, it was proving to be rather fun.

Margaret got back behind the wheel, wound the seat back a few inches and closed her eyes. A little nap, that's what was called for, after all the excitements of the day. Strange that her heart should be pounding with anticipation when all she was doing was having a rest....

She did not have long to wait. She smelt him before she heard him, a hint of citrus and musk, and she gave a little gasp, but kept her eyes squeezed shut. His voice started up again, gently at first and then growing more urgent, as if he really wanted her to understand the importance of what he was saying. Margaret wished she had worked harder at her Italian course, but she had a feeling that very little of this vocabulary would have made it into the pages of her text book. It would have needed an extra chapter – 'Romantic Encounters', perhaps, sandwiched between 'Ordering in a Restaurant' and 'Travelling by Train'. Her heart was thudding as she managed to work out that he adored her, that he thought she was gorgeous, that he wanted to kiss her mouth and her hair and several body parts that she couldn't translate ...... Shivers of pleasure were running down her spine, and she gave a little moan. In response, the low throaty voice grew still more passionate, and she soon abandoned any attempt to understand the words, and just savoured the deliciousness of the moment.

A lorry thundered past, jerking her back to her senses. What on earth was she doing? Suppose someone she knew saw her, lolling about in her car in broad daylight, a soppy grin all over her face? Margaret returned her seat to its upright position, put the radio on and turned up the volume. As she drove home, she tried hard to concentrate on Wagner. But it was no good. Her mind kept sliding back to those words, that voice, and after a few minutes she switched off the music, and waited. Nothing. Somehow she knew that she was alone in the car now, and she wasn't sure whether she felt relieved or disappointed.

Once in her kitchen, armed with a calming cup of tea, she decided it was time to apply some logic to the situation. One possibility was that she had gone crazy, but a second, more appealing, option was that the car was haunted. Houses could be haunted, couldn't they, so why not cars?

The logbook was in her handbag, and Margaret drew her breath in sharply as she read the words 'Giovanni Lucino' under 'Previous Registered Keeper'. There was a Bognor Regis address, and it took no time at all to get the phone number from Directory Enquiries. The woman who answered told her that Mr Lucino was no longer there, but gave her a number for his sister, Emilia.

And then it all began to fall into place. Emilia, on hearing that Margaret had bought the car, cast aside her initial reserve, and began talking very fast. Her accent was strong, but she spoke fluently.

'He died, Giovanni died,' she said. 'Six weeks ago. He was only forty three, and so alive, you know? So full of life and fun and laughter... I still can't believe he's gone. It was his heart, the doctors said he had a problem with his heart and we never knew....it would have been very sudden. He was in his car when it happened, with one of his lady friends, but fortunately not driving. She phoned the ambulance and then she ran away, I think she must have been one of the married ones...'

'One of the married ones?' echoed Margaret.

'Yes, well - Giovanni loved the ladies and they loved him, even when they shouldn't have. He was so beautiful, do you see?' Margaret did see. From her very short acquaintance with Giovanni, she could understand exactly how it had been.

'He flirted all the time, with all the ladies,' continued Emilia. 'He only lived in England a short while and he did not try hard to learn English – he said the ladies adored it when he spoke Italian to them.' She stopped and Margaret clenched her fingers round the phone, remembering the sound of that voice and feeling an absurd pang of jealousy.

'So I had to clear out his flat and get rid of his things and I decided to give Giovanni's funny yellow car to my son. And yesterday I was driving it to Brighton...' Emilia's voice became hoarse and she stopped.

'Please go on!' begged Margaret, although she had an idea what was coming. 'What made you sell the car instead?'

'He was there...' whispered Emilia. 'I kept feeling that he was there in the car and he wanted something and it was so painful.' Emilia sighed. 'I just couldn't bear it. I saw a garage with a big sign saying 'Part-exchange welcome', and I just did it. I didn't stop to think, I just did it. The man at the garage, he gave me a nice Escort instead, my son was very pleased, he did not want a yellow car ... but I've been so worried, maybe I should have kept the Fiat, maybe Giovanni is still there...?'

'It's alright,' said Margaret gently. 'I can feel him in the car too, but I don't mind at all. Actually, it's lovely.'

They talked a little more, and Margaret promised to take the utmost care of Giovanni's car. If ever he made his presence felt in any way that might be of interest to his sister, she would be sure to pass it on. Could she possibly have a photograph, to put a face to the beautiful voice?

The photograph arrived two days later and Giovanni was every bit as gorgeous as Margaret had imagined: wild black curly hair, a full, sensuous mouth and eyes to drown in. She bought a silver frame and carried the photo round the house with her, so that she could gaze at him and talk to him, whatever she was doing.

Giovanni sat on the kitchen table while she had her tea and toast in the morning, and he perched on top of the telly while she watched her favourite soaps. After a few days, she felt confident enough to carry him into the bathroom while she had, at his suggestion, a candle-lit bubble bath. Naturally, at night he kept watch on her bedside table. Margaret talked to him as she hoovered and dusted and tidied up around him, and her Italian was improving in leaps and bounds - but of course he could only speak back to her when they were in the car. She bought a gorgeous blue cashmere rug and some matching cushions, and the little yellow car became a love nest.

Margaret had found true love at the age of 58, and she had never been happier. From her in-depth study of romantic novels, she knew exactly what to expect from her hero, and Giovanni measured up in every way. He was almost too good to be true – passionate, attentive, sensitive to her every mood, and always, always delighted to see her.

Her life had changed dramatically. The neighbours were startled to see her out and about in her new yellow car at all hours of the day and night. Sometimes, she would just sit in the car in her driveway, smiling gaily and talking to herself. One night Mr Barlow from no. 42, who suffered from night cramps, saw her slipping out at 3 a.m to sit in her car in her dressing gown, and that settled it – she was officially declared batty by the other residents. Margaret was far too elated to care what people thought. On Giovanni's advice, she treated herself to some smart new clothes, high-heeled shoes and a stylish haircut. One memorable Monday morning she walked purposefully into Marks and Spencers, got herself measured for a bra (apparently she had been wearing quite the wrong size for years) and emerged uplifted in purple satin.

She had been living in Willow Crescent for most of her adult life, but it was only now that Margaret began to talk to her neighbours. She invited Lesley from next door in for a cup of tea, and astonished the milkman by initiating a conversation about the weather. She took to calling herself Maggie. She was still shy, and a little awkward, but there was a rosy glow about her that surprised everyone.

Margaret was entranced by her new state of happiness. She went to sleep at night smiling, and woke each morning eager to begin another day. She ordered a passport and studied the map and finally she was ready to go on her month-long Italian holiday. 'Yes, it is a long way to drive,' she agreed with Lesley when they met to discuss the arrangements for plant-watering. 'But I so love being in my car. And after all, I'm not in any hurry .... I shall take my time and enjoy every minute of the journey!'

An expert by now at working her shiny chrome coffee machine, Margaret pushed a cup of frothy coffee towards Lesley with a flourish. 'Now then, can I tempt you to an amaretti biscuit with your cappucino?'

Giovanni was sitting by the toaster and she smiled at him as she enunciated the Italian words in her best accent. It was probably a trick of the light, but she could have sworn that he winked back at her.

Do Me a Favour

I've always envied people who can stay asleep when they don't have to get up. At weekends, they can stay cocooned in their duvets and dreams for several more delicious hours; but my body clock is set for 7 am and at 7 am my eyes snap open, whatever day of the week it is. I know that if I try to go back to sleep I'll only get grumpy and irritated, my mind racing with all the things I could and should be doing if I wasn't just lying there.

So when the phone rang at 8.15 this morning I wasn't asleep. I was sitting on my bed painting my toe nails and lost in a daydream.

'Damn!' I exclaimed as my hand jerked sideways in surprise and a blob of Fuschia Pink landed on the sheet. I glared at the phone on the bedside table. I don't get many phone calls, and none at all at this hour of the morning. It was bound to be a wrong number. I decided to ignore it.

I held out until the fourth ring and then snatched up the receiver.

'Yes,' I barked, all ready to be rude and dismissive.

'Oh Jane, I'm so glad you're up - I need a big favour.'

It was typical of Chloe to assume that I'd recognise her voice. For a minute I was tempted to say, 'I'm sorry, who is this, please?' But it was too late. She was rushing on, her voice low and urgent.

'I've got myself in a bit of a mess, and I need you to bale me out. You see, I've been seeing someone most Friday nights for the past few months and I've always told Steve I was with you. But now he suspects something, and I need you to cover for me.'

I didn't know whether to be annoyed or flattered that she'd chosen me. I'd have to think about that later.

I wriggled my back into the pillows and pulled the duvet up over my legs, being careful to leave my tacky toes uncovered.

'What made him suspicious?' I asked. If I was going to get involved I wanted all the juicy details.

'Oh, he came across some undies he'd never seen me wear, and he tried to phone me a few times last night and my mobile was off, you know the sort of thing...'

I certainly do know. I am an avid watcher of soaps and fancy myself as something of an expert when it comes to marital shenanigans. I get so absorbed in fictional love lives that I rarely have time to mourn my own lack of action in that area.

'.... Anyway, it's fine, you just need to say I've been with you from about 8 till 12 most Fridays since September and he'll calm down. I've given him your number, so he'll probably phone later on this morning.'

What a cheek! She'd just assumed I'd agree without even asking me.

'And what are we supposed to have been doing on these Friday nights?' I inquired frostily.

Chloe didn't seem to feel the cold. 'I told him we play Scrabble,' she giggled. 'He loathes Scrabble and refuses to play with me, so when he goes off to his snooker club on Fridays, you and I have a few games of Scrabble over a bottle of wine.... I have to come to you because you've got a baby.'

'I've what?'

'Well, that's why you don't come here, you see. You've got a little baby and it wakes up and cries and stuff, so we have to be at your house.'

'Boy or girl?'

'What?'

'Is the baby a boy or a girl?'

'Oh, I don't know, a girl I think. It doesn't matter, he won't ask. He just might check you've got one.'

I looked up at the crack in the ceiling I keep meaning to paint over. I must have mentally painted that crack at least a thousand times. Scrabble on Friday nights with Chloe. It would have been fun, much more fun than staying in on my own watching telly. I love playing Scrabble. Once I even played against myself, which went surprisingly well. The final score was very close, I remember, because we were so evenly matched. I felt a sudden rush of anger. It was so unfair – she had everything, a jealous husband, a secret lover, looks, nice house, clothes, confidence - whereas my lonely life in this grotty flat was going nowhere...

'And did you tell him we met last night?'

'Yes, and we ran on rather late – that's part of the problem, I didn't get home till after 1 and Steve was waiting up for me. We had a row, and the only way I could get him to shut up was to give him your number...' Her voice dropped to a whisper. 'Look, I've got to go now, he's just finished in the shower. You're an angel! I'll phone you later to see how it went, okay? Bye bye.' She made a silly kissing noise and hung up.

I replaced the receiver, found the nail polish remover and started scrubbing at the sheet. As I watched the little blob spread itself into a messy pink stain I wished I'd left it alone. I could probably have picked it off once it was dry.... I re-annointed the cotton pad and persevered grimly.

It was all Chloe's fault, Chloe and her stupid lies. Why should I cover up for her anyway? What gave her the right to use me as an alibi, without even asking me first? And why had she chosen me, who she hardly knew, instead of one of her friends? It could only have been because she thought I was a pathetic mouse of a creature who would roll over and do her bidding, even if it meant lying. Someone less drippy would stand up to her. It would just serve her right if I refused to play, if her grubby little secret got her into trouble, maybe even wrecked her marriage...

I stopped rubbing and gave a little whoosh. It had suddenly dawned on me that I was in a pretty powerful position.

'She needs me,' I said out loud, giving up on the stain. 'This might just turn out to be my lucky day...'

My other favourite telly programmes, alongside soaps, are mystery thrillers, full of false alibis and blackmail and subterfuge. I've watched people being blackmailed often enough – maybe here was my chance to have a go.

I went into the kitchen, made myself a cup of instant coffee and sat down at the table. I needed to think this through. If I meekly provided Chloe with her alibi, that would be that. She'd carry on as before with the mystery lover – who was he anyway? – and after a few days of being extra nice to me, she'd have forgotten all about the role I'd played. She'd have got her own way as usual, and I'd have gained nothing at all. Unless I made my co-operation conditional.

For the second time that morning the phone made me jump. I stared at it, frozen with indecision, and after nine rings it fell silent. I breathed again. It might not have been Steve, but I wasn't taking any chances. I wasn't ready yet, I hadn't decided what to do.

I took a sip of coffee and thought about the day I met Chloe. I was pulling out of the staff car park during my second week at works when she rapped on my window. Her car wouldn't start, she was in a terrible hurry, could I give her a lift home? People like Chloe are always in a hurry; their lives are so full and so interesting that there aren't enough hours in the day for them. It turned out that I drive right past her road on my way home, so it was no trouble, no trouble at all. In fact I was flushed with pride at having gorgeous Chloe Phillips sitting in the passenger seat of my car, filling the air with her scent so that I felt quite giddy. She kept up a steady stream of gossip about people at work, flicking her long shiny blond hair back from her eyes as she laughed, and it was hard for me to keep my eyes on the road. She even sat beautifully, like a film star, with her knees together and her long legs leaning sideways,

I had admired her, from a distance, from my very first day at Pollards, although of course she had no idea who I was until she got in my car. We girls in accounts don't tend to have much to do with the sales assistants, and the ones like Chloe who work on the beauty counters are in a class of their own. They simply ooze superiority. I walk past them sometimes during my lunch hour and they look straight through me. I can see their point. Compared to them, I am nothing.

Last month I summoned up the nerve to apply for a sales job when a vacancy in Lingerie came up, but I wasn't surprised when I didn't get it. They said I was too valuable in accounts, but I knew the real reason was that I wasn't pretty enough. Women don't want to discuss cup sizes with someone who looks like me.

After that first lift, Chloe asked for my number, and during the past year I've helped her out quite a few times when she's been car-less. She would phone me at home the evening before to arrange the lifts – she didn't want to be seen at work talking to me. And I was always happy to oblige. I would rush out to the car after she phoned and carefully pick up all the sweet wrappers, polish the dashboard, change the CD to something trendier.

I got up from the table and shoved some bread into the toaster. I needed to make a decision. Was I going to help her or not?

If she'd been nicer to me at work I might have been feeling more charitable. But even after I'd started giving her lifts, she could only ever manage a tight little smile if I walked past her beauty counter. And she had the most amazing smile when she was being friendly; I'd seen her direct it at our boss, Nick Tranter. The toast popped up and at that same moment something clicked in my brain. Of course! I bet that's who lover-boy was. Nick Tranter, who I knew was married because his wife's calls came through to our office when his secretary was out. Sandra was his wife's name. She sounded really nice on the phone. Gentle, her voice low and hesitant. She always apologised for disturbing me, which I thought was very sweet of her. She was obviously a very nice person, who had no idea what her snake of a husband was up to....

I could hear my heart thudding. There was a lot at stake here. Not one but two marriages. Two people who would give a lot to keep me quiet...

I spread butter over my toast and took a big greedy bite. Where to start on my list of wants? A big chunk of money would give me loads of things, starting with a nice holiday. I could go to Tenerife, or the Costa del Sol, and come back with an amazing sun tan. Or maybe I could do up the flat – get some decent furniture, buy a comfortable bed, have the bathroom painted...

Or what about a more interesting job? Mr Tranter could see to that. My heart skipped a beat as I had the amazing idea of getting a job in the beauty department, working alongside Chloe. She could hardly ignore me then. I pictured myself in the regulation pale blue jacket, in the delicious pencil skirt with the slit up the back. I would have to get some high heeled shoes, and do something about my hair...

I was grinning as I walked along the corridor to the loo – and then I caught sight of myself in the mirror above the basin and my grin faded to nothing. I stared at my lanky hair, my podgy, pasty face, my uneven teeth. Who was I kidding? I wouldn't last a day in the beauty department. I simply hadn't the style, the confidence, the looks to carry it off. Chloe and her friends would snigger at me and it would be ghastly.

I wandered slowly back to the kitchen, feeling demoralised. So it was back to money then. But how much could I ask for without alienating Chloe? After all, I looked forward so much to our car rides; suppose she found somebody else to give her a lift, suppose she resented me for being so mercenary, and refused to ever speak to me again...

There was a loud knock at the door. Oh my God, Steve had come round to interrogate me. I'd never be able to lie to his face. I had to ignore it.

'Coo-eee!' Chloe's voice floated through the letter box. 'Open up, Janie, it's only me!'

Chloe was the only person who had ever called me Janie. I couldn't help it, I had to let her in.

'Sorry I'm not dressed yet,' I muttered, tightening the belt of my scruffy towelling dressing gown. Chloe, of course, looked as glamorous as ever in her designer jeans and leather jacket. She had a blue scarf casually draped around her neck, and she was holding a huge bunch of lilies.

'That's all right,' she replied graciously. 'I just popped round 'cos Steve said there was no answer when he phoned just now, and I wanted to check you were still okay with helping me out... Here, look, I bought you these!'

She thrust the flowers at me, and I took them, muttering a thank you. I couldn't think what else to say, so I just turned and led the way to the kitchen.

'Oh what a lovely kitchen!' enthused Chloe. 'I do like your curtains!' We both stood and looked at the curtains, which were lime green and garishly printed with yellow cups and saucers. My mother had made and hung them when I moved into the flat, declaring that they would cheer the place up a bit. Replacing them with something less horrible was yet another job I had never got round to doing.

I made myself turn to face her.

'Is it Nick Tranter?' I blurted, and knew at once that I had guessed right. Chloe's eyes widened briefly in alarm and she gave a nervous, breathy laugh.

'No, of course not!' she declared brightly. 'What ever made you think that? It's no one you know.'

I grunted, and moved towards the sink with my flowers.

'Honestly, Jane, you do have some funny ideas!' She laughed again, more confidently this time. And suddenly I wanted nothing more to do with this ghastly woman. I didn't want her gratitude or her money or to be involved in any way with her vile deceptions. I wanted her gone, out of my flat, out of my life. She was polluting my atmosphere.

'Do you want some coffee?' I offered limply.

'Oh no thanks darling, I really can't stay. I just wanted to tell you how grateful I am to you for helping me out! You must let me know what I can do for you in return. Would you like a free make-over next week? I could show you how to make the most of your skin tone."

After she'd gone, I hunted around for something to put the lilies in, and I had a little cry because I didn't have a vase. No one ever gives me flowers. In the end I cut the stems ridiculously short and stuffed the flowers into two jam jars and a milk jug. Than I went and did something I saw a boy do on the telly last week. He was supposed to be emotionally disturbed and to prove it he stood and banged his head against the wall. I had thought as I watched him that it looked curiously soothing, and it was. I stood in the hallway doing that for quite a long time, and then I ran myself a bath.

    I poured in a generous dollop of bubbles and lowered myself into the water. My head was hurting but inside a curious calm had taken hold of me. I felt pure and clean and righteous and it was wonderful. Perhaps this is why women become nuns, so they can feel like this all the time. I leant back against the plastic pillow and thought about Steve.

    I had only seen him the once, but he had made quite an impression on me. He came into the pizzeria at the end of our staff Christmas dinner to collect Chloe. He was tall and slim with dark hair and a lovely grin. Several people tried to make him sit down and have a drink, but it was clear that he only wanted to take Chloe home. She'd had too much wine and was being all silly and giggly and when he eventually persuaded her to her feet she could hardly walk, so he'd had to half-carry her to the door. I shall never forget the way he looked down at her, so loving, so protective, so indulgent. I couldn't imagine anyone ever looking at me with such kind eyes. She'd have a horrible hangover the next day and would be beastly to him but he wouldn't mind. Because he loved her.

    If I was ever lucky enough to have a husband who loved me I would love him right back. I would love him with all of my heart and honour him and keep myself only unto him till death did us part. I know I would. Chloe was despicable, shallow, selfish, amoral, and I was a thousand times better than she was. And so was Steve.

It is true that I enjoy watching the soap stars getting entangled in their silly deceitful love lives. They lie and cheat and make a mess of everything and hurt each other and it is all very entertaining. But it isn't real. When real people behave like that it isn't funny or even interesting. It is degrading and appalling.

I was drying myself when the phone started up again. I pulled on my dressing gown again and hurried into the kitchen.

I could do this.

'Hello,' I said.

'Yes, hello,' said a man's voice. 'Is that Jane? Jane Sargent?' I could hear the misery and my heart went out to him.

'Yes, that's right,' I encouraged him.

'This is Steve, Chloe's husband.'

'Yes, she said you would call me.'

'Er –yes, well I just wanted to check that she's been with you on Friday nights for the last few months.'

It seemed too cruel to just say no.

'Why, where do you think she's been?' I parried.

He coughed nervously. 'Well that's just it, I don't really know...'

'Do you think she's having an affair?' I asked gently.

'Look, do you think you could just answer my question?'

'I'd rather ask you one,' I replied, amazed at my boldness. 'Do you really think Chloe is the type of woman who would choose to spend her Friday nights playing Scrabble with a girlfriend?'

There was a pause.

'I guess not,' he said.

'I think that's your answer Steve,' I said. 'I'm sorry I can't help, but it wouldn't be right, you see.'

I waited for a bit, but he didn't say anything. There wasn't really anything to say.

'Goodbye,' I said quietly, and then I hung up.

I went into my bedroom and pulled on some clothes. I flung open the curtains and stood looking at the day. Wispy clouds were racing across the sky, the sun was shining, two bluetits were breakfasting on the bird table. It was all perfect, and I needed to get out there. I would go for a good long walk across the common and practice holding my head up high. Because that's what I would be doing on Monday when I walked past the beauty counter. I would look Chloe straight in the eyes and feel just a little bit sorry for her.

There was just one thing I had to do first. I stood on a chair in the kitchen and unhooked the ugly curtains. I folded them and slipped them into a carrier bag. There was a charity shop just down the road. There just might be someone out there with the same taste as my mother; or if not, they would make some very jolly dusters.

Alison in Marbella

The holiday did not begin well for me. I always get nervous at airports, and like to be there nice and early, in complete control. I was one of the first to check in, and then I settled down in Departures with a coffee and the paper and wondered whether it was too soon to text Graham. But he might want to know that I'd reached the airport safely, and perhaps he would text back a more coherent goodbye than the grunt he'd managed early that morning. A thorough search of my handbag and its many pockets failed to produce my phone, and that was when I remembered that I'd put it for easy access in the cubby hole in the dashboard of my car, where it undoubtedly still was. A little shiver of horror trickled down my spine. I had been a late-starter on the mobile phone front, but now that I had one I couldn't envisage managing without it.

    I groaned and looked at my watch. The gate was due to close in 20 minutes and there was no sign of Nicky and the girls. What on earth would I do if they didn't arrive in time? I was already having huge misgivings about this 3-day holiday. Fond as I was of my 16 year old god-daughter Emma, I really wasn't in the mood for silly girls and lots of giggles. Emma was quite loud enough on her own, but with 2 friends in tow, the noise would be ghastly. Would Nicky and I have enough time to ourselves to discuss the parlous state of my marriage? I needed her to listen carefully and tell me in her lovely commonsensical manner whether I was being silly or heading for the divorce courts....I squeezed my eyes shut and counted to 10. Then I tried to read the headlines, but my eyes kept sliding off the paper and up to the clock. I queued up to buy a bottle of water, and forced myself to smile at a revolting child who was attempting to play Peekaboo with me from behind its father's legs. I am not fond of children, so it's just as well I never had any. It's possible that the maternal instinct might have kicked in with the hormones, but somehow I doubt it.

The entire departure lounge was alerted to the arrival of Nicky and co. by the eruption of noise as they spotted me. 'She's over there!' and 'Oh my god, that was so lucky!' and 'Darling! How lovely to see you!' They all wanted to tell me how they had managed to take the wrong exit off the motorway. 'We tried to ring you!' was uttered several times, as if I were somehow to blame for the various calamities that had befallen them, resulting in them reaching the airport with 10 minutes to spare. I listened dutifully, nodding away, and I even managed an exclamation or two at appropriate places, but already I was wishing that I were travelling on my own. I wondered if I could slip in my earplugs without them noticing.

At last we were called to the gate, and ushered on to the plane, and I swear those girls didn't ever pause to draw breath. 'They're having such fun already!' Nicky said to me, her eyes dancing with delight. Thank goodness I'd checked in ahead of them and had been allocated a seat at the other end of the plane.

****

It was a peaceful flight, down my end of the plane, and I felt strong and capable as I climbed down the airplane steps into the Spanish sun. I smiled tolerantly when Nicky informed me that we'd just missed the bus and that we'd have to get a large taxi for an exorbitant price. Forty long minutes later we pulled up outside Nicky's flat and, my patience having been worn rather thin by their incessant chatter, I'm afraid I was a little short with Kirsty, who was being extremely silly in the lift. I caught the girls exchanging a grimace, but what did I care? Someone needed to instill a little discipline, and it obviously wasn't going to be Nicky.

My room, with its huge bed and en-suite shower room, was lovely. In fact the whole flat was lovely, much more luxurious than I could have hoped: leather sofas, tasteful pictures, beautiful tiles. I unpacked my things and changed into a cotton dress, and then made myself a cup of tea in the spotless kitchen. There was no milk, which was most annoying and reminded me why I generally prefer to stay in hotels. I was wondering whether I could be bothered to go out and buy some when someone's phone rang and my heart gave a flip. Graham! He'd managed to find Nicky's number and was ringing to see if I'd arrived safely! He did care about me, he was missing me already. I waited expectantly on the landing, but heard Nicky answer and knew that it was her husband, not mine on the other end. My eyes pricked with disappointment and envy. The girls were unpacking amidst gales of laughter, and I hovered in their doorway for a minute, but they didn't even notice me, so I wandered back downstairs again. I sank into a sofa with my cup of tea, which was nowhere near as black as my mood.

Nicky appeared and bustled about. Normally she would pounce on my misery and demand a full explanation, but all she did was ask if I'd mind popping to the shop for some milk, because the girls wanted some tea. The girls, the girls, already I was fed up with the girls.

But I did as she asked and worked very hard at keeping a smile pinned to my face as we eventually made our way to the beach and whiled away the afternoon on sun loungers. We had chicken salad and chips served to us by the friendly beach bar waiter and it should all have been lovely, but it wasn't. I had a headache, it was too hot, and there were too many people, most of them English and drunk. The conversations were not edifying. Our girls were discussing boys yet again, and a family from Birmingham was bickering over whose turn it was to get the ice creams. It got so bad that I very nearly offered to get them myself. Instead I went for a swim with the girls, and that was quite pleasant, except that the seabed was uncomfortably stony and I stubbed my toe. The sand shelved sharply down to the water, which made it very tricky to climb back up again, and I was quite sure that the girls were laughing at me. They were gorgeous in their skimpy bikinis and I felt old and fat and clumsy, so that by the time I made it back to my lounger the good effect of my swim had worn off and I was back in the doldrums again.

Fortunately, at that point I remembered my i-pod, and plugged myself in. No one but me needed to know that I had a weakness for Neil Diamond, and the next hour passed away happily enough. I must have dozed off, because the next thing I knew, we were packing up to go back to the flat. There was much discussion about how we were going to spend the evening. The girls wanted to go clubbing - surely they were too young? - and it was decided that Nicky and I would go on ahead to Puerto Banus, so that we would be nearby if they needed us when they came on later.

Now I'd be the first to admit that I know nothing about child-rearing, but doesn't a 16 year old who has been up since 5 am need to go to bed early? I myself had been hoping for an early night, after all the excitements of the day. But I clamped my mouth shut, and went off to don my best dress, a blue and green swirly number that Graham used to say he liked, back in the days when he noticed what I was wearing. He still hadn't phoned, although Nicky's husband had, twice, and so had Kirsty's mother. I tried to excuse him on the grounds that he didn't have the number, but surely a man who loved me would have rung Nicky's husband to get it. Well, I had my pride - I certainly wasn't going to weaken and phone him. I opened the bottle of rosé I found in the fridge and perched on the sofa to await the others. I was starving. My regular suppertime was at 7, and it was already half past. Waves of hilarity were emanating from the girls' room, and after a very long time they emerged, looking as though they had stepped from the pages of the magazine I was flicking through. Their dresses barely covered their bottoms, and their coltish legs were balanced precariously on 3-inch heels. With their cinched in waists and overmascaraed eyes they looked terrifyingly young and sexy. And so vulnerable. I badly wanted to pack them upstairs to scrub their faces and come back down in jeans and t-shirts, but of course I held my tongue.

'Well?' demanded Nicky as she presented the girls to me. 'Don't they look gorgeous?'

'Amazing!' I replied with as much enthusiasm as I could muster. 'Can you really walk in those heels?' The girls seemed to find this question inordinately funny and dissolved into giggles. There was still more silliness as Nicky attempted to monitor their efforts at creating their own supper from the groceries we'd picked up on our way back from the beach.

'Are we going soon?' I asked her. 'Only I'm not used to eating so late.' She gave me a sharp little look. 'I have to see that they're fed, you know,' she said crisply.' I won't be long.'

An hour later we headed off to Puerto Banus in a taxi, only to find that all the restaurants were full. We booked a table for 10 pm, and went to a bar where I bought us some sparkling wine in an attempt to cheer myself up. It didn't work.

'Come on then Ali,' said Nicky. 'Tell me what's up. You've been a right misery guts ever since we arrived.'

The tears appeared out of nowhere. Nicky fished some tissues from her bag and put her arm around me.

'Tell me everything,' she said, and her voice was gentler now. So I started to tell her, about my awful depression after the dog died that I couldn't seem to shake off, about Graham's irritation with me, about my suspicion that he was bored with me and was having an affair, about my loneliness and misery and feelings of self-loathing....

'Scuse me, love,' said a fat young man sporting a t-shirt that read 'Come and Get It Baby', as he attempted to squeeze past me to get to the door. I shifted my foot at just the wrong moment and instead of getting out of his way I tripped him up. Over he went, throwing the contents of his pint glass up in the air so that most of it landed on Nicky, and collapsing on his knees on the floor beside her. She really is an extraordinary woman. She wasn't shocked or angry, but just laughed as she helped him to his feet. He was all apologies and embarrassment but she waved him away with a big grin and dabbed vaguely at her dress with a tissue.

'Now then, where were we before we were so rudely interrupted?' she said. 'Ah yes, you were telling me that Graham is having too many evening meetings lately.'

'Don't you want to go to the Ladies and get that beer off your dress?' I asked, not sure whether to be impressed or appalled at her nonchalance.

'Oh no, it'll be alright,' she said. 'I'd much rather talk to you.' Right on cue, her mobile sang. It was Emma, with some complicated problem about keys to the flat, and by the time that was all sorted out, it was nearly 10.

'We'll talk in the restaurant,' said Nicky, as she took my arm and steered me through the crowds of people thronging the pavement. But we didn't. The restaurant was large and noisy and after a few bellowed exchanges we gave up and concentrated instead on our pasta. It struck me as a little odd that I'd come all the way to Spain to eat in a mediocre Italian restaurant, but I was too hungry to care. I wolfed down the spaghetti carbonara and most of the carafe of wine and shared a bowl of tiramisu with Nicky. Her phone pinged at regular intervals with text messages from the girls, who had arrived now and were busy sampling various bars. For some reason they felt the need to report back to their 'big sister' every time something interesting happened. I was feeling a bit tiddly after all the wine I'd consumed, and while I wanted to despise them for their lack of independence, all I could feel was envy towards Nicky for her obviously important role in their lives. When had anyone ever needed me like that? My eyes pricked again, and I quickly drained the last of my wine.

Nicky paid the bill, waving away my feeble attempt at getting to my purse. 'Come on then, let's go and find ourselves some fun too.' My heart sank. All I wanted to do was collect the girls and go home to bed. Was this why Graham was bored of me? Was there in fact something physically wrong with me, that made me so tired all the time? Maybe I had a terminal illness. When he found out, he'd be so ashamed of the way he'd treated me. I pushed my way along the pavement behind Nicky, imagining myself languishing on my sickbed, with Graham sitting beside me holding my poor wasted hand and apologising over and over.

The bars were not nearly big enough to hold all the people who wanted to be in Puerto Banus that night. The pavement was heaving with red-faced revelers, almost all of them British. It seems that if you are a certain kind of girl, you drag your friends to Marbella for a hen-do and make them dress up in silly costumes and proceed to get extremely drunk. The bride-to-be is distinguishable by the fact that she wears a short veil, but otherwise they all look the same in their basques and stockings and high heels. I shuddered as a very plump young woman, with her ample breasts on full display, cackled her way into me. My hen night had been a decorous dinner party at home, attended by my sister and two girlfriends and ending at 10.30 so that I could get plenty of beauty sleep. Obviously beauty sleep was very far from these women's minds; it was nearly midnight and things were just hotting up.

'There they are!' I followed the line of Nicky's arm and saw our 3 girls wobbling towards us and positively fizzing with excitement. For a minute I could do nothing but gape at their youth, their beauty, their vitality. And then I was caught up in the swirl of their laughter as they regaled us with tales of free drinks and funny men and gorgeous boys. Even the taxi ride had managed to be an adventure. They were young enough, bless them, to want us to accompany them to the next bar, and so off we went to be plied with glasses of perfectly revolting fizz and to cavort about to the music. Well, Nicky and the girls cavorted, while I did a bit of swaying and tried to keep smiling. Never in my life can I remember wanting a bed so badly.

At last it was decided that it was time to go, and we made our way to the taxi stand. As pre-arranged,

Nicky distracted the driver while Kirsty slid onto the floor of the back seat, because he would probably have refused to take all 5 of us in his standard car. And then of course the girls had to giggle helplessly all the way back to the flat and I couldn't help imagining in gory detail the damage that would be done to that delicate little unseatbelted body when he crashed the car. Whatever would Nicky say to the child's mother? But the taxi driver didn't crash the car and we clambered out unscathed. A short time later I was alone in my bed in the dark, overtired and miserable and certain that indigestion would keep me up half the night.

****

I did fall asleep eventually, and it felt like minutes later that I was woken by a loud knocking on my bedroom door.

'Only me!' sang out Emma, breezing into the room just as if she'd heard me ask her to come in. 'Mum said to tell you we're off to the beach, and she's left you her phone in the kitchen. Here's a cup of tea. It's 10.30 by the way.'

I managed a grunt, and she peered at me. 'Are you ok?' she asked. 'You look awful!'

'Didn't sleep well.'

'Oh, right. Well, you know where we are if you need us. See you later!''

She was gone. I sank back down on the pillows with a groan. Why hadn't Nicky come to see how I was? Wasn't she supposed to be my friend? Was I actually wanted on the beach, or was I just a terrible nuisance, a spoiler of fun? Suddenly I longed to go home, but then I remembered that home was where Graham and all my problems were. I didn't want to be here, or there, or anywhere that had me in it. Oh god. Maybe some tea would help. And then a fierce invigorating shower.

****

An hour later I was ambling through the narrow streets of the old town, feeling just a little chirpier. Nicky and the girls didn't need me, I had decided, but then I didn't need them either, so that was alright. I would have a gentle mooch about, perhaps treat myself to a pair of shoes or a scarf and a bite of lunch, have a bit of me-time before braving the giggling gang. I stopped at a cafe in a pretty square and ordered an Americano. At the table next to me a young English woman was admonishing a red-faced child. He looked as though he were about to scream or be sick, possibly both.

'Mummy is very sad that Ben doesn't like his truck,' she said. 'Mummy spent lots of money on it.' She held out the said truck to the boy wriggling in his buggy, and he grabbed it and hurled it to the ground. She drew in her breath sharply and waggled her finger at him. 'You know Mummy gets very cross when Ben is naughty,' she said, and when he stuck his little pink tongue out at her I wanted to cheer.

The waiter chose that pivotal moment to appear with Mummy's coffee, so war was postponed for a few minutes. When I next looked over, Mummy was busy texting and Ben was slumped sideways, fast asleep. The yellow plastic truck was still lying on its side in the dust, and I felt a pang of sympathy for it. I knew what it felt like to be unwanted.

I left the cafe and wandered off to look at the shops. There was an awful moment when my eye was caught by a beautiful purple and red leather dog lead in a shop window, and my fingers were on the door handle before I remembered with a painful lurch that I no longer had a dog to attach it to. Right next door was a tiny tapas bar and I stumbled in over the threshold. An old man was sweeping the floor and he gave me an enchanting smile, so that I immediately felt better. I was charmed to discover that there was no menu, only a counter with various tapas on display, so I pointed to three of the bowls and hoped for the best. The chorizo was delicious, and there was a tasty ratatouille and some potatoes in a spicy sauce. Perfect. I sipped at a glass of white Rioja and sat on at my corner table as the bar slowly filled up with diners. For the first time since arriving in Marbella I began to feel at peace with myself. It was entirely possible, I thought, that I had blown the whole Graham thing out of proportion, and that everything, in fact, would be alright.

The flat was empty and cool. I drank a long glass of iced water and stood looking Nicky's phone. If everything was fine between me and Graham, there was no earthly reason why I shouldn't phone home. When the answer phone picked up I felt a jolt of relief. I left a jolly message, explaining about my mis-placed mobile and saying I was having a lovely time. I put the phone back on the counter and went upstairs for a siesta. I would sleep all afternoon and wake refreshed and energised and ready for any amount of fun.

****

Nicky was waiting for me on the terrace when I eventually surfaced at 6.30, feeling light-headed and floaty. She put a vodka and tonic in front of me and I took a long drink and beamed at her.

'You're looking better,' she remarked. 'That sleep did you the world of good! I'm glad I didn't wake you when Graham phoned.'

My heart gave a loud purr of contentment, and I took another long slurp before answering.

'What did he say?'

'Oh we had a good long chat – he's a really nice man, your Graham. He said he was glad you were having this little holiday because you've been so miserable lately. He wanted to know how you were, if you were having fun. He's left lots of messages on your mobile, but of course you'd left it in your car! He said he was missing you. He's got some boring work do this evening, but he's not leaving till 8, so if you hurry you can catch him.

I hurried. He answered on the first ring, and he said all the right things, and so, for once, did I. When I had hung up I jumped to my feet and did a little dance around the elegant living room. I paused in front of the enormous mirror hanging over the fireplace and gave myself a thumbs-up sign. 'Here's looking at you kid,' I said.

****

Supper was on the seafront, and in my newfound mood of lighthearted gaiety I found it very amusing to watch the passagiato as we ate copious amounts of rather good paella. We were then entertained for too long by an aged Flamenco dancer who should have abandoned the whole idea twenty years ago. The girls of course found the spectacle hilarious and were probably as surprised as I was when I joined in the giggling.

'I know what we should do tonight, as a treat for Ali!' declared Nicky. 'Go to the Karaoke bar!' I cringed inside but managed to keep smiling as the girls chorused their agreement. Back in my youth I had sung in a band, but it was years since I'd performed in public. Nicky would be expecting great things of me. I downed my vino tinto in two gulps.

'That's a great idea!' I said, and was rewarded with a look of surprise from Emma. I'd show this goddaughter of mine that she had underestimated me. I'd show them all.

****

The karaoke bar was small and grubby and not the ideal venue in which to make one's come-back. There were plastic tables and chairs, a long sticky bar and no atmosphere at all. Never mind, I'd soon create an atmosphere. The only customers were a group of four 60-year-old women, obviously English, nursing halves of Guinness and looking very bored. We streamed through the door, me at the front, and I beamed at the weary compère with the mike. He was singing 'My Way' without much enthusiasm, and he broke off as we entered.

'Aha, some more ladies!' he cried. 'Can any of you sing?'

'Ali can!' shouted Nicky, giving me a shove, and there I was, in the middle of the room listening to the opening bars of Tina Turner's 'You're Simply the Best'. My heart was pounding with excitement but I wasn't the tiniest bit nervous. The feel of the microphone in my hand had melted the years away. I was 25 again, happy and carefree, with my whole wonderful life ahead of me.

The words were up there on the screen but I found I didn't need them. 'Better than all the rest!' I bellowed, and as I pranced up and down the length of the bar I saw that the four ladies were gazing at me with admiration. One of them raised her glass to me and I nearly burst with pride. The bar was filling up now as passers-by came in to see what was going on. The song came to an end too soon and I handed the mike back to the compère and plumped down at Nicky's table. Emma was open-mouthed with astonishment. 'I never knew you could do that!' she said, 'Please, please don't stop!' That was a very good moment.

One of the gang of four was pressing a glass of beer into my hand. 'That were bloody marvelous,' she said. 'You've perked us right up, you have. I hope you're doing some more?'

Well, why not? No one else seemed to want to, and the compère was more than happy, especially when everyone started dancing when I sang, 'She was just 17, and you know what I mean......' Nicky and the girls were surging around me and at one point I scrambled up onto a table to have more space to belt out the words. If only Graham could have seen me! I hardly paused for breath during the next hour, and the songs came fast and furious - 'River Deep, Mountain High', 'It's Raining Men', 'Mamma Mia' and finally my favourite, 'I Will Survive.' I caught Nicky's eye during the last song and she shone her great big generous smile at me and the words thumped their way into my silly self-indulgent brain. I would survive, of course I would, and I would go home and love my poor long-suffering husband and stop fretting about nothing.

And what's more, I would get off my backside and join the local choir, as I've been meaning to do for years, because when you have a voice like mine it is nothing short of criminal not to use it.

Daniel's Mother

Daniel unlocked the front door and I followed him into the flat, poised to enthuse. It was bound to be dark, damp and depressing, but I was ready to do my maternal duty and find something nice to say, something positive and encouraging. He had been in this flat for a full two months now, and this was the first time I had been allowed anywhere near it. It had probably taken him that long to get it presentable.

    I hadn't expected an inner door, complete with pretty stained glass panels. 'Gosh,' I said, and then, as the door was thrown open, I said 'Gosh' again. We were in a beautiful ultra-modern kitchen, with a gleaming silver oven and cooker hood and stylish maple cupboards. The worktop looked like granite, but surely it couldn't be, not in a cheap rented flat. Apparently Daniel had washed his dishes and put them away, a fact I was struggling to get my head round. It was all spotless.

    My eyes drifted up to the high ceiling from which hung not one, but two wrought iron chandeliers.

    'How much did you say you were paying?' I couldn't keep the sharpness out of my voice. It was all very frustrating. I had come along this morning relishing my mother-to-the-rescue role, bursting with helpfulness, and now I felt thwarted.

    Daniel was looking a bit shifty, I thought. 'It's – um- £450 a month,' he muttered.

    I opened the door to the large bay-windowed front room. 'Is that all?' I said. 'It seems far too little for all this!' I studied the immaculate paintwork, the bookshelves lining one wall, the halogen lights strung on wires across the ceiling. Then I looked at the black leather sofas, the flat screen tv, the elaborate sound system, and the pound signs were pinging up in front of my eyes. The rug on the floor must have cost £500 and as for the curtains....

I turned and fixed Daniel with my gimlet eye, and to my satisfaction he reddened. There. I knew there was something he wasn't telling me.

'Is there something you're not telling me?' I asked, as I had so many times before. Usually I had a pretty good idea of what that something was, but not this time. Perhaps he had decided to increase his teacher's salary by doing another job in his spare time, but what job, and why hadn't he mentioned it? Was it something shameful, illegal even?

'What do you mean?' he stalled.

I tssked, and swept out along the corridor and into the next room. When you only have one child, and an uncommunicative boy at that, it simply isn't an option to be one of those mothers who hold back and wait to be told things. I had to find out what was going on, and quickly. I opened the door to the bedroom. It was dominated by a huge bed covered with an elegant cream duvet cover. Now my Daniel is a lot of things but elegant isn't one of them. I revised my second job theory and substituted a flatmate. There had to be someone sharing this flat, this bed, with him. Someone extremely tidy, with lots of taste and lots of money. Who could she be, and why hadn't he told me about her?

Daniel came to the doorway. He was rubbing his nose, the way he always did when he was nervous. 'I –er– I'm just going to get some milk,' he said. 'Back in a minute. Have a look round if you like.'

I did like. The front door slammed behind him, and I began to hunt for clues. She liked candles, which was good.

It meant she was romantic, perhaps more likely to treat my poor boy gently when she tired of him. There was a beautiful mahogany chest of drawers in front of the window, and I pulled open a drawer full of men's briefs, then another one of black socks. They were curled up in neat little balls, something I had never known Daniel to do. She must be very fond of him, to be looking after his laundry so carefully. I pulled open a second drawer with more socks in it, different colours this time, and recognised a pair of thick brown socks that Daniel wore with his walking boots.

I then scuttled across to the wardrobe, wrenched open one of the mirrored doors and was startled to see a whole row of suits, jackets and shirts, some of them still in their dry cleaning wrappers. She must have bought them for him, but since when had Daniel taken to wearing suits? Last time I'd looked, he'd only possessed the charcoal grey one he wore to weddings and funerals. The other side of the wardrobe held more casual clothes, corduroy trousers, sports jackets. I saw the one I had given Daniel for his last birthday, in a lovely shade of greeny blue. And there at the end of the rail was his old grey suit. I gave it a little stroke, grateful that some things hadn't changed.

A third idea was fighting its way into my brain and I tried very hard to ignore it. Where did she keep her clothes? There must be another bedroom.

There wasn't. The only other door off the corridor led to the bathroom, gleaming white and immaculate, except for the towel Daniel must have left, as usual, on the floor. I picked it up and smoothed it out, my eyes fixed on the large medicine cabinet on the wall. In there would surely be face cream, tampons, make-up. I draped the towel carefully over the towel rail and moved very slowly to the cabinet. My heart was in my mouth as I pulled open the door to reveal aftershave, contact lens cleaner and mouthwash. Not a lipstick in sight. I sank down on the edge of the bath and gave a little moan.

How could I not have known? How could I have been so blind? I thought we had such a good relationship, that he told me the things that mattered. I thought I understood him. How long had he been keeping it from me? How long had he been pretending, producing girls at intervals, letting me tease him about them? Why hadn't he felt able to tell me? Was I so unapproachable?

He was back. 'Would you like a coffee Mum?' asked Daniel and I raised my head and looked at him. My beautiful boy. Tall, slim and sensitive. Kind, affectionate and funny. The light of my life, my pride and joy for the past twenty-four years, but someone, it seemed, who I didn't know at all.

'What I would like, Daniel,' I said, and my voice was gratifyingly calm and steady, 'is an explanation. I see you have two toothbrushes above the sink. Could you tell me who else is living here with you?'

'Ah,' he said. 'Yes, well, I've been meaning to tell you. Shall we go and sit down?'

I followed him into the front room and collapsed on to the nearest sofa. Opposite me I noted a well-stocked drinks shelf, complete with cocktail shaker, although the Daniel I knew rarely drank anything other than beer. Daniel sat on the other sofa and looked just the way he did as a young boy, waiting to take his dreaded piano exams. I clutched a suede cushion to my tummy for comfort because I knew of course what was coming. Bang go the grandchildren. The white wedding. The shopping trips and recipe-swopping with my daughter-in-law. Don't be selfish, think of him not you. This is when you have to be there for him, support him all the way. If you make a mess of this, you could lose him forever.

I looked down at my clenched hands, put the cushion down next to me and spread my fingers on my knees. I could do this, of course I could. My beautiful boy was still my beautiful boy, and the fact that he hadn't been able to tell me was my fault, not his. I should have been a better mother, I should have realised, I should have made it easier for him to be open and honest with me. But it wasn't too late. I would surprise him now with how enlightened and unprejudiced and liberated I was, so that in future he would feel able to tell me anything.

I smiled at him, a huge, loving, unconditional smile. 'I've worked it out darling, and don't worry, it's absolutely fine. In fact it's great!' The relief on his face was heartbreaking.

'I have only three questions,' I went on. 'What's his name, when can I meet him and, I know it's a little early in the day, but could I have a drop of brandy in my coffee?'

Christina

My yoga teacher thought I was called Christina. So that's who I was for an hour and a half on Wednesday evening. Actually, my name is Ann. That's Ann without an 'e'. And no one has ever called me anything else. 'Annie' would have been nice, but it's never happened.... Ann it is and always has been, until last Wednesday when I was suddenly transformed into Christina. Of course I should have put the teacher right straight away, but I was so surprised and delighted that the moment for correcting her passed, and then it was too late. But what did it matter? I was at a new class in a village I never normally set foot in, no one knew me or would ever see me outside of these 4 walls, so actually I could be whoever I wanted.

And I wanted, very badly, to be Christina. She sounded so confident, elegant and in control. Christina would have a lovely home with beech furniture and an island in the kitchen. She would have lots of friends to do lovely things with, and her fridge would be daintily filled with delicacies like guacamole and stuffed olives. Her husband would be kind and thoughtful and amusing and romantic, and he would sometimes run her a bath and surround it with candles, and take her out to dinner and call her 'darling'.

It was when we were doing 'downward dog', a position that I don't much like because it hurts my wrists, that the teacher paused next to me and said, 'Lovely line, Christina.' I flushed with pride and wobbled a little, but I kept my lovely line and I breathed into the pose just as

Christina would. And it was as Christina that I turned my attention to all my postures that evening. I pulled in my tummy and relaxed my shoulders and I concentrated very hard on my breathing. I made myself forget about my life, my husband and my home, all of which were very different from Christina's. I was so far away from being Ann that I even made a little joke when we were attempting the Eagle pose. 'I don't think I look much like an eagle', I said and to my surprise everyone, all 6 of the ladies and the teacher, laughed. That felt so good that I wanted suddenly to cry. Instead I smiled a Christina-like smile, the smile of someone who is accustomed to being witty.

My favourite part of a yoga class is the relaxation at the end. Some teachers cut it short, to a mere 10 minutes, but this new teacher understood how important it was. I glanced at the clock as we put our socks back on and arranged our rugs, and I saw to my delight that she had allowed us nearly half an hour. She lit some candles, turned off the strip lights and pressed a button on her machine to make some soothing music flow into the room. I felt the tension seep out of my body.

She has a beautiful voice, this teacher. Soft and gentle, with a melodic quality that means her words linger in your ears after she has fallen silent.

'Tonight I'd like you to think about the person you'd like to be,' she said, and I gave a little gasp of surprise. It was as if she knew that all evening I'd been pretending to be someone else. 'We all wish from time to time that we were better people, kinder perhaps, more aware. Or perhaps we just wish we were more organised, or had more confidence. Whatever it is about yourself that you would like to improve upon, just spend a few moments visualising yourself being this better person. Think about your daily life, meeting with people, doing what you normally do, but doing it better. Breathe slowly and deeply, and concentrate your energies into feeding this vision of the woman you would like to be....'

I had a head start on the others, so this was easy. All I had to do was behave like Christina. I saw myself strolling around the park in my lunch hour, instead of fitting in a scuttle to the supermarket. I saw myself laughing with the teachers in the staff room, instead of hiding in my classroom marking papers. I saw myself going off to the cinema with a friend instead of listening to Barry cursing at the football players on the Sports channel. I saw myself walking calmly out of the room when he yelled at me, instead of getting upset. I saw myself not being a doormat, and it felt wonderful. The tears threatened again, but they were happy tears, and I let them slide silently down the sides of my face. It did feel a bit strange having them trickle into my ears.

The teacher was calling us back to the here and now, and reluctantly I obeyed. I wiped my eyes with the back of my hand and yawned and sat up.

'Thank you for coming this evening,' said the teacher. 'I hope you've all enjoyed this practice and will take some of the energy away with you.' We nodded and smiled and thanked her in return. I rolled up my mat, put on my shoes and collected my bag. I filled in the form I had been too late to see to at the start of the class, and instead of Ann I wrote my new lovely name. As I handed it to the teacher, she smiled at me, and said, 'See you next week, Christina.'

'Oh yes,' I said, 'I'll be here.'

Ruth and Ruby

Ruth was feeling harassed. She had left her shopping list on the kitchen table and here she was in the supermarket, unable to remember more than two items. Tomatoes and mushrooms, she knew about them, but she was sure there were at least ten other things that she needed desperately. Calm down, she told herself. Just go up and down the aisles methodically and you'll remember what you need. And if you don't, you'll just have to come out again, that's all. Or go without. It's no big deal. Why do you have to make such a fuss about things? She sighed. Lately everything seemed so much harder, fraught with difficulty. Even the simplest of tasks, like a trip to the supermarket, made her feel insecure and fretful. It was as if she were taking some sort of test every minute of every day, and she was conscious of failing badly at all of them. Perhaps she had come off those yellow pills too soon, she hadn't felt right for days now. The doctor had told her to take it slowly, but as usual she'd thought she knew best. She promised herself she would take a pill when she got home.

She was standing looking at the yoghurts when the small boy crashed the trolley into the counter, right next to her. It narrowly missed running over her foot and Ruth leapt back in surprise, before realising that there was a baby in the seat of the trolley. After a collision like that, it probably had whip-lash, the poor little mite. The baby wasn't making a sound, and just stared at her with mildly surprised eyes. Ruth wondered why it wasn't yelling. Perhaps it was brain-damaged, too dim to realise that something frightening had just happened. She hesitated, not sure what she should do next, when all at once she was shoved out of the way. 'Oh god, oh god,' said a young woman as she hurriedly unstrapped the baby. 'It's alright,' said Ruth, 'the baby's fine, it's not hurt.'

The woman ignored her and turned to the little boy. 'How many times have I told you,' she hissed, 'never, never pull on the trolley, you could have hurt Molly.' She was peppering the baby with kisses. 'Poor baby,' she cooed, 'poor Mollykins.', s she strapped her back into her seat.

Ruth hovered, waited to be acknowledged. It was true that she hadn't actually done anything to help, but she would have done if she'd been given the chance. And the woman had shoved her very rudely in her haste to get at the baby. At the very least she was owed an apology for that. As the woman fussed over the still silent baby, Ruth smiled down at the boy and he scowled back. The young woman looked at her then and her eyes narrowed. 'Come here Jack,' she said, 'you know you mustn't talk to strangers.' And with that she marched off, one hand on the trolley handle and the other on Jack's back.

Well really! thought Ruth. Some people have no manners, no manners at all. And how will that poor boy grow up to have any if he's not allowed to return a smile? She felt very aggrieved as she dumped a pot of Greek yoghurt in her basket and tried to remember if she needed any milk.

She was still sulking as she started down the biscuit aisle. Some shortbread to have with her cup of tea, that might cheer her up. It was then that she noticed the little girl. She was clutching a packet of Jammie Dodgers, and silent tears were streaming down her too-pink cheeks. Ruth paused in mid-reach. What was wrong with mothers today? This was the second neglected child in the space of two minutes. Had she been fortunate enough to have had a child, there was no way she would have abandoned it in a trolley or left it behind in the biscuit aisle. She would have been a dutifully attentive mother at all times, of that she was quite certain.

'Hello', she said, smiling down at the little mite, whose jumper, she observed, had a large orange stain on its front. The child drew herself back against the wall of biscuits and stared at her, a mixture of fear and suspicion in her eyes. I probably do look a bit weird, Ruth thought. I didn't feel right this morning, I may even have forgotten to brush my hair. She patted at her head, and as she feared, it felt more than usually unkempt. She looked around for the child's mother but the aisle was empty apart from the two of them. She tried again.

'Hello, she repeated,' have you lost your mummy?'

'Mummy's horrid,' said the child. 'Ruby hates Mummy.'

'Ruby! What a pretty name! My name is Ruth.'

'Ruby - Ruth,' said the little girl slowly, 'Ruby - Ruth. Nearly same.' Her smile, when it finally came, was delightful, and Ruth beamed back at her. Her mind was racing with possibilities. The woman who had such poor parenting skills that she could lose this defenceless little girl needed to be taught a lesson. She needed to understand that if you were lucky enough to be given the responsibility of looking after a child, you had to wash its clothes and know where it was every minute of the day. She, Ruth, would have done those things admirably, and it was so unfair that she had never been given the opportunity. Well here was her chance, and if it resulted in her and Ruby having a few hours of fun, and the child's mother being given a short sharp shock, then that was obviously what she should do. It wasn't as if she had anything else on that day. She could look upon this as a bit of essential social work.

She glanced at the packet of biscuits in Ruby's hand. 'Those are nice biscuits,' she said. 'Shall I buy them for you?'

'Mummy said no,' replied the child and her lower lip wobbled at the injustice of it.

'Well Ruth says yes!' announced Ruth, and she grabbed the biscuits and placed them in her basket. 'Come on then, let's go to my house and eat them with a nice glass of juice.' She held out her hand and Ruby slipped hers into it.

It was so easy. Ruth and Ruby marched up to the self-service checkout at the front of the store, processed the few items in Ruth's basket and were out of the shop less than five minutes after they had met.

Ruth's heart was racing with excitement, as they trotted along Fore Street, and she thought she might be grinning idiotically. She tried to think about the consequences of what she was doing, but she couldn't seem to get past the delightful prospect of having a little girl sitting at her kitchen table. A little girl whose own mother didn't deserve her. Just a few hours, what harm could it do? They would have a lovely time together, just chatting, maybe watching a bit of telly. She could give Ruby a bath and wash her hair, that would be nice. She made herself move on to afterwards. Just a few hours of fun and then she would take her to the police station and say she had found her wandering around. What a heroine she would be! Her name would probably be in the local paper, she would be famous as the woman who found the little girl.

Across the road from them stood Dr Jameson, waiting to cross the street on his way to a house call. He was surprised to see Ruth Grayson out and about, and with a young child in tow. He wasn't aware of her having any connection at all with children, and he had assumed her psychosis kept her more or less house-bound. Perhaps he would call on her later, just to check that all was well. She certainly looked happy enough today, not at all like the last time he had seen her.

A shadow crossed Ruth's mind and she frowned. What about when they questioned Ruby? Wouldn't she be bound to tell them that Ruth had taken her from the supermarket? Perhaps she could persuade her to keep it a secret, a special secret just between the two of them. Was such a young child capable of keeping a secret? They were approaching the steps to Ruth's basement flat, and she pushed the bad thoughts away. She would just concentrate on enjoying herself for the next few hours and not worry about anything. That was one of her problems, that she worried too much.

'Here we are!' said Ruth, with studied jollity. 'This is where I live, would you like to come in?'

Ruby had grown quiet as they walked along. 'Where's my mummy?' she said, trying to pull her hand away from Ruth's, 'I want my mummy.'

'Mummy's very busy just now, she asked me to look after you for a bit,' replied Ruth. She gave Ruby a gentle push, so that the child had to reach out for the railing. 'That's it, hold on to the railing as you go down the steps. You can meet my pussy cat, you'll like her, she's called Prudence.'

That seemed to do the trick. Ruby carried on down the steps and stood unprotesting while Ruth hunted through her bag for her key. Her breath, she noticed, was ragged and she felt rather sick. Nothing a nice cup of tea can't sort out, she told herself.

Once inside the flat, with the door bolted and the kettle boiling, Ruth felt a bit calmer. She looked at the clock on the dresser. 10.40. She would look after Ruby for two hours, and then she would take her to the police station at lunchtime. The only person to be put out would be the child's mother, who badly needed to be taught a lesson. Jack and Molly's mother might hear about the missing child and she too would be more careful in future. All in all, this was turning out to be a good day's work, thought Ruth, as she placed a cushion on a chair so that Ruby could sit up at the table. She lifted the child up and grimaced as the scent of unwashed hair and damp underpants assailed her nostrils. A bath was a very good idea. Now if she were my little girl, she would smell fresh and pretty all day, just as a little girl should. The mother was probably too busy watching daytime telly to carry out her maternal duties.

As if she could read her mind, Ruby whined, 'Where's my Mummy, I want my mummy.'

'I told you, Mummy's busy, I'm looking after you for a little while.' Ruth tried to soften her voice. 'Now then, where did I put those biscuits?' she said. She opened the packet and carefully placed four on a plate. Before she had a chance to offer them to Ruby, the child reached out and grabbed one, stuffing it into her mouth as though she were afraid it would be taken away.

If there was one thing Ruth couldn't bear it was bad manners. Quick as a flash she pulled Ruby's hand from her mouth and then gave it a hard smack. The child's eyes welled up with tears and she began to howl, bits of half-chewed biscuit falling from her mouth onto the table.

'Oh don't be so silly,' Ruth snapped,' that didn't hurt!'

'Did, did, did,' sobbed Ruby. 'Mummy, MUMMY!'

It was the shrieking that pushed Ruth over the edge. After all she had done, all she was trying to do, to be repaid like this was simply intolerable. She could feel beads of sweat breaking out at her hairline, and the headache that had been threatening all morning now took hold with sickening force. She glared at the child who was at that moment looking particularly unappealing, with her little red face screwed up in anguish, and a long bead of snot dangling from one nostril. It was more than Ruth could bear.

'Stop that horrible noise!' she bellowed, and when that only served to increase the volume, she hoisted Ruby off her chair and carried her under one arm out of the kitchen. The child was wriggling furiously and yelling at full volume, and as a flailing leg caught her thigh Ruth suddenly saw the answer. Still clutching Ruby, she pulled open the door to the understairs cupboard and hauled out the hoover and three cardboard boxes. Then she shoved the child in, slammed the door shut and pushed the boxes up against it.

'NO!' came a muffled scream from behind the door. 'No! It's dark! No!'

Breathing heavily, Ruth slid down in front of the boxes. Her heart was bouncing around in her chest and her mouth was so dry that she couldn't swallow. Pills, she needed her pills.

Behind her the screams had subsided now into whimpers. She'd be getting tired now after that little display of temper, thought Ruth. She just needed to be taught some manners; like all children she would soon learn how to behave if given some strict guidance. After all, she' herself had been shut in the coal shed often enough as a child and it had never done her any harm.

With a huge effort, Ruth clambered on to her knees and stayed on all fours for a minute, struggling to get her breathing under control. She shut her eyes and pretended she was watching her yoga dvd. In for four, hold for four, out for four, she muttered. Behind her, Ruby was cranking up the volume.

217

Ruth got to her feet and dragged over the cast iron umbrella stand. She planted it in front of the boxes and tested the door. Good. What she needed now was to lie down. Just for half an hour, and then she would take the penitent child to the police station and say she had found her in the park.

'I'll be back in a minute Ruby,' she called. 'You be nice and quiet and I'll let you out very soon.'

Ruth ignored the muffled screams from the cupboard. Her legs were trying to buckle under her but she made it into her bedroom at the end of the corridor, and collapsed onto the bed. Her pills were in the drawer of her bedside table and with a shaking hand, she tipped several onto her palm and swallowed them. She lay down on the bed and closed her eyes. The little girl seemed far away now. So far away.

In the darkness Ruby eventually gave up on the screaming and instead set about making a little nest out of a garden chair cushion and 2 blankets. She curled up with her thumb in her mouth and after a few hiccupping sobs she was fast asleep.

****

The ring at the doorbell forty minutes later failed to get a response. Dr Jameson paused on the doorstep, wondering if he should ring again. If Ruth was taking a nap, which was highly likely, then it would be better not to wake her. He could phone after his afternoon surgery instead. But then, he might forget, and there had been something unsettling, even a little manic, about the way Ruth had been striding along with that child in tow. Something didn't feel right. He pushed again on the white button marked Grayson.

Ruth raised her head and groaned. She received so few visitors that a doorbell ring had the status of a special event, even in her current befuddled state. She couldn't just ignore it. She pulled herself up from the bed and groped her way along the corridor. She slid back the bolt and opened the door, and her mouth fell open.

'Ah, Ruth!' said Dr Jameson, said, registering with some alarm her dishevelled state and dull eyes. 'I'm so sorry to have disturbed you. I was just passing and thought I would make sure that you were alright.'

She grunted, still confused. He had never called on her uninvited before.

'I saw you earlier you see, with a little girl.... I just thought I'd check that everything was ok. I know that things have been difficult lately...'

Ruth shook her head in an attempt to clear its fogginess. He'd seen her with the child. This was terrible. She had to think of something to say to him, she had to get rid of him and then get rid of Ruby.

'Hello Doctor,' she said, her words a little slurred. She gripped the door hard as she concentrated on speaking clearly. 'Yes, that was my little niece; I must have been taking her back to her house when you saw me. I'm fine, just having a little nap. Children can be so tiring can't they!' She tried a laugh, but it came out more as a cackle.

'Indeed they can,' he replied. 'I'll be on my way then, sorry again for waking you. Goodbye.' He wasn't happy about the way she looked, but he was expected over at the police station, something to do with a young woman in need of a sedative.

Ruth watched until he had reached the top of the steps and then she re-bolted the door. She went into the bathroom and splashed her face with cold water again and again, until her head felt a bit clearer. The woman staring back at her in the mirror looked quite mad, she thought. Mad and just like a witch. A slow smile spread across her thin lips as a plan began to form itself.

'Prudence!' she called. The cat usually came when summoned, but not this time. She must be outside. Ruth took the box of cat biscuits from the kitchen cupboard, opened the back door and shook the box. As if by magic, a slim black shape slid over the neighbour's fence and came to rub against Ruth's legs.

Ruth bent down to scratch her behind one ear. 'Biscuits in a minute,' she said. 'First you can do something for me.'

With the cat at her heels, Ruth went into the corridor and pulled the umbrella stand and boxes away from the cupboard door. She opened the door and roughly shook the bundle of sleeping child. 'Wake up, Ruby,' she said. 'Time to go home now, time to go to Mummy.'

Ruby gave a squeak and tried to scramble out of the doorway, but Ruth was blocking her passage. 'Mummy!' squealed Ruby, 'I want Mummy!'

'And you shall go to Mummy, very soon,' said Ruth. 'But I need you to understand something first.' She fixed her eyes on the little girl, who whimpered. 'You see this pussycat?' asked Ruth, pointing at Prudence. Ruby nodded. 'Well once upon a time, she was a little girl just like you.' Ruby's eyes were like saucers now, and her thumb flew back into her mouth. 'She was a little girl who did a terrible thing: she disobeyed me. She came to my house, just like you have today, and I told her not to tell anyone that she'd come here. But she was so naughty, that she did! She told her mummy that she'd been to my house and so when it was dark I crept into her bedroom and I turned her into a pussycat. Because I'm really a witch and I can do anything. I turned that little girl into this cat and now she has to live with me forever and she can never see her mummy again.'

Ruby gave a strangled whimper. Ruth brought her face down inches away from her's and the child whimpered again. 'Do you want to be turned into a cat, Ruby?' hissed Ruth. 'No!' shrieked Ruby. 'No, no, no!'

'Then this is what you must do,' said Ruth, straightening herself up. 'You must walk with me sensibly to the police station, and we will go in and talk to the nice policeman at the desk. He'll ask you lots of questions and you'll say that you went out of the supermarket all by yourself, and I found you just now in the park. You must never ever say that you came to my house. Do you understand?' Ruby nodded.

'And what will happen to you if you say you've been with me all the time?'

'You'll make me be a pussycat!' wailed Ruby.

'That's right, and don't you ever forget it. One little whisper about meeting me in the supermarket or coming to my house and Poof! you will be a little pussycat just like poor Prudence. A little tabby cat, that's what you could be. Or would you rather be ginger?' Ruth laughed at the stricken look on Ruby's face.

'No!' said Ruby and she burst into tears. Ruth went into the kitchen and tossed some cat food into Prudence's bowl. 'Good girl,' she said, 'that worked a treat.'

Then she unbolted the door and grabbed Ruby's hand.

'Come on then, it's time to go. Stop that silly crying, or I'll be cross. Hold my hand while we walk along the road, and remember, I'll be watching you and listening to what you say, always and forever.'

Ruth opened the door, and walked outside with Ruby's hand clamped in hers. She pulled the door shut behind her and the two of them started up the steps. Conscious this time that people might be on the look out for a small girl, Ruth planted a confident smile on her face and mentally practiced her story as they walked. 'Oh, it was nothing,' she imagined herself saying, 'I just happened to be in the park at just the right time! Such a dear little girl, I'm just glad to have been of service. A photo? Oh go on then, if you must!'

The police station was halfway down the next street. They went through the main door and up to the desk, where a young policeman with a bad case of acne was looking through some papers.

'Hello officer,' said Ruby, 'I've just found this little girl playing on her own in the park – she says her name is Ruby. I thought I'd better bring her straight here.' The young man leapt to his feet, and leant over the counter to look at Ruby. 'Oh that's great!' he said, grinning wildly, 'That's so great, hang on, I'll get the sergeant.' He disappeared and a few seconds later Ruth and Ruby heard a whoop of delight, as a plump young woman burst through a door and threw herself on her knees in front of Ruby, squeezing the child to her and laughing and crying. 'Thank god,' she kept saying, 'Thank god, where have you been?'

Ruth jumped in. 'She was playing in the park', she said. 'On the roundabout. I stopped because there didn't seem to be anyone with her, and when I asked her where her mummy was, she said, 'In the shop.' So I guessed she'd wandered off, and thought I'd better bring her here.'

'Thank you, oh thank you,' said Ruby's mum, 'you are an angel, thank you so much! God, you don't know how much this means to me! '

'Well hello again Ruth,' said a man behind Ruth and her grin froze. She knew that voice. She turned very slowly, and the colour drained from her face. She put a hand out to the counter to steady herself.

'Once I've checked the little girl over,' said Dr Jameson, in a voice that was steely calm, 'I think I'd better come in with you to the interview room. I imagine there will be some explaining to do.'

Maureen

Maureen is such a gentle name. She sounds like a librarian, a softly spoken, short plump woman in unflattering glasses, with an earnest and careworn expression. She probably looks after her invalid mother and has never had sex.

But the Maureen I know is not a bit like that. My Maureen has had plenty of sex, and during the last 3 months it has been my husband she's been having it with. My Maureen is tall and slim and likes to toss her long brown hair. Whenever I've seen her she has been smiling. Well, I'd be smiling too if I had someone to adore me and take me out to lunch and buy me roses.

The funny thing is that although I know a lot about her, I'm not sure she knows I exist. After all, married men often forget to tell their mistresses that they have a wife at home. I expect that at the time it doesn't seem important. They would have other, more pressing things on their minds.

Stephen is in many ways a very simple man. Since he would never dream of looking at my phone messages, he assumes that I behave the same way. And so, whenever he goes for one of his lengthy soaks in the bath, which is at least 3 times a week, I catch up on what he and Maureen have been up to and are planning next. That is how I've managed to watch her while she waits for Stephen at the station, in Waterstone's café, at the Italian restaurant that used to be my favourite. Before it became theirs.

One of Stephen's greatest faults is that he is never on time. It drives me crazy but Maureen doesn't seem to mind. Last Thursday she and I waited 35 minutes for him in the garden centre, and when he eventually sauntered up, grinning from ear to ear, she beamed at him. From my vantage point behind the bird tables I watched in amazement as she threw herself into his arms, just as if she hadn't seen him for weeks. Although I knew for a fact that they'd had dinner at Piero's the previous evening.

Perhaps this was true love, I mused, as they studied the display of home-made cakes in the café, standing hand in hand. Perhaps it was churlish of me to feel such ferocious hatred for this woman who was making my husband happy in a way that I never had. But I couldn't help it. I didn't love him enough to want him to be happy. I wanted him to be as miserable as I was, because otherwise it wasn't fair. Which is why I had to get rid of her.

This proved to be very simple, because I knew she liked to do her shopping on Thursday nights after work. All I had to do was lurk in the wine aisle in Tesco's and then approach her, with a sad, brave smile on my face, as she wondered whether to splash out on a bottle of Chateauneuf du Pape.

'He's not worth it,' I said, and I told her who I was and that I'd seen her with Stephen. She was so shocked that I had to make a grab for the bottle before she dropped it. I put it back on the shelf while she struggled to compose herself.

I was pleased that she made no attempt to pretend that they were 'just friends'. Quite the opposite, she kept saying, 'I'm so sorry, I had no idea,' and I realised that Maureen was in fact rather a nice woman. I decided not to hate her after all. It wasn't her fault that she had trusted my cheating husband.

Apparently, Stephen had told her that he lived with his sister who had learning difficulties and was nervous of visitors, which is why she couldn't visit him at home. And she had believed him! I had to laugh when I heard that, but Maureen wasn't smiling. She didn't look so good when she wasn't smiling, and up close as I was, I could see that her skin wasn't very good either. She was older than I had realised, and her teeth were a bit yellow. That made me feel so much better. I patted her on the hand and said, 'Never mind dear, you'll find someone else in no time!' and she looked up at me with her big brown eyes swimming with tears, and for a minute there I almost felt sorry for her. But then I remembered those text messages that no decent woman should ever allow herself to write, and my heart hardened again.

'I won't see him again,' she said in that husky voice that men seem to like. 'I can't tell you how sorry I am.'

'Thank you,' I said, and I tried to sound mournful and a little pathetic, although actually I was feeling very smug. 'There is just one thing – would you mind not telling Stephen that you heard it from me? Perhaps someone else could have told you he was married? Only I wouldn't want him to hate me, you see.'

'Of course I won't. I'll just send him a brief message ending it and saying someone at work told me. And then I won't ever contact him again.'

I offered to buy her a cup of tea then, to help her get over the shock, but she said she wanted to go straight home. She just abandoned her trolley in the middle of the aisle and headed off. I had a good poke about and decided that her shopping was much more interesting than mine, so I swapped trolleys and made my way to the checkout.

Stephen would be very surprised when I presented him with venison pate and pork medallions and gorgonzola for supper. But a special meal would be just the thing to cheer the poor dear up after his bit of bad news.

My Next Life

I have no idea why I'm so terrified of water. Deep water, I mean. Obviously I can do the washing up without flinching, and take a quick shower – but suggest that I go on a boat or in a swimming pool and I'm a quivering wreck. I haven't had a bath for years. I wish I could say that I fell in a river when I was four and nearly drowned. But I didn't. Nothing as exciting as that has ever happened to me.

So I have no excuses. But there is always the possibility that I had a terrifying watery experience in a past life. Malee is quite convinced that she had a past life and will have a future one. She's Thai and beautiful and Buddhist. I overheard her explaining it all to Sandra Crabtree at the last AGM, when we were standing in a queue for a cup of watery coffee. Sandra is the Chairperson of our fundraising committee, one of those women who's forever rushing about doing good things. Ever since I eavesdropped on their conversation I've been thinking a lot about the possibility of other lives. I find the whole idea enormously appealing. It helps to accept the fact that you're not making much of this life if you can imagine that you were hugely productive and admirable last time round. Or will be next time. It sort of takes the pressure off. Perhaps it explains why Malee is always so joyful and smiley and not worried about anything. She probably thinks that next time, or the time after that, she'll be admirable, so she's happy to swan around in this life not wasting her time worrying, but enjoying everything she does to the full.

I don't know how to set about lodging a request, but if at all possible I'd like to come back as a cat. An English tabby cat, please, in a warm comfortable home, with regular meals and not too much fussing. Just think how uncomplicated my life would be - no bills to pay, or things to buy, or people to try to form relationships with. Cats don't seem to need relationships, which must be very liberating for them. And better still, they don't appear to suffer from guilt. My Barney, for instance, will spend all day sleeping on the sofa if he feels like it. Which he usually does. Whereas I feel guilty if take a nap on a Sunday afternoon – unless I'm poorly of course. Then it's alright – just. Sometimes I think Barney has a much better life than me.

Especially today, when I've got myself all churned up because of my inability to just say no. I'm terrified because I've let Malee talk me into doing something I'd give anything not to have to do. I was so surprised, you see. There I was last Friday, minding my own business, trying to steer a reasonably straight course out through the supermarket doors with my wayward trolley, when Malee appeared out of nowhere and grabbed me by the arm.

'Frances!' she exclaimed, flashing me that wonderful smile. She has perfect pearly white teeth. "How lucky that I've bumped into you!' I resisted the urge to look round to see who she was talking to. She had said my name. She really did mean me. Despite the fact that my hair needed washing and I was wearing my gardening trousers.

'Are you free tomorrow morning?' Malee asked. Her hand was still resting on my arm. My brain had gone numb and I failed to produce an answer, but that didn't seem to matter. Malee rushed on, while I fixed my eyes on her rings. She had four on her left hand and six on her right, all of them gold with sparkling stones.

'Because the Bay Tree Hotel is running a special offer at their pool this week, and it ends tomorrow!' she explained to me, her eyes like lychee stones shining with enthusiasm. Malee likes nothing better than to spread her happiness around, and she was so caught up in her own excitement that she completely failed to notice that I'd gone pale at the mention of the pool.

'As a member I can take a friend along for a taster session and it's absolutely free - they'll even give us a complimentary cup of coffee afterwards!'

It was that word 'friend' that did it. I was thrilled to have that label attached to me, so thrilled that I forgot to say 'No thank you, I don't like swimming,' until the time had long passed for saying such things. I see Malee every two months or so at committee meetings (I take the minutes and she has interesting ideas), but it would never have occurred to me that she might think of me as a friend. I couldn't say no to her, because I wanted her to like me as much as I like her and that means I couldn't be a wimp.

When she finally paused for breath, I slipped in the fact that I couldn't swim, and Malee's incredulity was something to behold. She gasped theatrically and her lovely eyes widened, while I grinned apologetically back. She makes the most of her eyes, and always wears lots of mascara and eyeliner. At one of our meetings, I remember, the mascara was a startling bright blue. The shade exactly matched her soft clingy sweater and I was so distracted by the sight of her opposite me that I made a pathetic job of the minutes that day. I scribbled nonsense and left out vital details, and when I emailed them to Sandra she sent them back with lots of amendments and asked me in a most unfriendly way if I was coming down with flu.

Malee was adamant that I should leap into a pool at the first possible opportunity and discover how delightful swimming could be. If I held on to a polystyrene float, I would, she assured me, come to no harm. She told me where and when to meet her the next morning. Just like that. It was more like an order than a request, which is another reason I found it impossible to say no. And then she glided away, leaving me standing in the supermarket entrance with my trolley, feeling rather dazed and trying to remember where I'd left the car.

 I know I could have phoned her when I got home and backed out with some excuse – but I was frightened of losing that beautiful label so soon after receiving it. Our friendship, so newly formed and fragile, might just crumble away to nothing if I rejected her offer. Also, I have to admit that I was very interested in seeing what she looked like in a swimsuit. She has such a lovely face, round and completely wrinkle-free, with plump well-defined lips that I have to force myself not to gaze at. I suppose you could say I have a bit of a crush on Malee.

 I tried to imagine what the next day would be like, and in my head I visited the changing room rather than the pool. We would chat, I supposed, in a girlie, giggly way about nothing in particular, as we slipped out of our clothes and into our swimming costumes. The idea made me feel quite faint - I hadn't undressed in front of anyone since I'd been at school. Maybe there would be little cubicles, that would probably be better. And I could have my costume on already, under my clothes. And then my thoughts leapt forward to the bit afterwards, when we would be sitting in a cosy sitting room in pretty chintz armchairs, sipping our complimentary coffee and planning our next outing together. Perhaps we could go to the cinema, or visit the botanical gardens? In this way I managed to get through the afternoon. I was restless, nervous, excited, but not in a bad way.

After supper though, the fear kicked in. I went in search of my one and only swimming costume and found it scrunched up at the back of the wardrobe. It has, of course, never been near any water - I only use it for sunbathing in the back garden. When I'm not at the office I spend hours in the summer stretched out on my lounger, soaking up every feeble ray the sun deigns to send my way. At my age and with my figure a bikini is out of the question; I need to look respectable in case Frank from next door pops his head over the fence to comment on the weather or his runner beans.

I pulled on the navy costume and forced myself to have a critical look in the dressing table mirror. It's not a very big mirror, and I had to keep tilting it to get all of me in. It was not at all a pleasurable experience. I hadn't realised that over the years the swimsuit had gone a bit bobbly and that it sagged around the bum. If it had ever had any tummy-firming properties, the washing machine had long since dissolved them away. I promised myself I would start on that diet, in earnest this time. But I had to get the swimming pool nightmare over with first. For a frantic moment I wondered if I would have time in the morning to rush into town and buy a new swimsuit, but I knew that getting myself to the hotel would be as much as I could manage. I couldn't burden myself with anything more.

I fetched my friendliest towel, pink with white spots, and then spent the evening playing fast and furious games of Scrabble on the internet, which of course allowed no time at all for scary thoughts to crawl into my brain. I think I'll gloss over the ghastly night. I did get to sleep eventually.

****

The aged swimsuit is laid out ready over the frame at the foot of my bed, and it's the first thing I see when I turn on the light this morning. Terror clutches at my heart. The second thing I see is the alarm clock telling me that I've overslept. My haste gives me little time to dwell on the ordeal that lies ahead. I'm on automatic pilot. Shower, dress, feed cat, find keys, go.

I've often passed the Bay Tree Hotel on my way to town, but this is the first time I've ever ventured inside. My legs seem to be made of rubber as I negotiate the stone steps leading to the front door. This is probably my last chance to make a run for it. Exactly how far am I prepared to go in my quest for this friendship? Do I really think I can go through with this terrifying experience? Won't I just make a complete fool of myself and ruin everything? I hesitate, with my hand on the huge brass door knob.

'Morning, Frances!' calls Malee as she hurries up behind me. She giggles excitedly as together we push the heavy door open. Her breath smells all lemony, and her black glossy hair swings forward and strokes my cheek for a moment. I want to touch its silkiness but of course I don't.

The hotel lobby is small and dark and stuffed with potted plants. There is so little light that they must be plastic; they're pretending, just like me, trying to pass themselves off as the real thing. Well, they don't fool me, not for one second. Malee pushes her arm through mine, which makes my heart lurch about a bit, and propels me past the desk. A plump receptionist is talking crossly into the phone, her face pink with indignation. She glances up for a moment and then turns her back on us, and I can't help feeling a little wounded by her indifference. This is such a momentous day for me that I want the world to sit up and cheer me on as I perform this act of extraordinary courage.

'This way to the pool!' Malee sings out as we head off down the corridor. Her voice, like everything else about her, is very inviting. It's low and a little husky, and her Thai accent makes everything she says sound exotic. The corridor becomes too narrow for us to walk side by side and she moves ahead of me. All at once I am in a black fog of panic. Her coat is bright orange and I pretend it's the sun and I follow it reverently, through the double doors and down the stairs. I force myself to take slow deep breaths, and to think of nothing. Then we're standing in a bright white room in front of a desk. There's a nasty smell in the air which I guess is chlorine. The back wall is made of glass and on the other side of it is the pool. I quickly avert my eyes from the sight of so much water.

'Oh good, you're here!' says Malee to an elegant thin woman seated in a chair reading a magazine. She has lots of blond curly hair which is piled loosely on top of her head, and her coat is long and velvet. She is exactly the kind of person I would expect to be a friend of Malee's and suddenly I feel dull and dowdy and completely boring. The Friend gets to her feet with a lazy smile, and tosses her silky scarf over her shoulder as she and Malee hug each other. Malee and I have never hugged. I wonder if we ever will? It's probably too late now. It's the sort of thing you have to do from the beginning.

'Frances, this is Susanna.' The Friend smiles graciously and I manage to nod at her, but I am engulfed in a wave of misery. Susanna is sophisticated, confident, beautifully dressed. Even her name is classy. How stupid of me to have thought I could ever be in the same league.

The young woman at the desk is looking very bored.

'We're here for the taster session,' Malee tells her, with one of her lovely smiles. 'I'm a member – here's my card – and I've brought two guests along.'

'Only one,' says the girl flatly.

'I'm sorry?'

'Only one guest allowed for the taster session. It says so here.' She points to a poster blu-tacked to the front of the desk.

It feels as though a shower of golden light is pouring down over me. I want to whoop for joy but instead a weird, tinkly, mad-sounding laugh emerges from my throat.

'Oh dear, what a shame!' I cackle. 'Never mind – you two go on, I'll do it another time.'

I don't give Malee or Susanna an opportunity to discuss this. I don't even look at them. I've been given a second chance to make what is so obviously the right decision and I just grab it and run – up the stairs, through the doors, past the rude receptionist who is still fretting on the phone, out of the front door into the cool November air.

I pause at the foot of the steps to get my breath back. I am flooded with an overwhelming relief that I don't have to get into that pool. I don't know how I would have made myself do it and now I don't have to. I feel as though the hundred rubber bands that were squeezing my heart have burst open and I can relax and be me again. I am trembling all over and I can't stop grinning. I probably look half-witted but there's no one to see. Except a cat. Padding up the gravel drive towards me is a large tabby. I stoop down and stretch out my hand and slowly, nonchalantly, he comes up and graciously allows me to scratch him behind his ears. I am flattered and soothed by his purring, and settle myself down on the step.

'Hello, old chap,' I say. 'You wouldn't agree to go swimming, would you? Even if the loveliest pussycat in town invited you. You'd think it was an appalling idea. Well, so do I.'

He approves of this, and rolls over onto his back for more tickling. I feel like purring myself.

'Frances?' It's Malee, coming down the steps, her face all smiling concern. 'Please come back! I'm sorry I didn't know about the one person rule – but of course I'll pay for you to have a swim.'

I feel calmer now, more feline. I keep my fingers busy on Tabby's tummy as I smile up at Malee. Why don't I just tell her the truth?

'That's very kind, but really I'd much rather not swim. Actually, I'm frightened of water and I was dreading it.'

Malee crouches down next to me and puts her hand on my shoulder. 'Oh you poor thing, I had no idea! Why didn't you say?'

'I don't know,' I reply, abandoning the truth this time. 'I suppose I thought I ought to try to overcome it.' That's good, that makes me sound very brave and admirable.

'Well!' she says, shaking her head in wonder. 'Bravo for making the effort! I promise I won't mention swimming again. But it's a shame – I hoped you could help me with Susanna. She can be such hard work, always banging on about her awful ex-husband. I thought with you there, we might be able to talk about something else!'

We both laugh then, a lovely easy companionable laugh. I don't know what to say. I am flooded with happiness and my eyes are pricking. I rub the cat's tummy too roughly and he gets to his paws with a little grunt and slinks away round the back of the hotel.

'I'd better go and have my swim,' says Malee, as she stands up. 'Will you be at the meeting on Wednesday?'

'Yes,' I say, 'I'll be there. 6 o'clock.'

'Well, maybe afterwards we two can go for a drink, make up for today?'

'That would be lovely,' I reply. I am savouring the sound of that phrase 'we two'. We say our goodbyes and Malee disappears back inside the hotel.

I make my way down the drive, shoulders back and head held high, feeling at least a thousand times happier than the last time I trod this gravel. Suddenly this life is looking pretty good. But if I'm coming back as a cat next time it wouldn't hurt to get in a bit of practice right away. When I get home I think I'll join Barney on the sofa for a nice long snooze.

Printed in Great Britain
by Amazon